T0089044

PENGUIN CLASSICS

THE MARTYRED

RICHARD E. KIM was born Kim Eun Kook on March 13, 1932, in Hamhung, Korea. He attended schools in both modern-day North and South Korea. After the division of Korea in 1945, he escaped to the South and during the Korean War served in the Republic of South Korea's army, being honorably discharged as first lieutenant, infantry in 1954. He immigrated to the United States soon after and attended Middlebury College. After receiving master's degrees from Johns Hopkins University and Harvard University, as well as a master of fine arts from the University of Iowa, Kim shot up to literary prominence with the publication of his first novel, *The Martyred* (1964). Critics praised the book for its complex take on religious faith and humanity, citing Kim as a successor to Fyodor Dostoevsky and Albert Camus. The book was nominated for the National Book Award. Following the success of his debut novel, Kim published two more books: *The Innocent* (1968), a novel, and *Lost Names* (1970), a collection of loosely autobiographical short stories. The latter became a staple in contemporary Asian American literature. Through the 1980s, he published a number of essays, including "In Search of Lost Years" (1985) and "In Search of 'Lost' Koreans in Russia and China" (1989). Mirroring his literary success, Kim also had a distinguished academic career, teaching at the University of Massachusetts and Syracuse University before becoming the Fulbright professor of English at Seoul National University in 1981. He received fellowships from the Iowa Writers' Workshop, the Guggenheim Foundation, the Ford Foundation, and the National Endowment for the Arts. Kim also founded the Trans-Lit Agency, representing American authors in the Korean publishing market. In the 1980s, Kim shifted his focus toward journalism, working as a columnist at a number of Korean daily newspapers and producing and narrating documentaries for KBS-Seoul TV. He died on June 23, 2009, at his home in Massachusetts.

HEINZ INSU FENKL was born in 1960 in Incheon, Korea. He is a novelist, translator, and editor. His autobiographical novel, *Memories of My Ghost Brother*, was named a Barnes & Noble

Discover Great New Writers selection in 1996 and a PEN/ Hemingway Award finalist in 1997. He is coeditor of *Kori: The Beacon Anthology of Korean American Literature* and *Century of the Tiger: One Hundred Years of Korean Culture in America 1903–2003*. His most recent book is *Korean Folktales*. He serves on the editorial board of *AZALEA: Journal of Korean Literature & Culture*, published by Harvard University's Korea Institute.

SUSAN CHOI was born in Indiana and grew up in Texas. Her second novel, *American Woman*, was a finalist for the 2004 Pulitzer Prize for fiction. Her first novel, *The Foreign Student*, won the Asian American Literary Award for fiction and was a finalist for the Discover Great New Writers Award at Barnes & Noble. With David Remnick, she edited an anthology of fiction entitled *Wonderful Town: New York Stories from "The New Yorker."* In 2004, she was awarded a Guggenheim Fellowship. Her most recent novel, *A Person of Interest* was a finalist for the 2009 PEN/Faulkner award. In 2010, she was awarded the PEN/W. G. Sebald Award for a fiction writer in midcareer. She teaches creative writing at Princeton University.

RICHARD E. KIM

The Martyred

Foreword by
SUSAN CHOI

Introduction by
HEINZ INSU FENKL

PENGUIN BOOKS

PENGUIN BOOKS

Published by the Penguin Group

Penguin Group (USA) Inc., 375 Hudson Street, New York, New York 10014, U.S.A.

Penguin Group (Canada), 90 Eglinton Avenue East, Suite 700, Toronto, Ontario, Canada M4P 2Y3
(a division of Pearson Penguin Canada Inc.)

Penguin Books Ltd, 80 Strand, London WC2R 0RL, England

Penguin Ireland, 25 St Stephen's Green, Dublin 2, Ireland (a division of Penguin Books Ltd)

Penguin Group (Australia), 250 Camberwell Road, Camberwell, Victoria 3124, Australia
(a division of Pearson Australia Group Pty Ltd)

Penguin Books India Pvt Ltd, 11 Community Centre, Panchsheel Park, New Delhi–110 017, India

Penguin Group (NZ), 67 Apollo Drive, Rosedale, Auckland 0632, New Zealand
(a division of Pearson New Zealand Ltd)

Penguin Books (South Africa) (Pty) Ltd, 24 Sturdee Avenue, Rosebank,
Johannesburg 2196, South Africa

Penguin Books Ltd, Registered Offices:
80 Strand, London WC2R 0RL, England

First published in the United States of America by George Braziller, Inc. 1964
This edition with an introduction by Heinz Insu Fenkl and a foreword by Susan Choi published in
Penguin Books 2011

The author gratefully acknowledges the help given to him during the writing of this book by the Mary
Roberts Rinehart Foundation.

The excerpt from Hoderlin's *The Death of Empedocles* is from *The Rebel* by Albert Camus, translated
by Anthony Bower. Used by permission of Alfred A. Knopf; a division of Random House, Inc.

PUBLISHER'S NOTE

This is a work of fiction. Names, characters, places, and incidents either are the product of the
author's imagination or are used fictitiously, and any resemblance to actual persons, living or dead,
business establishments, events, or locales is entirely coincidental.

LIBRARY OF CONGRESS CATALOGING IN PUBLICATION DATA

Kim, Richard E., 1932–
The martyred / Richard E. Kim ; forward by Susan Choi ; introduction by Heinz Insu Fenkl.
p. cm.
ISBN 978-0-14-310640-1
1. Korean War, 1950–1953—Fiction. I. Title.
PS3561.I415M37 2011
813'.54—dc22 2011007045

Set in Sabon

To the memory of Albert Camus,
whose insight into "a strange form of love" overcame for me the
nihilism of the trenches and bunkers of Korea

"And openly I pledged my heart to the grave and suffering land, and often in the consecrated night, I promised to love her faithfully until death, unafraid, with her heavy burden of fatality, and never to despise a single one of her enigmas. Thus did I join myself to her with a mortal cord."

—Friedrich Hölderlin
The Death of Empedocles

Acknowledgments

The author gratefully acknowledges the help given to him during the writing of this book by the Mary Roberts Rinehart Foundation. The lines from Hölderlin's *The Death of Empedocles* are quoted by permission of Alfred A. Knopf, Inc., from *The Rebel* by Albert Camus, translated by Anthony Bower.

Contents

THE MARTYRED

Foreword

In the fall of 1998, after a reading I had given in Manhattan, an older gentleman, gray-haired, in a suit, approached the table at which I was signing copies of my novel for a procession of well-wishers who were mostly my friends or the friends of my friends. This man was neither, and he bent toward me with a hesitant formality. He had been, he said, some three decades before, a sales representative for George Braziller, publisher of *The Martyred* by Richard E. Kim. I knew the book, surely? A hot flush of fraudulence lighting my cheeks, I assured him I did. By this lie he was visibly gratified. Of course I would know it. Given that Kim had been the first true Korean American writer, and one of such prominence—thunderously praised for *The Martyred*, comfortably lodged for five months on the *New York Times* bestseller list of 1964, nominated for the National Book Award, compared to Bellow, admired by Roth—and given that I was now a Korean American writer myself, he had expected I'd know the book well, that it would have unique meaning to me. Then he pressed a first edition in my hands. I took it home and put it on a shelf, where it remained, unread, accreting emotions of inadequacy and guilt particular to it but applicable to many other realms in my life, for the next dozen years.

Perhaps it was inevitable, given this introduction, that I would attempt to dismiss Richard Kim as the sort of overbearing older relation one wants to avoid. All these years walking around with a Korean last name, scribbling and publishing stories—and now just as success is in reach, this grandfather whom no one has mentioned turns out to have done it all first, and is crashing the party? Richard E. Kim had never been discussed at the Asian American reading group, he had never appeared on the syllabus—but all this petulant casting of blame veiled my shocked insecurity. I had just spent the better part of a decade researching a novel about the Korean War, yet here was *the* groundbreaking work on the subject, and I'd never heard of it.

History offers some clues as to why. After publishing three works of fiction in only six years, from 1970 to the end of his life in 2009, Kim never published a novel again. And in the post–*Woman Warrior* era in which I grew up, enthralled by identity politics, Kim was certainly well out of style. But I preferred other explanations for my ignorance—I was a bad "daughter" who never tried hard enough; Kim was a bad "father," almost certainly (was I guessing or hoping?) a practitioner of fussy, florid, dated prose—all of which were related. All my explanations had to do with relatedness itself, with my confused Koreanness, and Richard Kim's. I consigned Richard Kim to my menagerie of family problems. Even up to accepting the invitation to provide this foreword, I continued to relegate Kim in this way. Like the journey abroad that will force one to visit the doddering aunt to whom one never writes, writing this foreword would force me to belatedly fulfill my obligation to Kim. And so it was the bad daughter who sat down to read, a dozen years late by her own estimation—but merely a reader who stood up some five hours later, in a state of most potent elation, all prejudgments of the book and its author dynamited to dust.

Richard E. Kim's *The Martyred* is no more "about" the Korean War than *Antigone* is "about" the civil war in Thebes. Such utilitarian preoccupation with subject matter as I was guilty of before reading *The Martyred*—it is "about" the Korean War, I must read it, it might contain some little fact about jeeps I don't already know—denigrates the work of art as surely as particular attention to the author's ethnicity denigrates the author. The work of art need not be "about" anything because it is "about" everything. In *The Martyred* Kim forges a drama of such devastating universality that an electri-

fying sense of recognition binds us to the page, and the universality of the novel is not merely a happy accident of its aesthetic
success. Clearly Kim meant this as a fundamental aspect of its
design. Though this is a novel of war, Kim steers clear of combat, limiting his settings almost entirely to interiors, and his
characters to men of letters, whether they be pastors, military
intelligence officers, or military propagandists. Though this is
a novel of the war in Korea, notorious for the seesawing chaos
of its lines, which lurched up and down the full length of the
peninsula with such frequency and rapidity that those in the
rear would find themselves abruptly ahead of the front, and
vice versa, Kim chooses the sustained (and it would turn out,
highly uncharacteristic) lull of the late fall of 1950, before
China entered the conflict. His characters, at their desks, on
their cots, are allowed to stay put. They stoke fires. They brew
tea. They attend briefings. And, hardly before we've seen it
coming, they embroil themselves, and us, in a conflict of principles so urgent and so impossible to solve, the very muscles of
our souls ache from the effort. Though this is a novel of Korea,
specifically of Pyongyang just before it is abandoned by the
United States and its allies to the Communist forces, Kim
blankets scene after scene beneath a slashing, stinging, blinding, numbing snowfall, with the result that every physical par-
ticularity, every distinguishing detail, is erased. The choice
earned him vitriol in Korea for being inaccurate—Pyongyang
received no snowfall in 1950—but these critics were missing
the point. *Of course this is Korea, and Koreans,* Kim is telling his readers, *and of course, whoever and wherever you are,
it's your society, and you.*

Throughout his life—which had begun in Japanese-occupied
Korea, and survived a civil war, before concluding in an ad-
opted homeland where he achieved prominence writing in his
third language—Kim implied to interviewers that he never felt
entirely at home. Perhaps the existential purity of *The Martyred* to some extent arises from this unease, from Kim's reluc-
tance, conscious or not, to author a novel "too" Korean, or
"too" soldierly. Yet I doubt it. Nowhere does this novel waver
with uncertainty. In Kim's prose not a word or phrase fails in

its task. At one point, near the end, I felt the walls of my throat growing thick with emotion, and tears flooding my eyes, but was so immersed in the stream of the story I could not pinpoint what had provoked my upsurge of emotion. I went back and reread:

> A cool breeze drifted toward the land from the darkening sea. The long shadow of a flagpole stretched up the sloping garden. The grass felt chilly against my palms.

It had been that cold grass, against the narrator's palms, that had moved me to tears! For it had been such a long, grueling winter, so full of death for both bodies and souls, that to feel a touch of life against the skin was almost overwhelming. This is a writer in perfect control of his craft, who can move us to tears by the touch of a grass blade. How humbling to reflect that *The Martyred* was Kim's first book. But how wonderful, as the erstwhile bad daughter, to find that here is no neglected grandpa at all, but a master, and masterpiece.

SUSAN CHOI

Introduction

1.

In 2000, when I contacted Richard Kim to include one of his stories in the anthology of Korean American literature I was coediting, he was feeling like an old Confucian man of letters. When I asked him if he was working on any new fiction, he told me that it was time for the younger generation, those with more energy and political enthusiasm, to write meaningful literature. He was disappointed at what literature had become in the twentieth century in America, and he felt resigned to taking a distant backseat to watch, to see whether this new generation could make literature the voice and the conscience of the people.

What he said to me struck deeply, and I took a much closer look at my own role as a writer—more specifically, as a Korean American writer caught in many of the same dynamics as Kim himself. My coeditor, Walter Lew, and I ended up selecting the story called "Is Someone Dying?" from Kim's loosely autobiographical collection, *Lost Names*. We chose it for its vividness, its honesty, and its historical realism as it depicts the period, toward the very last days of World War II, when the Japanese and Koreans both knew that Japan was losing. More important, we picked it for its unexpectedly sympathetic representation of the Japanese, a point of view entirely uncharacteristic of Korean writing, in which the Japanese are almost uniformly demonized as colonial oppressors. Kim's perspective was honest in a way that cut through consensus and convention into a difficult ethical and moral turf most writers fear to tread. Indeed,

Kim's whole career is characterized by this tendency, and that is why he is not only one of the central Korean American writers, but perhaps the most difficult and most ambitious.

For a few years before his death in 2009, Richard Kim enjoyed a new surge of popularity with the rerelease of *Lost Names*, which had originally been published in 1970. Although most of its new readers classified Kim with the growing number of famous Korean American writers like Chang-rae Lee (*Native Speaker*), Nora Okja Keller (*Comfort Woman*), and Susan Choi (*Foreign Student*), who were most visible at that time, Kim is of an entirely different, older generation. He was tolerant of the audience's ignorance of the history of Korean American letters, and he spoke to audiences of his own experiences and how they informed his writing, representing a deep and authentic connection to modern Korean history, culture, and language—something that most of the younger Korean American writers find difficult to do. Part of this was because his own life was directly affected by the tragedies and traumas of the Korean War era (after all, he had escaped from the North Koreans and served as a liaison officer at the U.S. 8th Army Headquarters); but more important, it was because he understood his role as a writer in distinctly Korean terms.

In the late seventies and early eighties I was searching for my own identity as a writer—a male writer, writing in English, whose formative years were spent in Korea speaking Korean and living in volatile times—and there were only two who could serve as direct role models: Younghill Kang and Richard Kim. Younghill Kang had died in 1972. His works include *The Grass Roof*—an autobiographical novel about his childhood in Korea that ends with his departure for America—and *East Goes West: The Making of an Oriental Yankee*, a complex novel that participates in the genre of the ethnic immigration novel while also simultaneously critiquing it. Kang's novels, published in the early 1930s, were not only the first Korean American literary works available to the American readership, they also added a new dimension to the immigrant narrative by refusing to play into the theme of the oppressed Oriental finding happiness in America. Kang's narratives, thinly veiled autobiography, were both candid and realistic in a way that was unusual for their time. Kang's interest in folklore was particularly meaningful for me because I had come from a family of storytellers and was studying anthropology. When I wrote my first novel, *Memories of My Ghost Brother*, which deals with my childhood and ends with a departure for the West, I placed myself in a literary lineage that began with Kang.

Even while I consciously explored Kang's themes, I was repeatedly drawn to Richard Kim's novels, which were more thematically challenging. Kim's central character in both of his novels is an army officer, a man who has left the academic life behind because he sees the military as the salvation of Korea. Kim's subject resonated with me deeply, partially because I took the opposite path and decided to become a writer and scholar after struggling with the difficult legacy of my own father's military service in Korea and Vietnam. Kim wrote of the complex dilemmas of the Korean War and the reconstruction era—periods close to my experience and those of my family. *The Martyred* and *The Innocent*—which seem especially timely today—explore military and civilian relationships and the legacy of hidden secrets, addressing profoundly important and dark moral, ethical, political, and philosophical issues. Ironically, Kim, unlike Kang, saved his childhood reminiscences for the end of his fiction-writing career, making the collection of fictionalized stories in *Lost Names* particularly poignant and nostalgic for those who know Korean history.

Together, Kang and Kim form the foundation of the Korean American literary tradition. All of the later writers, including the older writers like Gloria Hahn (who wrote under the pen name Kim Ronyoung) build on their legacy. Hahn, in *Clay Walls*, wrote of the immigrant experience during the Japanese colonial era, relying on the readers' knowledge of what would happen later in history. Chang-rae Lee's second novel, *A Gesture Life*, and Nora Keller's *Comfort Woman* also look at the period just before Korea's liberation from the Japanese, and Susan Choi's first novel, *The Foreign Student*, features a main character who leaves Korea shortly after the Korean War to become a student at a university in Tennessee. It was not until his fourth novel, *The Surrendered*, that Chang-rae Lee (whose father was born in North Korea) addressed Korean War themes directly. While Younghill Kang's works refer back to the cultural and aesthetic values of the old Korea traumatized in becoming modern, Richard Kim's works document that trauma from inside the political and military culture. It is Kim's novels that resonate with special relevance now, when American combat troops have just withdrawn from Iraq and we prepare to mark our tenth year in the war in Afghanistan.

2.

The Martyred, Kim's first novel, was originally published in 1964 by George Braziller, Inc. It spent fourteen weeks on the bestseller list and was nominated for a National Book Award. Only a couple of months after its publication, the March 20 issue of *Life* magazine featured a piece on Kim, noting: "Currently in its fourth printing, the book is selling 1,000 copies a day." Since his editor had expressed little hope that the book would sell, Kim was especially stunned by both its critical and commercial success.

A look at the bestselling books of 1964 provides a possible reason for the fabulous success of *The Martyred*, which made number seven on the fiction list. Among the other top ten fiction titles were John le Carré's *The Spy Who Came in from the Cold*, Leon Uris's *Armageddon* (a thriller about Berlin in the years following World War II), Irving Wallace's *The Man* (about the intrigue surrounding America's first black president), and Ian Fleming's *You Only Live Twice* (the James Bond novel set in Japan). Postwar politics and cold war intrigue were clearly in the air, but that holds largely true for many of the thrillers and espionage novels published even today. By odd coincidence, one of the other novels on that year's list was Louis Auchincloss's *The Rector of Justin*, which is a biographical novel about the headmaster of an Episcopalian boys' school in New England called Justin *Martyr* (emphasis mine). But a look at the nonfiction list shows why Kim's book was so resonant with the American psyche. The number one book on the top ten list was *Four Days*, which is about the death of JFK, whose assassination in November of the previous year had been an international trauma. Three others were devoted to JFK, and one—*Profiles in Courage: Memorial Edition*—was by JFK himself. Number nine on the list was *Reminiscences* by General Douglas Mac-Arthur, who had a decade earlier been in the constant limelight because of his controversial handling of the Korean War (he had been relieved of command by President Truman in 1951).

Perhaps it was this perfect storm of Kennedy's figurative martyrdom, the recollection of America's most recent troubled war, and the one in Vietnam just beginning to take center stage in the media that explains why American readers would find the novel deeply unsettling, cathartic, and oddly comforting—though few would explain it in those terms.

In June 1963, the Vietnamese Buddhist monk Thich Quang Duc had immolated himself in protest of the Diem regime, and the image of him dying in flames was still fresh in the American psyche when, only three weeks after the military coup that established a new government in South Vietnam, President Kennedy was shot in Dallas.

The conditions were ripe in the American consciousness for a book called *The Martyred*, one examining precisely the kinds of difficult issues Americans were living with, but one that looked at these issues from a safe distance in another country, in a previous war whose veterans were quietly hidden in the culture in a way that veterans of future wars could never again be hidden.

The Martyred won accolades from major writers and public figures, including Pearl S. Buck (whose novel about Korea, *The Living Reed*, had just been published the previous year), Philip Roth, and Edward Seidensticker, the noted translator of Japanese. *The Martyred* was published in more than fourteen other countries ranging from Japan to Burma, and it was eventually produced as a TV drama and a stage play (in 1964), a critically acclaimed film (directed by Yu Hyun-mok in 1965), and an opera in 1982 (composed by James Wade) that played to packed houses every night during its run at the National Theater in Seoul.

3.

The Martyred is set during 1950–51, the first year of the Korean War. Its quiet and elegant opening sentence is somewhat deceptive—the Korean War was one of the most volatile and fast-moving wars in modern history, its battle lines shifting so rapidly that units often found themselves lost behind enemy lines, and civilians were permanent refugees, fleeing from one part of the country to another, not knowing whether they would see UN or Communist forces around the next bend in the road. The war began at dawn one Sunday in June 1950. By September, the Communist North Koreans had driven all of the southern forces to the very tip of the peninsula in a tiny area called the Pusan Perimeter. The situation seemed entirely hopeless. But then, in what is considered one of the most brilliant military maneuvers in history, General Douglas MacArthur orchestrated an amphibious invasion of the coastal city of Incheon, cutting the North Korean supply lines and effectively destroying their army. Between September and October, the North Koreans were driven far north, beyond the 38th parallel, to the Manchurian border.

As the novel opens, winter is approaching in the city of Pyongyang, the capital of North Korea, and in the brief reprieve before the imminent Chinese assault (which will entirely turn the tide of the war by late November), South Korean military intelligence must investigate the execution of twelve Korean Christian ministers by the hands of the Communists.

The narrator of the novel, Captain Lee, is an up-and-coming officer in South Korea's military intelligence. He learns from his commanding officer, Colonel Chang, that the North Koreans had originally arrested fourteen ministers and that there are two survivors. Lee is to interview them, to learn the truth about the death of the ministers, and—through his implicit understanding of Colonel Chang's strange and conflicting directions—ultimately turn the story into useful propaganda. For Chang, the case would publicize North Korean atrocities and also serve to show that the South Korean military is newly sympathetic to Christians.

Lee's investigation is maddeningly difficult, and through the course of the novel he faces one profound problem after another. He sets out to pursue what he sees as a straightforward truth, only to be confounded by its intricate meanings in the context of a fundamentally corrupt war. As the story unfolds, Kim addresses the questions of truth and lies, good and evil, honor and duty, and loss of faith in one's god. Young Captain Lee must grapple with the conflict between his quest for the truth and the combined falsities of political utility and religious mythmaking.

To the contemporary American reader, conditioned by Hollywood films that resolve difficult moral and ethical conflicts conveniently through gunplay and large explosions, Kim's relentless pursuit of difficult themes may seem puzzling or foreign at first. But that is because the recurrence of themes in *The Martyred* is recursive—each time the questions are raised again in the fraught conversations among the key players and in the mind of Captain Lee, they arise with a new degree of complexity. In the end there is no easy resolution. What we see, instead, is a kind of moral, ethical, and spiritual relativity played out before our eyes. Each of the central characters believes himself to be doing the right thing in the face of profound moral dilemmas. Each is pushed into his decision, fully cognizant of the compromise he makes—and perhaps even of the apparent contradictions in his behavior. Kim permits the reader to empathize with each point of view, not allowing Captain Lee's role as narrator to privilege him as the moral compass.

Colonel Chang, Captain Lee's commander, is an old pro at manipulating facts to fit the needs of the military. (In the novel this is portrayed as a kind of explicit deception that we would characterize in these more jaded times as "spin.") Chang, though he has assigned Lee the task of investigating the ministers' murders, also guides the outcome, often rather heavy-handedly, but always several steps ahead of Lee, who is not permitted a view of the bigger picture. While he does not order Lee to lie himself, Chang's actions suggest he is leading by example through the habit he has of sending mixed messages that imply he wants a particular outcome. Lee finds Chang impossible to read, and even into the very end of the novel he continues to surprise.

Hann, one of the two surviving ministers, goes mad with the trauma of witnessing the executions; in his frail physical and psychological state, he harbors some dark secret that the other survivor, Shin, knows but will not reveal. The theme of lost faith is central to *The Martyred*, and as Lee pursues Shin to learn the truth, the plot is made more complex by the presence of two other characters: Koh, a chaplain who has abandoned his congregation to serve the military, and Lieutenant Park, Captain Lee's best friend, whose father was the leader of the twelve slain ministers. Koh initially arouses Lee's (and our) suspicions, and Park appears at first to be resolute in his estrangement from his father and in his rejection of his father's faith. Both of these characters will lead us deeper into a world full of apparent contradictions.

But the most complex character, by far, is Minister Shin, who is hailed as a hero by the local Christians. He is a brooding, dark, and tortured presence who at first lies and says that he was not witness to the executions, claiming divine intervention. But he is like Dostoevsky's Raskolnikov of *Crime and Punishment*, and he cannot keep himself from speaking to Captain Lee, the very man from whom he wants to conceal the details of his guilt. Shin's behavior is so profoundly enigmatic that Lee cannot understand it, but in a series of charged conversations he begins to infer what Shin is trying to convey. Shin knows that it is faith, not reason, that the people need. In that sense, he ironically inverts Marx's critique of religion: "Religion is the sigh of the oppressed creature, the heart of a heartless world, and the soul of soulless conditions. It is the opium of the people." Shin gives the masses precisely the opiate they need and crave in their time of despair, even when he himself no longer believes. Jacqueline Reditt's piece on Kim for the *Christian Science Monitor* in July 1982 ran under a headline that encapsulated the theme of *The Martyred*: "Korean-American Opera: Using Deception to Fight Despair." Ultimately, it is Shin's existential crisis upon which that theme is built. He is the figure that permits Kim to dramatize the elaborate and ironic intersections of religion and politics, how the parallel interests of church and state can operate simultaneously for the benefit of the people and at the people's expense.

Toward the end of the novel, the South Korean army, in cooperation with the American military, abandons the civilians of Pyongyang just as they had abandoned Seoul at the outset of the war. Pyongyang had been spared bombardment earlier in the war for its cultural and historical importance (much as the cities of Kyoto and Prague were spared bombing during World War II). Though the novel does not describe it, Kim's readers in the late sixties would remember that Pyongyang, captured by MacArthur's forces in mid-October 1950, would suffer the most devastating destruction of the war: bombed by 1,400 aircraft until the entire city was flattened, leaving nothing but a moonscape with a few husks of buildings punctuated by thousands of mysteriously standing chimneys.

Though we experience the story through Captain Lee's eyes, thereby identifying with him and understanding the demands of his role as a junior officer in the South Korean army, Lee himself does not escape moral complicity in the end because he has remained silent while witnessing deception layered upon deception. One would expect *The Martyred* to end with a note of tragic bitterness and pessimism given the story line, and yet Lee's feeling at the end is "a wondrous lightness of heart," a mood that seems entirely antithetical to his experience. How can that be?

4.

The key to understanding *The Martyred* is offered cryptically by Kim himself. He dedicates *The Martyred* to Albert Camus, whose work, he says, helped him overcome "the nihilism of the trenches and bunkers of Korea." Kim also begins *The Martyred* with an epigraph—lines from Hölderlin's *The Death of Empedocles*, which Camus himself quoted in *The Rebel*— whose essence is "I pledged my heart to the grave and suffering land, and . . . promised . . . never to despise a single one of her enigmas."

Kim drew upon Camus carefully, and he refers both explicitly and implicitly to a range of Camus' works, creating an unexpectedly rich parallelism—not just in alluding to Camus as subtext, but in illustrating a kind of deeper, synchronistic resonance he felt for Camus. For instance, Kim's characters are what Camus would term men of "balance" (*messure*), who know their limitations as men. Kim's world in *The Martyred* (and in *The Innocent*, which also features Lee as the narrator) could be characterized as one that illustrates the godless indifference of the universe—the nihilism attributed to Camus' early work. And yet, like Camus, Kim is able to move beyond nihilism by embracing and transcending the many enigmas portrayed in *The Martyred*.

Kim also identified with Camus because they were both displaced individuals. In the way that Camus always considered himself a French Algerian, Kim saw himself not as a Korean or an American, but as a Korean American, an interstitial person living in a kind of permanent "exile."

In May 1982, when Kim was in Korea as a Fulbright professor, he said to the *New York Times*, "I think I had a psychological problem living in the States and writing in English about Korean characters and settings. . . . I had the problem of writing in two cultures, being neither here nor there. I always had a kind of exile problem; now I finally have peace of mind, and I've been very productive." Later, discussing his book *Lost Names*, he said, "'Lost Souls' . . . was at one point my working title. I like 'lost' because it has a lot to do with my sense of my generation. . . . Kind of like I am now. I don't belong. Born in Korea, moved to Manchuria, back to the North, then to South Korea. Didn't belong in either place. Then to the military, where I didn't belong. . . . For a while I thought about it, then I gave up. . . . I'm lost, lost between two cultures, two worlds, neither North nor South Korea, not Korean or American. I felt that way always, even as a little kid."

Camus was likewise forever an "exile," born in French Algeria, writing in a divided France during the Vichy period of

World War II, and always longing for his Algerian home and its "Mediterranean" qualities even while he was one of France's most distinguished intellectuals. In support of the French Resistance in 1944, Camus wrote anonymously in the opening editorial of the first Parisian issue of the journal *Combat*:

> Nothing is given to man, and the little which is his to conquer is paid for by unjust deaths. But that isn't where his greatness lies. It lies in his decision to be stronger than his condition. And if his condition is unjust, he has only one means to rise above it, and that is for he himself to be just.*

The passage is uncannily resonant with the themes of *The Martyred*—it could well have been the voice of the narrator, Captain Lee.

Kim's work is among the finest literary explorations of Camus' often misunderstood idea of the absurd, which is the "enigma" central to Camus' philosophy and integral to *The Martyred*. Philosophically, the absurd has little to do with its common English usage, which is a dismissive way of suggesting a lack of coherence or meaning. Camus' absurd refers to the modern condition characterized by an uncomfortable (and perhaps irresolvable) sense of contradictions. For Camus there is no cosmic order created by a god—nor is there a necessity for such order. It is by beginning to comprehend the inherent absurdity of the human condition that we begin to understand that the progression from life to death (with nothing beyond) is all predicated on the disjunction between the inherent human desire for clarity (and meaning) and the fundamental meaninglessness of the universe. This seems to be a clear recipe for nihilism on the face of it, but in Camus' and Kim's work, one sees the dramatic illustration of how the absurd—which for Camus is the beginning of the existential question—results in an unexpected and transcendent understanding of the human condition. Captain Lee, in the face

* Translated by David Zane Mairowitz in *Introducing Camus* (New York: Totem Books, 1994), p. 90.

of the most profound suffering, injustice, and enigma, perse-
veres with his integrity intact. Even in a condition that appears
to be morally ambiguous, he remains a fundamentally just
individual.

5.

Richard E. Kim (Kim Eun Kook) was born in Hamhung, the
second largest city in North Korea, in 1932. He grew up in an
intensely Christian family in what he recalled as a "Chekho-
vian life—landowners with an apple orchard called 'New Life'
Orchard." His father was imprisoned by the Japanese during
the colonial period for being a local leader in the nationalist
movement; in 1945, his father was imprisoned again, this time
by the Communists for counterrevolutionary activities. His
grandfather was a Presbyterian minister, one of the many who
were shot by the Communists for refusing to abandon their
churches. Kim's family eventually escaped to South Korea, but
only after a grueling two and a half years.

Kim enrolled at Seoul National University, but he had not yet
begun his studies when the war began. The Sunday morning in
June 1950, when the North Korean army marched unopposed
into Seoul, he was still asleep; he woke up to find that troops
had already occupied the city. Like many of the men who were
left behind by the South Korean retreat, he was picked up and
conscripted into the Communist army, but he was able to escape from the holding area. He hid out for a time in the hills to
the east, where he witnessed the historic amphibious invasion
of Incheon by UN forces that year in September.

Later, like Lee, the narrator of The Martyred, Kim joined
the South Korean army and served as a liaison officer at U.S.
8th Army Headquarters in Seoul. He was aide-de-camp to the
undersecretary of defense and to the commanding general
of the U.S. 7th Division, Arthur Trudeau. Kim claimed that
he learned English by watching American films that were
screened at the mess hall, and although he was not primarily
an interpreter, he was sometimes called on to do translations.

After the end of the war, in 1954, he was able to immigrate to the United States and enroll at Middlebury College through the help of Charlotte Meinecke, the dean of Colby Junior College, who served as a consultant to the Korean Ministry of Education.

At Middlebury, Kim received a B in freshman composition; he never completed his bachelor's degree because he did not take a required science course, but he studied history and political science. He went on to get an MA in writing at Johns Hopkins University, during which time he decided that he would become a novelist. With the help of the poet Paul Engle, he got a fellowship to the MFA program at the Iowa Writers' Workshop, which is where he wrote most of *The Martyred*. Later, he studied Far Eastern languages and literature at Harvard and would go on to teach at the University of Massachusetts at Amherst, and at Syracuse University.

From 1981–83, Kim was also a Fulbright professor at Seoul National University (where his studies had been interrupted by the Korean War). He earned many awards throughout his life, including fellowships from the Ford Foundation, the Guggenheim Foundation, and the National Endowment for the Arts. In addition to fiction, he wrote essays, journalism, and narration for documentaries. He also founded a literary agency to represent American authors in Korea and was instrumental in getting Korean publishers to honor international copyrights.

After the great international success of *The Martyred*, Kim continued Captain Lee's story with *The Innocent*, which can also be read on its own. *The Innocent* did not fare as well as *The Martyred*—the critical response was a total about-face that seems, at first, quite baffling. But the social and political climate in America had changed quite radically in the four short years between the two books. The Kennedy assassination, followed by the intense media coverage of the Vietnam War, made it difficult, if not impossible, for critics to appreciate a novel that dramatized a coup d'état in which Americans were complicit behind the scenes. *The Innocent* was read with the horrific images of the 1968 Tet Offensive still fresh in the

American mind, and though the novel was about Korea, its reference to the horrors of war and postwar political machinations did not sit well with readers—the themes were simply too close to the reality of the American involvement in Vietnam. In Korea, *The Innocent* was met with stern criticism by the *mundan* (the South Korean community of intellectual literary critics), but for a different reason. They took it to be a sympathetic fictionalized portrayal of Park Chung-hee, who had come to power through a similar coup d'état and remained a de facto military dictator until he was assassinated in October 1979.

Lost Names, a collection of loosely autobiographical stories from Kim's childhood, received a much warmer response from reviewers when it was published in 1970. Among Kim's vocal supporters was Pearl S. Buck, who said, "I think it is his best book. . . . If this young man continues to do as well as this, he will someday be worthy of the Nobel Prize for Literature." Many critics saw the publication of *Lost Names* as restoring Kim's reputation. When it was reissued by the University of California Press in 1998, he was invited to speak at a summer institute sponsored by the Five College Center for East Asian Studies.

Kim had always been circumspect about whether his works were autobiographical and was often critical of readers who assumed they were. But in the interview he gave in the summer of 1998 to Kathleen Woods Masalski at Smith College, he touched on how complex that issue actually was for him:

> Everything in the book actually happened. It happened to me. So why am I always insisting it's not autobiographical? I think because of the way I used the things that actually happened. You have to arrange them, mix them up. Above all, it's interpretation of facts, of actual events—some thirty or forty years later. . . . I like to separate the actual events from the emotional, the psychological. One shouldn't confuse the actual events with the inner events. . . . A lot [of readers] think everything is exactly as it happened; but we put our own interpretation on

events. I didn't invent any actual events. . . . but everything else is fiction. That is very important to me.

The stories were read primarily as memoirs—perhaps not exactly in the way Kim had originally intended, but with an understanding of how they were linked to the truth of experience. It was deeply meaningful for Kim to see them appreciated by readers a half century after the experiences he described.

Now, with the release of *The Martyred* as a Penguin Classic, the poignant irony in Kim's work and career seems more profound than ever. In 1982, while he was in Korea, he said to the *Christian Science Monitor,* "My feelings here are very intense. I think of my generation during the war, I look at the young people here today—I hope . . . they won't repeat history." He was speaking about the Koreans who were attending the opera of *The Martyred,* whose themes are once again most timely here in America thirty years later.

We have had our own fabricated martyrs in recent years, associated with troubled wars, and Americans are more skeptical than ever of political administrations, which we now know to willfully deceive their people. History does repeat itself, but perhaps by illustrating that fact while hoping for the opposite, while at the same time ironically being part of the very process of repetition, writers like Richard Kim can ameliorate, if not interrupt, that unrelenting cycle.

HEINZ INSU FENKL

Suggestions for Further Reading

FICTION

Lost Names: Scenes from a Korean Boyhood (New York: Praeger, 1970; Berkeley: University of California Press, 1998).
The Innocent (Boston: Houghton Mifflin, 1968).

NONFICTION

"Notes from the Underground," *Koreana Quarterly*, vol. 12, no. 3 (1970), pp. 24–27.

The Martyred

1

The war came early one morning in June of 1950, and by the time the North Koreans occupied our capital city, Seoul, we had already left our university, where we were instructors in the History of Human Civilization. I joined the Korean Army, and Park volunteered for the Marine Corps—the proud combat outfit that suited his temperament. In a short time—because junior officers died very fast in the early phase of the war—we were trained and battle-tested, and we both became officers. We survived, but we were both wounded. The shrapnel of a mortar shell had grazed my right knee during the defense of Taegu, and a sniper had shot Park in his left arm in the mopping-up operation in Seoul after the Inchon landing. We both spent some time in the hospital, were both promised medals, and were returned promptly to our respective duties.

Park, who was then a first lieutenant, went back to combat duty somewhere on the eastern front, but I did not rejoin my antitank company. Someone in the Army accidentally discovered that I had been a university instructor and decided to transfer me to an intelligence unit. When I came out of the hospital in Pusan, I was sent to Seoul, where I was put in charge of a section in the Army Political Intelligence, and was made captain, temporarily, in due conformity with the table of organization.

In the second week of October, the United Nations Forces captured Pyongyang, the capital city of the North Koreans. We moved our headquarters to that city and established ourselves in a four-storied gray marble building. My office, which was on the third floor, looked across the street at what re-

mained of the Central Presbyterian Church. This was a strange
coincidence. It was Park's father's church; he had been its minister for nearly twenty years.

I knew very little about him; although Park was a close friend
of mine, he had seldom talked to me about his father. Which
was to be expected. His father had disowned him and, in turn,
Park had denounced his father. Mr. Park was, according to his
disowned son, "a man of fanatical faith," who had "harassed"
him "day and night with his self-righteousness, with his exaggerated faith, and his obsession with his equally obsessive
God." On the other hand, Park had become an atheist after his
return from a university in Tokyo, and abandoned the Christian faith in which he had been brought up. I suspected that he
would not have denounced his father had not Mr. Park told his
congregation, one Sunday morning from his pulpit, that his
son had gone over to the Devil and that he had asked the Lord
His forgiveness for severing all earthly ties with his son. That
was about ten years before the war.

Park was aware that his father was missing from Pyongyang; I had informed him of the disturbing news soon after I
moved to the city, and I had done so in an unsettled frame of
mind. I had come to Pyongyang in a good mood; for the first
few weeks I was in a state of buoyancy, partly because of the
exciting novelty of finding myself in an enemy city that our
victorious army occupied, and partly because of the irresist-
ible enthusiasm and affection with which the people of the city
greeted all of us, their liberators. Many of my fellow officers
were natives of Pyongyang and, in the midst of that delightful
emotional chaos following the liberation, they were able to
stage melodramatic yet heartwarming scenes of reunion with
their families, relatives, and friends, or for that matter, with
anyone whose face they recognized.

I had no acquaintances in the city, and sometimes I felt
vaguely envious of these officers. It was at such times that I
felt an urge to go to see Park's father, though I told myself I had
not the slightest excuse for doing so. I thought of many reason-
able ways in which I might call on him, yet when I imagined my-

self actually knocking on the door of his home and introducing myself as a good friend of his son's, I could not help feeling a peculiar sort of fright. Then I found out that the Communist secret police had arrested him shortly before the war; and when Army Intelligence let it be known officially that "an unspecified number of North Korean Christian ministers" was reported missing and that the Army "believed them to have been kid-napped by the Reds," I even felt relieved—shamefacedly, of course. So I wrote to Park about it at great length, but his reply contained nothing but irrelevant matters—just as I expected—things about his command, about his men, and even about his future plans, but not a word about his father.

Across the street the church bell clanged. I opened the window. From the white-blue November sky of North Korea, a cold gust swept down the debris-ridden slope, whipping up here and there dazzling snow flurries, smashing against the ugly, bullet-riddled buildings of Pyongyang. People who had been digging in the ruins of their homes stopped working. They straightened up and looked toward the top of the slope, at the remains of the nearly demolished Central Church, and then at the gray carcass of a cross-topped bell tower where the bell was clanging. They gazed at one another as though they un-derstood the esoteric message of the bell. Some old women knelt down on the ground, and the old men removed their dogskin hats and bowed their bare heads.

The bell was quiet now. The people were back at their labor, working as silently and stubbornly as they had day after day. Ever since I arrived in the city, I had been watching these people. Occasionally, I saw them drag out of the debris some shapeless remains of their household goods or, sometimes, a dead body, which they would quietly carry away on a hand-pushed cart. Then they would continue digging in the crumbled mess of brick, boards, and chunks of concrete.

I closed the window and returned to my desk. The potbel-lied, rusty coal stove in the far corner of the room gave off plenty of heat, but I shivered as I settled down in my chair. It was as if a cold hand had stroked my nape as stealthily as the tip of a soft, soft brush.

Park's father was dead; I had just learned of his death from my commanding officer.

2

Colonel Chang, the Chief of Army Political Intelligence, had summoned me to his office on the fourth floor. Seated in his swivel chair behind his desk under a dusty chandelier, he did not show any sign of recognition when I stood before him. His subordinates were accustomed to the way he kept them waiting in his presence, sometimes for as long as five minutes. He was a stout man in his late forties, with a head as bald and shiny as a Buddhist monk's, and with a bulbous nose that dominated his straw-colored small face. He began rocking back and forth in his chair, and peered at me through his glasses.

The junior officers at headquarters were not inclined to take Colonel Chang too seriously, though they admitted he was a baffling character. Since it was standard procedure in an intelligence unit not to keep in the personnel file the record of its commanding officer, his past was obscure. Those who despised him said he had been a sergeant in the Japanese Army during the war in the Pacific; those who disliked him said he had been a notorious soldier of fortune in China; and those who did not care one way or the other said he was just one of those professional military men. No one seemed to know precisely how he happened to be enjoying the rank of a full colonel in such a young army as ours, though everyone assumed he was longing for a star.

At last he motioned me to take a seat and, bringing his swaying chair to a stop, said gravely, "I want you to start an investigation of the missing ministers."

"I beg your pardon, sir?" I said, to cover my surprise.

His thin lips curled. "You recall those Christian ministers

who were reported missing. We've had a big break. Our CIC was able to round up a few Reds who had something to do with the missing men." He rummaged through the clutter of papers on his desk. "They were all shot the day the war started."

"A mass execution!"

Casting me an indignant look, he said, raising his voice, "I call it mass murder."

"Yes, sir."

"Now, there's a problem. The findings of the CIC are conflicting. We are not so sure about the exact number murdered."

"Then they didn't shoot all of them."

"No, no, I am not saying that. However, one source of information claims there were fourteen, the other says twelve. Unfortunately, both sources of information are no longer available. We seem to have an impetuous CIC."

"You mean the prisoners were killed?"

Colonel Chang ignored my concern. "Now if we are to assume there were fourteen ministers and all of them were shot, and if we can't round up any other sources of information, well then, it means there are no witnesses. All we can say is that fourteen were murdered."

"But, if I may say so, sir," I said, "we can't say they were murdered, or how many. We can only say that an undetermined number of ministers disappeared."

"I am glad you said that, Captain. I knew you would come around to it, and that's why I want you to work on the problem. The Chief of Army Intelligence just called to tell me that it belongs in the area of political intelligence, and I can hardly disagree with him."

"You are suggesting that it may be good material for propaganda," I said. "A grave case of religious persecution by the Communists. Of international significance, if I may add, sir, particularly in America. In short, we may be able to exhibit to the entire world the Korean chapter in the history of Christian martyrdom."

"All right, all right. I am not suggesting anything," Colonel Chang said impatiently. "Now, let me return to the problem. It's a simple matter of arithmetic. If we assume there were

originally fourteen ministers, and if we take into account the
claim that only twelve were shot, then it is possible two have
survived, is it not?"

"Of course."

"As you know, it is impossible for us, at this early stage, to
check every single living Christian minister in North Korea.
But the curious thing is that there are two in Pyongyang, right
this minute, who were imprisoned by the Reds. Actually they
were still in prison when we took the city. It is an interesting
coincidence, don't you think, however hypothetical it may be?"

Something in his manner—perhaps it was the sudden, quick
gleam in his eyes, or the way he tilted his bald head—impressed
me that he knew more about the two ministers than he was
willing to tell me.

"Well, what do you think of this possibility?" he asked.

"Hypothetical, as you say, sir," I replied.

He was pleased with my response. "Good. Now, I want you
to go and see these ministers, Shin and Hann, and tell them
about our problem. Be tactful about it, because I don't want to
create the impression that I am handling Christians roughly.
Christians in this country are quite influential these days," he
said with a faint smile. Then, after a pause, he continued with
an undisguised tone of acidity. "Everyone seems to be Christian nowadays; it seems fashionable to be one. From the President to cabinet ministers, generals, colonels, all the way down
to privates. Why, even the Army has to have Christian chaplains, just to please the American advisors. Ah, well, you can
see my difficult position."

"Yes, sir."

"I am not suggesting that these men had anything to do
with the murder, or that they were originally included in the
murder plan. Also, I have no intention whatsoever of implying
that I am suspicious of the circumstances relating to their fortunate survival, although it may be highly desirable for me to
be so; that is, from the point of view of an objective intelligence analysis. Their fortunate survival, Captain Lee, please
note my word. Anyway, officially speaking, I am merely asking you to see them and inquire, yes, inquire politely, if they

would be kind enough to enlighten us concerning the exact number involved in this mass murder; that is, if they know anything about it at all, you understand?"

I felt confused, but I said, "Yes, I fully understand."

He seemed delighted. "Good. That's what I like about you. Civilians seem to have a keener sensibility in affairs of extreme delicacy," he said, smiling. "Oh, incidentally, one of them, Hann, I believe, is presumably crazy."

"You mean—he is not well?"

The colonel darted a sardonic glance at me. "Forgive my indelicacy, Captain Lee," he said. Then he stood up, grabbed a pad of paper from the desk, and strode over to the window. "That is all," he fairly shouted.

The church bell clanged.

Colonel Chang swore. "I can't stand that bell! Clanking, clanking day and night! Intolerable!"

"Sir," I said, "the minister of that church . . ."

He cut me short. "He's dead."

3

I was waiting for my driver to bring the jeep to the sentry box outside headquarters. Whenever a whistling gust whipped past the box, spraying a silvery mist of pulverized snow, I could hear the bell clanging, clanging over the slope, and I could visualize Colonel Chang banging on his desk, swearing as he glared out of the window. I asked the sentry to tell my driver to wait for me, and walked toward the church.

There had been an alley off the street between houses and shops leading up the slope to the church. Nothing was left standing now. Houses had been smashed to bits in the bombardment, and their ruins buried the alley; a wooden board that said CAMERAS, soiled and cracked, hung lopsided from the remains of a shattered shop. A trolley car crawled along the street, clanking, flashing cold, blue sparks. An Army jeep drove past, its loudspeaker blaring out an unintelligible message. Loose wires were lashing at a prostrated lamppost.

In the rubble, people were still digging, and when I started up the slope, a few of them stopped working and looked at me. An old man followed me, keeping several paces behind, but when I came close to the front of the church, he came abreast of me. We exchanged perfunctory bows. He wore a black coat, but he had no gloves, and he rubbed his hands together, blinking in the sun and in the wind that ruffled his white hair.

The Central Church was rather small and was built of red bricks. A flight of stone steps led up to two dirty marble columns, above which was the bell tower, with a golden cross on its top. The exterior of the tower was torn open and the black iron bell could be seen hanging precariously inside, its rope swaying loosely in the wind. Beyond the columns, two white doors, now dusty and broken, stood wide open, one of them wobbling on its loose hinges as though it would collapse at any moment. Through the open doors the interior of the church was dimly visible. Either a bomb or an artillery shell had blasted the middle section; the pews had been tossed about, twisted and smashed, though the altar had been left intact.

A shrieking wind swirled about us for a moment. The bell clanged. I looked up at the tower and saw the rope violently jerking, to and fro, up and down. I turned to the old man, who shrugged his shoulders.

"What's the matter with the bell?" I asked him.

"The bell?" he muttered, squinting his blinking eyes.

"Don't you have anyone to take care of it?"

"Why, I don't see anything wrong with the bell, do you?" he said, rubbing his eyes. "Nobody touches it. The wind comes and rings the bell."

"Why don't you church people do something about it?"

"You can't get up there. The stairway is almost gone, and it's too dangerous to use a ladder. The tower may crumble at any moment."

"But I still think you ought to do something about it."

"We're waiting," the old man mumbled. "We're all waiting for our minister to come back to us. Any day now, because we're winning the war, they say. When he comes back, maybe he can do something about the church"—slowly he focused his bleary eyes on mine—"and maybe he can do something about the bell, too. Who knows?"

"You know what happened to him, don't you?" I said.

"No, we don't," he said. "Yes, we do, but we aren't sure, nobody is sure, what's happened to him. He was taken away by the Communists some time before the war broke out, and that's the last thing we've seen of him. 'Don't worry,' we tell each other, 'he will come back.' Any day now. Yes, any day now. He will come back."

I hastily echoed his sentiments. "Yes, any day now."

I moved a few steps closer to the threshold of the devastated church. It was then that I saw someone inside. Though the pews were strewn about and the debris from the broken roof was piled over them, the rear white wall with its small, shattered stained-glass window was still there beyond the altar. The left balcony had fallen halfway down, and was hanging loosely, almost touching the front edge of the altar. It was there, directly beneath the twisted balcony, that I saw the prostrate gray figure of a man, with his bare hands stretched out over his head, clutching at the edge of the barren altar. I looked at the old man beside me, but he only shrugged his shoulders and pointed a finger to his shaking head. "A madman," he whispered. "I don't know who he is."

"Well, you'd better tell him, I mean tell someone to stop him from getting in there. He may kill himself."

"He comes around here once in a while," the old man said. "I talked to him once. He just stared at me—you know the way they look at you—almost frightened me. You know what he said? 'I come here to pray.' That's what he said. Well, he didn't sound like a madman to me. So I let him do whatever he pleased."

Then, suddenly, the man came out of the church, saw us standing there, and leaped back inside, turning to peer at us suspiciously through the doorway. I stepped forward. The old man grabbed my arm, whispering, "No, no." But I could not restrain myself from shouting, "Listen! You'd better come out of there. It's dangerous. You may kill yourself there!"

To my astonishment, he cried, "Go away!" There was a pause and he said, "Go away!" once more and disappeared.

I might have dashed into the church after him, had not my companion held onto my arm, begging me to leave him alone. Then I heard the man laughing, and I was . . . yes . . . dumbfounded when his laughter was followed, a moment later, by a wail like that of a hungry, abandoned baby, a piercing cry that mingled with the clanging of the bell. I told the old man to inform the proper authority, though I had not the vaguest notion as to who the proper authority might be. He paid me no mind, and when I left he was on his knees in the dirty snow.

I hurried across the street back to the sentry box, dismissed my driver, and drove off.

4

The solitary house stood at the top of a hill that commanded a wintry view of the city of Pyongyang and the Taedong River. I drove up the winding road that ended halfway up the hill, parked the jeep and walked the rest of the way. A gravel path, almost hidden in the snow, led to the front of the two-storied gray house through shrubs, stubby, crooked pine trees, and a dilapidated garden cluttered with piles of dirty snow. A small balcony with iron rails was supported by two short pillars of gray stone.

I knocked on the white front door, which was finally opened by an old woman, who let me into a dim hallway. She peered at me warily, wiping her chapped hands with her apron. She told me that Mr. Shin was not at home for he usually spent his day at his church downtown, that he was busy, very busy, and that I could leave my message with her. She was blocking my way, as it were, firmly planting herself in front of me in the hushed hallway.

I asked her, then, if I could see Mr. Hann. "How did you know he is here?" she said, surprised, and even frightened, I thought.

"Are you from the police?"

I told her I was not, that I was an army officer. But why did she ask me if I was from the police? She ignored my question.

"Anyway, he isn't feeling well. I ought to know," she said. "I am his nurse."

So I ventured to ask her if she minded my paying my respects to him.

She gasped in protest.

"I promise you that I shan't take too much time," I said.

"Well, he isn't home either," came the prompt reply.

"But you told me he is ill."

"He isn't a sick man. He can go out for a walk, can't he?" she said as though she were pleading.

I looked at her closely, but her eyes did not meet mine. I decided to leave. I told her I hoped I might have the pleasure of meeting the ministers some other day. She gave me an appreciative glance and asked me who I was. Would I care to leave any message? When I said no, she seemed relieved and asked me where I was from. Was I a Christian? I said I was not, but I had gone, when I was small, to the Sunday school of a neighborhood church in Seoul. I told her that I was sorry I had disturbed her, and I turned to go away. But as I touched the cold brass doorknob, I found myself impulsively swinging around, facing her. "What would you say if I told you I saw Mr. Hann this morning at the Central Church?"

"No!" she said. "Not there!"

"Yes!" I was about to tell her what I had seen when I heard someone on the stairway. I collected myself and looked up.

A man garbed in a black robe stopped halfway down the stairs, waiting for the nurse to withdraw, his dark eyes looking down at me. Then he came straight to me.

"Mr. Shin?" I said.

"Yes. Forgive me. I could not help overhearing. You wanted to see me?"

I took off my helmet and introduced myself.

As soon as we were seated in a bare, dusty room—there was no furniture other than a few brown wooden chairs, nor any sign of heat—he said quietly, "You say you have seen Mr. Hann?"

"Do you think I might have seen him?" I said, feeling ill at ease.

"It is possible." Mr. Shin drew his garment tightly around him. His Adam's apple twitched as he adjusted his long neck to the robe. There was a hollow look in his unshaven face, and his large, feverish eyes gazed steadily into mine. "Yes, it is possible."

He coughed—a dry, racking cough that convulsed his thin

frame. "I have been worried about him," he said. "He went out last night and hasn't come home yet. This is the first time he has stayed out so long."

"Didn't you look for him?"

"We couldn't go out last night. There is a curfew, as you know. Unfortunately, I am ordered to be in bed by my doctor, and I couldn't send the nurse out for fear she might lose her way. So I have been waiting for the janitor of my church, who comes here once a day, but he hasn't come yet. I am only hoping that Mr. Hann hasn't troubled the authorities and that he will come home any minute."

"The nurse told me he is ill," I said. "Is he seriously ill?"

Mr. Shin did not reply.

"Is there anything I can do?" I did not know why I said it.

"Why should you care for us?" he asked, frowning slightly. "We hardly know you."

"Why should you be surprised?"

"Aren't you here to . . . how shall I put it . . . to interrogate me?"

I did not like the tone with which he deliberately stressed the word, interrogate. "No," I said.

"But you are from Intelligence."

"Yes, but I am not an interrogator."

"Sorry. I did not mean to offend you," he muttered, stirring in his chair. "What do you know about me?"

"Not very much and that only superficially."

His pale lips formed a semblance of a smile. "Well?"

"You are forty-seven years old, and Mr. Hann, twenty-eight. You were both arrested by the Communist secret police on June eighteenth, seven days before the war started; and on the same day, other Christian ministers were also arrested." I told him what I had been briefed on by CIC. "You were about to be shot when our Infantry arrived, and you were set free from prison."

"Are you a professional intelligence man?" he asked. "If so, I don't mind telling you that I disdain your profession."

I told him about my academic career, to which I would return as soon as the war was over.

"You interest me," he said. "But I suppose you want to find out something from me, whatever it may be?" He crossed his arms over his chest, hunching his shoulders as he coughed.

"We are concerned about the other ministers," I said. "I assume you know they were kidnapped by the Communists." I paused and studied his face, which remained expressionless. "I can tell you that the Army knows that much. There is no evidence about the kidnapping, even about the fact—well, we established it as the fact—that they were arrested. We would like to know why they were arrested in the first place."

"Need there be any special reason for the Communists to arrest Christians?"

"Were you with them?"

"I beg your pardon?"

"When you were arrested you were all together, weren't you?" I suggested boldly. "As a group?"

"Yes," came the unhesitant reply, to my surprise.

"Then you must know what happened to the others."

"No, I don't."

"But you were with them."

"Yes. You want to know why we were separated." He looked up at the white, cracked ceiling, from which dangled a naked light bulb, then back at me again. "That I wouldn't know."

"We know that you and Mr. Hann were moved to the prison on June twenty-fifth, the day the Communists invaded the South," I said. "Why did they move just the two of you?"

"You *are* interrogating me, aren't you?"

"No. I am merely interested to know what has happened to the other ministers."

"Why through me?" he said wearily. "You know that we were separated. Then how do you expect me to tell you anything about them?"

"I thought perhaps you might be able to tell us something about their fate."

"Don't you know enough about it already?" he said, looking at me sternly.

"Kidnapped?"

"That's right."

"Do you believe it?" I raised my voice. "That they were really kidnapped and that they may be alive somewhere?"

"Do you?" he said.

"No," I confessed. "No, I don't."

"Neither do I."

"Then you believe they were executed?"

"Yes."

"When?"

"I don't know."

"How many ministers?"

"There were fourteen of us."

"Then two survived?"

"And I suppose you want to know why we two were not shot?"

I waited for his reply; but I was hardly prepared for what he declared a moment later:

"It was through divine intervention."

I remained silent.

"You don't believe in God, do you?" he said, and lowered his eyes.

"No."

"Then call it luck," he said resignedly.

Mr. Shin asked me if I had driven to the house, and if so, would I mind giving him a ride into the city. "Would you be kind enough to take me to the Central Church? I don't want to impose on you, but I would appreciate it."

He left me to get his coat, and came back wearing a black overcoat and carrying a gray one on his arm. We walked silently down the hill to my jeep, and drove into the city.

It was almost dusk when we reached the church. The curfew was near and the streets were deserted except for a few uniformed passers-by. A jeep prowled by, its loudspeaker reminding people of the curfew and of the nightly blackout.

Mr. Shin did not want me to come with him inside the church, and without a moment's hesitation he disappeared through the dim, gaping mouth of the open doorway into the dark interior.

In a little while he came out with the man I had seen that

morning, who was now wearing the gray overcoat. When they came down the steps, at the bottom of which I was standing, the man saw me and stopped. Mr. Shin said to him gently, "It is all right. He is our friend. Would you like to meet him? Why, of course," and he turned to me, his face serene. "Captain Lee, I would like you to meet Mr. Hann."

The young minister looked at me blankly, with a faint smile on his emaciated face.

I do not know what it was about him that pierced my heart, but suddenly I felt again the same rage I had experienced earlier in the war. A few miles south of Pyongyang we had discovered a cave on a mountainside. Several hundred political prisoners had been forced into the cave by the retreating Communists, who then machine-gunned the prisoners and sealed the mouth of the cave by dynamiting it. I was in charge of a detachment to dig open the cave. For hours we dug; spectators were gathering— farmers from a nearby village—photographers, Korean and foreign—radio announcers, clutching their microphones. At last we made an opening barely large enough for me to squeeze through into the black mouth of the cave. Something gave way under my boots—I had stumbled on a corpse. With a shiver I stood dazed in the darkness, nauseated by the hellish stench of decomposition and excrement, aware of faint groans and a whimpering that seemed no longer human. Something touched my arm; in a frenzy, I seized it, a human hand almost skeletal, and edged toward the opening and out into the world, pulling, carrying, dragging a man. And there he was, out in the flooding sunshine, lying on his back, his hollow eyes wide open, his spent flesh shrouded in tattered, rotting clothes, oblivious of everything around him as though his soul had not been dug out of the cave with his body. And I, too, was oblivious of every- thing, everyone around me as I squatted down beside him. Then I came to and saw them, those photographers, and heard the sharp, metallic clicking of the shutters of their cameras. A strange, terrible shame seized me, and I crouched over the man, staring into the limbo of his leaden eyes, as if trying to shield with my body the mute dignity of his suffering from the non- chalant prying eyes behind the cameras. "Captain, would you mind," someone shouted, "would you move away so I can get a better shot of him?" Out of the bloated toothless mouth oozed dark, yellowish liquid, and flies, those flies, swarming, buzzing, buzzing, eerily mingled with the hysterical voices of the announcers, and "Captain, let me get a good shot of him." Then I thought someone pushed me away, and blind with rage I snatched a shovel from the hands of a soldier and began smashing the cameras, chasing those cold eyes from my man, the flies, those terrible flies . . .

In silent humility, I touched Mr. Hann's cold, cold hand.

He turned his face to Mr. Shin, who nodded to him; then, suddenly he staggered, and almost collapsed.

I drove them back to the foot of the hill, and walked with them to the house. The nurse came running out of the front door and led the young minister inside.

Mr. Shin cordially shook my hand before I left. But I had scarcely taken ten or so steps away from him when I stopped and turned around.

He was still there, standing in the bleak garden, a shadowy figure in the blurring twilight.

"Mr. Shin?" I called out to him.

"Yes?"

"The other ministers—they were all murdered shortly before you were moved to the prison. Did you know?"

He was silent.

"Mr. Shin?"

"Yes?"

I hesitated for a moment, but I knew I had to ask him. I said, "Your god—is he aware of the suffering of his people?"

He turned around without a word, and withdrew into the dark, solitary house.

5

The black, cold November night shrouded the city outside. It was singularly quiet. I did not hear the sound of the usual troop movements or of the convoys of supply, only occasionally the faint whining of a lone jeep, or the distant humming of a formation of bombers. Alone in my office I sat on the edge of the camp bed near the coal stove that glowed in the shadowy halo of the candlelight. The night was getting deep, but I was in no mood for sleep. The windowpanes rattled, and the faint clanging of the bell slipped into the room, permeating my consciousness. I picked up the crude iron bar from the coal box and poked the lava-like coal in the stove, sending up a hissing blaze. The undulating light and the enveloping darkness gnawed at each other spasmodically, and gazing at the hypnotic, wavering blue core of the candlelight I knew only that I was at a loss; and that was a pity.

That certainly was a pity because the next morning when Colonel Chang exclaimed, "Divine intervention! What does he think he is, a saint!" I could not help laughing with him, however momentarily, half amused and half uncomfortable.

"Divine intervention, eh? Oh, well, let him have his way," he said, good-naturedly.

I was surprised and even puzzled by his extraordinary geniality, for I had expected him to fly into a rage over my report on the visit to the ministers. However, he behaved extremely well, and even managed to put me off my guard by indicating that he was not at all annoyed with the outcome of my interview with Mr. Shin. I had anticipated some sort of violent reaction from him upon learning that the two ministers had been with the other twelve shortly before the execution. Yet all he said was: "Yes, yes." Then he swiveled in his squeaking chair and laughed again: "You really must have scared the devil out of him! So—he had to hide behind his god, eh? Well, well, young fellow, that's good work, very good work, indeed."

His confident manner and indulgent laughter disturbed me. "I don't think I did anything to scare him, sir," I protested. "Besides, I don't think he was scared of anything. He looked more tired than anything else."

"Ah, you don't understand. Of course, he was scared. But remember, he is a preacher and he knows how to put on a good act—theatrical, if you know what I mean. Of course, he was scared," he said, with a wave of his hand. "I knew it, I knew it."

"Sir, I hope you are not suggesting that they collaborated with the Communists," I said.

"Well, what do *you* think?"

"It is very difficult for me to suspect that they could have betrayed the other ministers."

"Why not?" he asked, with a peculiar, cold smile on his face that for some reason at the moment made me think of him as a gambler. He leaned back in his chair. "Well, why not? Because they are Christians? You are not a Christian."

"No, I am not, but that's beside the point, sir. I don't think the Communists needed any collaboration, because they wanted to murder the prisoners anyway. There wasn't anything really against the ministers, as you know yourself, sir. What I mean is that there were no justifiable charges against them. So, why should the Communists have needed informants or collaborators?"

"Of course the Reds had no charges," he said, as though he pitied my naïveté. "But that's beside the point, if I may borrow your expression. When you don't have charges, you manufacture them. It's as simple as that. So they manufactured charges against the ministers, then they needed someone to confess—that's right—confess and bear witness to the charges. It's all very simple."

"You mean the two ministers were forced to confess?"

"Possibly."

"We don't have any evidence for that."

"No, we don't."

"Then what do you suppose we ought to do?"

"Just wait."

I was quite tense by then, and I felt as though I were struggling to disentangle myself from a web. "Wait for what, sir?"

"Confession."

"I don't understand."

"I am waiting for them to confess."

"Confess what, sir?"

"That they gave their confessions to the Reds."

"Then you really think that's how they survived."

"Can you think of any better explanation," he said, "apart from his nonsense about divine intervention?"

"Good luck, perhaps," I muttered.

"More nonsense."

I felt desperate, without knowing precisely why. I said as calmly as I could, "Then you ought to arrest them."

Colonel Chang chuckled. "My dear fellow, you don't think I am as stupid as that, do you?"

"No, I don't."

"Look here, I have no intention of downgrading Christians. Why should I go out of my way to discredit Christians, whose interests, after all, coincide with ours in this war? On the contrary, I intend to do my best to protect them, to boost their morale, and to promote their interests."

"Then why do you have to have such a strong suspicion about the ministers?" I said. "After all, even if they confessed to the manufactured charges, we can reasonably assume that they were forced to do so, and that it doesn't really constitute an act of treason. At least, not in my opinion, sir."

Tilting his head, he gazed at me through his thick glasses. "What about in the opinion of their god?" he said.

I shook my head helplessly. "I wouldn't know about that."

Suddenly dispelling the air he had been affecting of harmless good nature, he snapped, "No, you don't. But I do! I tell you, I do!" He paused, and pointed his finger at me. "Put yourself in

their place and think about the martyrs—those twelve ministers who were murdered in cold blood. Can't you see what
these two must be going through? Well, we'll forget about the
crazy one. Now, don't misunderstand me. I am not trying to
hound this man, Shin. By no means. I want to help him."

"Help him!"

"For the sake of justice, I want to hear his confession. But I
won't turn that against him. No, I won't. I mean to protect
him and I'll do all I can to keep it secret. I am sure the Chief of
Army Intelligence won't have any objection to that. That's
right. I'll protect him, I'll make him a hero, and I'll even cooperate with him for the cause of Christianity in North Korea."

"But suppose, sir, suppose, he has nothing to say?"

Colonel Chang leaned forward, his eyes shining darkly.
"We shall then appeal to his conscience," he said.

6

Curiously enough Colonel Chang had not told me to see Mr. Shin again, nor had he intimated that I should do so on my own initiative. In the next few days, I saw the colonel several times but he gave me no inkling as to the unresolved problem concerning the ministers. His behavior puzzled me, finally disturbed me. Meanwhile, I was busy with my routine activities; I attended regular staff meetings, wrote innumerable pamphlets for the Army's Troop Information and Education Bureau, and prepared a few speeches for the chief, one of whose jobs it was to speak to groups of civic-minded people in the city.

As the month of November progressed, the Korean Infantry and various U.N. troops on the western front were busily engaged in the final stage of mopping-up operations near the Yalu River, across which stretched the endless expanse of the frozen plains of Manchuria; on the eastern front, the U.N. Infantry and the American Marines, encountering little opposition, steadily made their way toward the Tumen River near Siberia. The demoralization of the North Korean Army was swift and complete; the war was virtually coming to an end. Everyone was cheerful and hopeful, and was convinced that it would be all over by Christmas.

Then one cold and windy afternoon, I received the following letter from Park:

I am still alive, in case you wondered. At least I know I am alive right this minute. We are moving fast these days, too recklessly fast, perhaps. We hardly stop anywhere long enough to think about where we are going. Well—I just survived my first hand-to-hand combat. But my CO was killed, so they made me a temporary captain and put me in charge of the company. What happened is—we got into a bayonet fight with a company of North Koreans in a valley. Both sides charged and it was all right for a while—just a regular hand-to-hand combat. Then somehow everything got all mixed up, and it was wild. The trouble was that it was pitch-black night and that we all spoke Korean. Devil only knew which side we were killing. Everyone was shouting in the same language, "Who are you? Who are you?" For a while the bewilderment was simply staggering. Then, something—panic, terror, you name it—snapped, and everyone was killing everyone else. All of a sudden, a hand grenade exploded, and that did it. We scattered in all directions, throwing grenades behind us. But that was nothing. Some idiot had called for artillery fire, and shells started pouring down out of the black sky. It was a deep, rocky valley, squeezed in by steep cliffs, and I just wonder—if you had been up on top of one of those mountains and had been able to see what was going on down there in the black bottom of the valley—I just wonder how you would have felt? But why am I writing you all this? I don't exactly know. Perhaps, I am frightened of myself. It depresses me to suspect that I am the very source of my horror. Will write again. Take care of yourself. . . .

Park's letter had been written nearly two weeks before, and it did not give me the faintest clue as to the location of his unit. I wanted to write him, but I knew my letter would take more time to reach him than his letter had to find me. I thought I would take advantage of my position and make use of the direct telephone of the Intelligence Communication Service. For this, I needed the assistance of the Marine Corps liaison officer assigned to our headquarters. I went down to his office.

The officer, a husky, young lieutenant who limped noticeably, made notes of Park's name, his serial number and his unit's number, and assured me that he would let me know as soon as he could how to reach Park. He was usually cheerful and sociable, with clear brown eyes and a quick boyish smile; but while he attended to me that afternoon, he was quiet and businesslike. I did not tell him more than was necessary, and he was scrupulous enough not to ask me any questions.

When I thanked him for his help and turned to go, he stood up from his chair and detained me. Then he closed the door of his office and came to where I was standing. His behavior aroused my curiosity. He looked at me for a moment, scratched the back of his head and his cropped hair, and smiled sheepishly. "Captain Lee," he said, "I really don't know if it's all right to tell you this."

I returned his smile. "Well?"

"It's about this Captain Park," he said.

"Yes?"

"You are not the only one who wants to contact him. Colonel Chang is also interested in him."

"Colonel Chang?"

"Yes. He was down here about four days ago and asked me to locate Captain Park . . . well, he didn't know the officer had been promoted then."

"What did he want?"

"That's the point. It was supposed to be very important. Of course, I don't have any idea what he was up to. It wasn't that he wanted to call him, though." The lieutenant frowned and went on to tell me that, after he had located Park for Colonel Chang, the colonel had communicated with the Chief of Naval Intelligence. "It was, you know, sort of hush-hush," he concluded. "I really don't know if I should have told you about this."

I told him it was all right, he was not violating any security regulations.

"So, you see, when you asked me about the same officer, I just couldn't help wondering about him," he said. "Who is he? Is he involved in something? Oh, I talk too much. Never mind, Captain. I won't ask you any more questions."

I assured him that it was all right with me, that Park was a friend of mine, and that I wanted to call him only for personal reasons.

He was relieved and said, beaming, "Oh, that's fine. Tell

you the truth, I do it myself sometimes, I try to contact fellows I know all over the country. You know, just to keep in touch." He told me how, out of two hundred or so who had been trained and commissioned with him, only forty-seven were still alive; they were, most of them, college students who had volunteered. There was a feeling of kinship between us; we both had been in an academic environment before the war; we chatted, oblivious to our present status, about our universities, and our future plans. Then we talked about our experiences in the war; and he was telling me how he had been wounded by "a God-damned Russian mine," and how those "quacks"—those medical students in uniform—had been scared to death at the first aid station and had almost "chopped his knee off" and so on, when we heard a knock on the door.

It was my orderly. I was wanted by Colonel Chang. I thanked the Marine lieutenant for his help, and headed for the colonel's office.

On my way upstairs, I could not help feeling that I was like a helpless spectator, vainly conjecturing about the elusive performance of a magician. At the same time I was indignant, for I felt the colonel had encroached upon my private life by deliberately bypassing me in undertaking affairs that had something to do with Park.

Colonel Chang, upon seeing me enter his office, gestured that I should take a chair and wait until he was ready for me. I could not but think that he had already guessed what was in my mind. For a few minutes he engaged himself in a mute examination of papers on his desk. Then, shoving the papers aside, he raised his smooth bald head and said, as though speaking to himself, "Well, well, how do you like that?"

"Sir?"

"This man, Shin," he said, shaking his head as if he was overwhelmed by a sense of helpless resignation. "I simply don't understand him."

"What's the trouble, sir?"

"I've had CIC do a quiet opinion poll, so to speak. You know, just asking some Christians about the two ministers. Well, they all say the same thing—that the two were separated from the others by the Reds, so they had no knowledge of what became of the twelve ministers. How do you like that, eh?"

"Perhaps it's the truth."

With a grin, he said, "It's not as simple as that. The point is that this man, Shin, has told his congregation in plain words that he and the other one, Hann, hadn't seen the other ministers again after they had been separately interrogated by the Reds. What do you think of that?"

"I suppose his congregation, or for that matter, all the Christians in the country, would like to know what happened to the ministers and they would ask him about it. It seems to me only natural under the circumstances."

"Natural indeed," he snapped. "And they would believe whatever he tells them, wouldn't they? If they are all good Christians, that is."

"I suppose, sir," I answered helplessly. "I don't expect they would seriously think their minister was telling them a lie from his pulpit."

"Well said, Captain. Very well said."

I was not ready to leave. I stood up but lingered for a moment, groping for the right word with which to begin my own cross-examination, as it were, about Park. Colonel Chang looked up from his desk at me, as though he were genuinely surprised to see me still there, and said good-naturedly, "That is all, Captain. Thank you for coming."

I gave in and made to go, when he said casually, "Tomorrow is Sunday, isn't it?"

"Yes."

"Oh, good. I thought you and I might attend the service at Minister Shin's church tomorrow."

7

"But why are you telling me about it?" said Mr. Shin, slowly raising his head.

I had decided, after my supper at headquarters, to go to see him. I had no clear idea why I wanted to see him, except for a vague feeling of restlessness. I still did not have the slightest notion, even when we were sitting face to face, as to what had convinced me of the necessity to drive all that way to the hill. So I sat quietly, for some time, merely looking at Mr. Shin, who maintained, to my great relief, an air of immeasurable serenity.

"I suppose I should be grateful to you for letting me know where I stand," he continued slowly, "but, frankly, I don't quite understand why you should go out of your way to do me this favor." He looked at me calmly, covering his mouth with a handkerchief. He was coughing with much difficulty, with his lean shoulders hunched and twitching; he looked weary and his eyes were deeply sunken. The coughing stopped and he said, "To be sure, I don't mean to say that I am not grateful. It is just that I don't understand you."

"Neither do I understand myself," I confessed.

"I expected to see you again, of course," he said, "but not under these circumstances." He looked at me as though he doubted the sincerity of my motive for coming to see him.

I felt uncomfortable, and I said awkwardly, "I hope you don't still consider me an interrogator."

"It makes little difference to me. I don't mind if you question me." His manner was cool and deliberate—at least it seemed so to me.

"Is there anything more I can learn from you?" I said, slightly vexed with myself, for I wished I had not come. "Haven't you told me all you know about the murdered ministers?"

He did not respond.

"I can understand your feeling toward those whose business it is to interrogate, prosecute, and execute people," I went on. "Perhaps you judge them all alike, regardless of whether they are North Koreans or South Koreans or whatnot. But I assure you that within our organization, as far as I know, there are many decent people who would like to be of help to others, well, to others like you." I stopped and felt I was blushing a little.

"Are you trying to help me?" he asked. "Why?"

"I don't know." I said. "Perhaps, I need your help more than you need mine. Who knows?"

"To tell you frankly, I don't blame your colonel," he said, pausing for his coughing to stop. "On the contrary, I consider it his duty to form such opinions about me. I should have done the same had I been in his place."

"Are you suggesting that he has justifiable reasons for suspecting you?" I said, frowning.

"But of course," he said. There was no indication of sarcasm in his placid, matter-of-fact air.

"You don't really mean that, do you?"

"Why not? After all, do not forget that a Christian, a clergyman, is also a human being. He should be examined in the same light of human passion, and on the same scale of human frailty as any other man would be. I don't consider myself or any other clergyman necessarily capable of not succumbing to physical and spiritual torture."

It was the first time I heard him speak so forcefully, though his voice was subdued and his manner unruffled; he spoke without looking at me, only staring into the empty, cold space before him as though he were addressing someone invisible, hovering over me.

"As you know," he continued, "Mr. Hann and I were about to be shot when the prison was captured. But that makes little difference. We survived, and the survival of any political prisoner in a Communist prison is an extraordinary thing in itself. Particularly, in our case, it was a near-miracle. But miracle is a difficult word to understand these days, and when we survived while twelve ministers were executed, the meaning of the word becomes ambiguous. Therefore, it is natural that a suspicion should arise."

"But you are innocent of the suspicion, aren't you?" I blurted out. "I assume you have told me the truth."

He stirred in his chair. "I have told you all that I can tell you."

"You are innocent, aren't you?" I repeated.

"Yes."

"Then you told me the truth."

"I speak the truth of my conscience, Captain."

"Am I not capable of judging the truth?"

"Don't you realize," he said gravely, "that you are speaking of the fact of man, and I of the truth of my faith?"

"Then you believe you are innocent in the eyes of your god."

He seemed startled by my words, and he gazed at me intensely for some time; then he lowered his eyes and said quietly, "It is for Him to judge me."

Mr. Shin came to the door with me. I asked him about the young minister and was told that he was well taken care of by a doctor and the nurse; beyond that, he would say nothing. I wanted to do something for him, and I was on the point of telling him that he should not hesitate to ask me for help, when he said, "Do you know, by any chance, a young man of your age, Indoe Park?"

"Do I know him!" I exclaimed. "He is my best friend."

For a moment, he stared at me as though he regretted that he had asked me about Park. Then he said quietly, "The last thing I heard of him was that he was teaching in Seoul at the university where you taught before the war. I thought you might have known him."

"We were always together," I said. "We taught the same subject. But how do you know him?"

"I suppose you must know about his father," he said.

"Yes, I do."

"I knew both of them. You may say, I was a family friend. How is he now?"

I told him about Park, adding that I had just received a letter from him that afternoon.

"Does he know?" he asked.

"No. I haven't told him."

"I understand both of them," he said. "I understand your friend as I understood his father. Very proud, so passionately proud. Yes, I understand them." Then he was silent; and I knew he did not wish to detain me any longer. I was bidding him good night when we heard a knock on the door. I looked at Mr. Shin; he nodded, and I opened the door.

A man in uniform walked into the dimly lit hallway and glanced at me in surprise, as though he had not expected to find another man in uniform there. His outward appearance was nearly identical to mine: combat boots, a parka, a steel helmet, though he did not wear a pistol nor any insignia. He did not seem to have recognized my host, who was standing quietly behind me. "I would like to see Mr. Shin," he said gruffly. "I am Chaplain Koh of the Third Brigade. I am an old friend."

I stepped aside so that he could speak directly to Mr. Shin. The chaplain came forward and looked closely at the minister. He was a tall, thickset man, and his steel helmet, pressed down to his eyebrows, blurred his profile with an uneven shadow, save for his dented chin. He seemed only now to recognize Mr. Shin and exclaimed, "Why, it's you! I could hardly tell it was you! My Lord, what suffering you must have gone through!" He thrust out his hand, but Mr. Shin did not respond, and the big, stubby hand remained suspended in the air as if it were suddenly frozen. Then he grabbed the minister's arm, and said, "Good Lord, you need a doctor to take care of you!"

Mr. Shin violently brushed his hand aside. He stepped back and said sternly, "Do not touch me." He coughed violently. The nurse appeared in the background.

"What's the matter? Are you ill?" cried the chaplain; and turning to me, "Is he all right? Is he ill?"

"I do not wish to see you," said Mr. Shin, agitated. "I bid

you leave my house. You know as well as I do why I do not wish to see you."

I looked at Chaplain Koh with vague feelings of hostility, but he did not seem to be shocked or angry. Rather, he appeared to have anticipated Mr. Shin's behavior. He was silent for a while, then said politely, "Yes, I know. I understand how you feel about me. But I have something very important to tell you and as soon as I finish telling you about it, I'll leave."

"Then speak," commanded Mr. Shin.

The chaplain glanced at me as though begging me to leave them alone.

I turned to Mr. Shin. "Is there anything I can do for you?"

"No, thank you," he muttered. "Good night."

8

Late Sunday morning, Colonel Chang and I drove to Mr. Shin's church, which was not too far from our headquarters. We parked the jeep in a deserted alley off the main street, and started to walk. About thirty paces from where we left the jeep, there was a narrow, gradually ascending path barely wide enough for us to walk shoulder to shoulder. Along both sides there were rows of shabby, flat houses of gray stone and dirty plaster. Beneath the soft new snow under our feet lurked the old snow as hard and slippery as ice. Colonel Chang had much difficulty walking up the winding path.

When we looked back we could see first the snow-covered roofs of the houses we had passed, then those of the other houses farther away, and then the streets down below. Soon we found ourselves in a clearing, face to face with a small wooden gate, beyond which a footpath led us to two flights of stone steps cleared of snow. There, above the steps, on a massive expanse of flat rock, stood the towering church of red brick, with four ponderous marble pillars and large stained-glass windows aglow in the sun. The cross-topped belfry perched high above the blinding snow on the roof, its many bells ringing, vibrating in the sunny air. To the left of the church, near the edge of the rocky clearing, ran an iron fence, and a steep precipice swept downward. The bells stopped ringing.

We were late for the service. It was very quiet; not a sound from within the church, nor from the traffic down below reached our ears. Perhaps the congregation was praying, I suggested to the colonel.

He turned to me. "Quite a church, isn't it? I understand it can seat well over a thousand people."

"It is lucky to have survived," I remarked. "Nothing seems to have touched it at all." I could not help comparing the fates of the two churches in the same city, the devastated church of Park's father, and Mr. Shin's, which somehow had managed to survive the tribulations of war.

"It has nothing to do with luck," Colonel Chang said. "We saved it quite intentionally. Didn't you know that this church saw one of the bloodiest battles? The Reds had an antiaircraft battery up here, certainly a very convenient location, although it's extremely vulnerable to aerial attack. Of course they had an artillery observation post here, too, when we reached the other side of the river. They knew we were not allowed to do any damage to this church. It was an idiotic decision when you look at it from a purely tactical point of view, but the strategic value of saving the church was greater than smashing it for an immediate tactical gain. It was supposed to be a symbolic gesture on our part. But the Reds could pinpoint their artillery fire practically at any target, and that was too much for us when we had to cross the river and take the city. So we threw in a detachment of commandos, who climbed up here—Heaven knows how—and took the post and held it, with our aerial protection, until we crossed the river. So that's how this church was spared. Can you imagine," he glanced upward, "that a Red was right up there in that belfry, directing artillery fire against us while we were trying to save the church and by so doing save his life?" He cluck-clucked, shaking his head. Then he said that we should go in and join the congregation. We seated ourselves in one of the rear pews.

The interior was somewhat like that of a grand theater, with rising rows of pews, plastered pillars that supported the balcony, and many aisles leading to the altar with an elevated pulpit. Under the expanse of white ceiling, from which a dozen or so crystal chandeliers were suspended with gilded chains, the congregation was bowed in prayer, immobile as though the freezing air had turned it into a multitude of lifeless statues. I looked for Mr. Shin but I did not see him behind the altar, where four white-robed elders sat on high-backed chairs. One of the chairs was unoccupied. I glanced at Colonel Chang, but his face remained expressionless. I looked at the altar again, in time to see one of the elders disappear into the right wing of the church and come back.

Then the prayer was over, there was a rustling of clothes and discreet coughing in the congregation, and I saw the elder, who had returned, lean toward the others. Presently, one of them mounted the pulpit, on which a giant Bible lay open, and announced the singing of a certain hymn. Colonel Chang reached for the rack on the back of the pew in front of us, and picked out a hymnbook, which he opened and handed to me, motioning me to stand up. We rose as the pipe organ began to play the prelude, but I did not join in the singing although the Colonel urged me to, indicating with his plump finger the proper passage. He observed my behavior with obvious enjoyment; once he even chuckled.

During the singing, the same elder went into the wing again, returning to his seat only at the end of the hymn. Colonel Chang reached out for the rack again, picked up two small square envelopes, and asked if he could borrow some money from me. I gave him some change, which he put in an envelope, explaining that these envelopes were for the use of those who did not wish to reveal the amount of their offering. He handed me one.

The service progressed, but Mr. Shin still did not appear. An elder read a passage from the Bible, then spoke to the congregation. It was with the greatest regret, he said, that he had to announce the sad news that Mr. Shin was unable to be present, due to a sudden illness. He proposed that the congregation pray for the health and speedy recovery of the minister who had suffered much at the hands of those who were against the will of God.

Colonel Chang sprang to his feet and stalked out of the

church. I hastily followed him and when I had closed the weighty front door behind me he was already approaching the gate. I ran down the path and came abreast of him. Together, we descended the hill in silence.

It was only when we reached the jeep that he spoke. "Too sick to preach!" he snorted.

9

A series of conferences and briefings occupied the afternoon until well past four o'clock, when, at last free and alone, I shut myself up in my office and gazed out the window. In the last rays of the setting sun, the tip of the cross over the gray bell tower glowed faintly, and snow flurries swished about the ruins, some chasing after the jeeps and trucks, some sweeping along the edge of the streets. Shadows crept upward on the slope, invading the mutilated church, then the bell tower, and as the jagged silhouette grew darker, a somber silence enveloped the city. The wind had subsided, no sound came from the bell as the sun swiftly disappeared, and then it was evening. I headed for Mr. Shin's house again.

The nurse met me. Her hair was neatly combed and her clothes unruffled, but she seemed weary and at a loss as to what to do with me as she held open the front door, neither letting me in, nor shutting me out. We looked at each other mutely in the dim light for a moment, then she smiled shyly, shaking her head. She let me into the hallway and hushed me. She opened the door of the room where I had sat with Mr. Shin the night before, and motioned me to follow her in. Her manner flattered me a little, though I felt uneasy. I asked her if Mr. Shin was ill.

Her small eyes became smaller and narrower, wrinkles gathered about them. In the harsh light of the naked light bulb, her face looked, for a second, like a shriveled death mask. "It's worse than that," she said.

"Did you send for a doctor?" I asked.

"What can a doctor do for him?"

"He was coughing badly last night."

"He's been spitting blood," she said, shaking her head.

I felt alarmed, for I had not suspected that Mr. Shin's illness was so critical. "You should have told me about it sooner," I said. "We must do something."

"I don't know what we can do," she said. "He won't take medicine. He only tells me it's not the doctor's medicine he needs."

"Can I see him? You must let me see him at once."

"I can't. He's been praying since last night and fasting too. I stayed up all night in case he needed me; he hasn't slept, he hasn't eaten, he hasn't even called me. He's still praying upstairs, I am sure."

We were both quiet for a while.

Then she said, "It's all because of that man!"

"You mean the chaplain."

"Yes, the man who came to see Mr. Shin last night. They were shouting at each other after you left. I didn't know what to do. Then Mr. Shin started coughing. I could hear it even in the kitchen; he was coughing terribly. I told the man to leave the house."

"Had you seen him before?"

"No, I don't know him personally, but everyone knows what sort of a man he is," she said. "He had a church here, but one night he ran away. He just bolted, without telling anyone about it. That was a year or so before the war."

"Didn't he have a family?"

"No, he was all by himself."

"Was he, maybe, in trouble with the Communists?"

"Who knows? The next day, the Communist police took four young men of his church and nobody saw them again. Now he's back as an Army chaplain and all that. You see, Mr. Shin had good reason to get upset and angry." She paused. "Anyway, after he ran away, they asked my son to tend his church."

I interrupted her. "Your son?"

She was taken aback by my sudden question, realized what she had said, and became confused.

I muttered an apology. "You were saying?"

"Mr. Shin told me you know Mr. Indoe Park?"

"Do you also know him?"

"No, I've never seen him but I've heard much about him. I knew his father well."

"Then you know what their relationship was."

"It was sad," she said. "Do you know how your friend feels about his father now? Is he still angry with his father, do you think?"

I hesitated for a moment. "No, I don't think he is," I said.

"I am so glad to hear that. You see, my son lost his father when he was seven, so I had to work to send him through school. He went to a missionary school here and became a Christian, and was baptized by your friend's father. My son wanted to be a minister, so Mr. Park helped him through the seminary. He was always kind to us and when my son finished the seminary, Mr. Park himself ordained him. Then all of a sudden this war." She broke into sobs.

I could not help saying, "You have been speaking to me about Mr. Hann, haven't you?"

She covered her face with her chapped hands. "Yes, I am his mother," she said.

10

When I returned to headquarters, I was met by my orderly. I was wanted by Colonel Chang, who had a visitor with him. After making a routine check with the duty officer, I went upstairs to the chief's office and found them standing near the stove. When they both turned to me, I could not fail to recognize the visitor; it was Chaplain Koh. I was not at all surprised to see him there with Colonel Chang; I was, perhaps, more amused. He appeared to recognize me and I thought he looked puzzled as he scrutinized me while the colonel introduced us. We shook hands. Neither of us spoke a word. The coal stove emitted a stale air; it was stifling in the hot and smoky room.

"He is an old acquaintance of mine," the colonel said, "and it might interest you to know that he is a good friend of Mr. Shin's." He turned to the chaplain. "Aren't you?"

Chaplain Koh smiled at me, and said, "A pleasant surprise, indeed, that Mr. Shin is a mutual friend of ours. He and I went to the same seminary and we were ordained together. Have you been acquainted with him long?"

"I wouldn't call myself a friend of Mr. Shin's," I replied. "I don't know him well enough."

"I see," he said; then, after a pause, "I am afraid he hasn't fully recovered from his past suffering. I assume you know that he was in a Communist prison. It seems to me my poor friend feels quite mortified that he survived the Reds' persecution. . . . I mean that he . . . you know, the twelve martyrs . . ."

I looked at the colonel.

"He knows all about it," the colonel said, to me. Then to the chaplain, "That's a pity. He shouldn't feel that way."

"Ah well, I can understand him," said the chaplain. "I would feel the same way if I were in his place."

"You clergymen," the colonel said, shaking his head.

"After all, my dear military friends," said the chaplain, "we clergymen share a stronger spiritual bond than yours, if you don't mind my telling you so." He smiled.

"I can hardly disagree with you there," the colonel said. "I am sure Captain Lee feels the same way. The fellowship in the service of God ought to mean more than the fellowship in the service of a state—if you believe in God, that is."

I spoke to the colonel. "I was told that you wanted to see me, sir."

With a nod, he said, "I want you to look after the chaplain. He is going to be with us for a week or so, and I want you to make sure he is comfortable here."

"I hope I won't be a burden to you," the chaplain said to me.

"I asked him to represent the Army," said the colonel.

"I beg your pardon, sir?" I said.

"The Christians are planning a joint memorial service for the twelve martyrs, and several ministers who are on the preparation committee asked me for help. Of course, I promised them that I would do all I can."

"But, Colonel, how do they know?" I said.

"About what?"

"About the twelve, sir."

"Oh, that. I've told them."

"You haven't made it public yet, sir. Are you going to announce it officially?"

"Sooner or later."

"What about the two ministers?"

"What about them? Is there anything you want to suggest?"

"Nothing in particular, sir. I merely wanted to know what you propose to do with them." I turned to the chaplain. "Excuse us, but we are talking about Mr. Shin and Mr. Hann."

"Is there anything wrong with them?" the chaplain said, frowning.

"Nothing that I know of," said the colonel.

I could not help wondering what his game was now.

"Captain, you and the chaplain will represent the Army for the memorial service," the colonel continued. "Of course, both of you will be on the preparation committee. He will cooperate with the ministers in the city and you'll take care of, say, logistic problems. We'll discuss it in more detail later on."

"It will be my great pleasure to work with you," the chaplain said to me.

"I am sure it will be a very rewarding experience for both of you," the colonel said.

"Is that all, sir?" I said.

"The chaplain is going to use my office for his temporary stay, so why don't you get him a camp bed." He looked at the chaplain. "I hope you don't mind sleeping here. We'll try to get you a more comfortable place in a day or so."

I asked the colonel, "Sir, do you think, perhaps, I should contact, say, the local YMCA? I should think that they might be able to find a better place."

"Please don't trouble yourself about me," said the chaplain. "After all, I am in the Army and I am used to sleeping anywhere. I should hesitate to trouble the Christians here. They have enough problems of their own and I don't want to impose on them. Please don't worry about me. I'll be most comfortable in this room."

"Yes, we in the Army can take care of ourselves," the colonel said, "Not that Chaplain Koh doesn't know anyone in the city. He had a church here before the war, in case you didn't know, and that's how I got to know him."

"Colonel Chang saved my life," the chaplain said.

"At that time—a year and a half ago, wasn't it Chaplain?—I was in charge of the Army's Intelligence network in the Pyongyang area, and my old friend here was invaluable to our operation. Do you realize that he was more daring than any of the men I sent here? Why, I even had to slow him down!"

"Now, now, let's not get into that," said the chaplain. "I only did what my conviction dictated, that's all."

Colonel Chang chuckled. "Captain, do you know that I had to have my men kidnap him? Can you imagine my men spiriting him out of Pyongyang?"

"Now, really," the chaplain said, with a sudden, severe frown.

Colonel Chang ignored his protest. "The truth of the matter is that the Reds got wind of our operation. We learned that from a double agent we had planted in their Counterintelligence. They were about to take a crack at our network. It all happened so fast I barely had enough time to tell the chaplain to get out. To my surprise, he refused to go underground. Too proud, you know. So, I had to kidnap him, so to speak, and whisk him off to the South."

Chaplain Koh fixed an impassive gaze upon the colonel.

Colonel Chang shrugged. "I couldn't let them shoot you, could I? You were too valuable to be made a martyr."

"Martyr? Were there any casualties?" I said.

Colonel Chang waved his hand. "Ah, enough of the past."

Chaplain Koh looked angry, but he said quietly, "Yes, Captain, we had casualties. I had to abandon four men. They were all shot later by the Reds."

"Enough, enough," said the colonel. "I couldn't do anything about it. I did my best." He turned to the chaplain. "And there was nothing you could do either. . . . Come, come, we should be more concerned with what we have to do right now. And that reminds me of the talk I've had with several Christian leaders here. I regret to say that they don't have any constructive ideas. They don't seem to have the fighting spirit. Now, that's why I asked you to come here, Chaplain. They need a man like you to help them stand on their own feet."

Chaplain Koh looked preoccupied.

"We must revive the Christian church here, and they need our help," Colonel Chang went on. "They need moral support from the South Korean Christians and from the Army, too. More than anything else, they need leaders who can initiate vigorous action. You see, they are suffering from the loss of their leaders. And I am sure the memorial service will help them greatly. Let's understand this: after all, we are all fighting Communists and in this joint operation, you might say, we need each other. We help Christians, and they help us."

"It was very good of you to have initiated the idea of the memorial service for the Christians," said the chaplain matter-of-factly.

Colonel Chang continued placidly, "The twelve martyrs are a great symbol. They are a symbol of the suffering Christians and their eventual spiritual triumph. We mustn't let the martyrs down. We must let everyone witness their spiritual victory over the Reds."

"The Christians here are still suffering from the sickness left by the persecution," the chaplain said quietly, as though speaking to himself.

Colonel Chang tapped him on the shoulder, smiling. "Ah, they need new wine to fill the old bottles."

Standing between them, with my back turned to the smoky stove, I had no other desire at that moment than to go to bed.

The Marine lieutenant called me shortly after I returned to my office. Park had been transferred to Marine Corps Headquarters a few days ago, but the lieutenant could not locate him there. He was on leave. No one seemed to know where he was.

11

When Chaplain Koh came down to my office, a little past midnight, I had just finished working on the weekly report and was about to retire. He was still in his uniform. He apologized for disturbing me when I offered him a chair near the stove. I asked him if there was anything he wanted me to do for him. He replied that he was well taken care of. For a moment, we looked at each other without a word, then he shook his head and blurted out:

"You surprised me. I've been thinking about you ever since Colonel Chang left me in peace."

I could not help smiling. "So he left you in peace."

He grinned. "As you know, I saw you at Mr. Shin's last night. Should I have recognized you in the colonel's office?"

I shrugged.

"Why didn't you mention that you had seen me?"

"And why didn't you?" I asked.

"I was too busy speculating. I thought you didn't want Colonel Chang to know that you were at Mr. Shin's last night."

"I don't see why you should have thought so," I said. "But, anyway, that was very considerate of you."

"Oh, but it was you who was considerate of me. After all, you saw me caught in an embarrassing position at Mr. Shin's, and when I saw you tonight, I needed time to think."

"We are very thoughtful of each other, aren't we?"

"Then we are friends," he said, smiling.

"Would you like to be?"

"Ah, you are a hard man," he said. "I understand that you used to be a university instructor."

"Yes."

"I hope the Army hasn't succeeded in corrupting you."

"Why do you say that?"

"What I mean is," he said, clearing his throat, "I hope you are not yet capable of being too cynical or too blindly professional."

I did not respond; somehow, he managed to surprise me.

"I know, I know," he said, nodding. "You want to know where I stand."

"Perhaps," I said.

"I can see that you respect Mr. Shin very much. Now, now, don't try to deny it. I know you said you hardly know him, but I know better. Or perhaps I should say I know Mr. Shin better. I respect his judgment and he seems to think highly of you. He told me about you, by the way. I am not trying to flatter you, nor am I trying to convince you that Mr. Shin shouldn't have treated me the way he did. He was quite justified in his evaluation of my past conduct."

"If you don't mind my telling you so," I said, "I am hardly interested in your past conduct."

"Ah, you should be, you should be, with good reasons. Many people used to think I was a Communist informer. I don't need to say that they don't think so anymore. But they despise me. Some still think I was a shameless coward who ran away from his church. Some think I defiled the vocation of ministry by engaging in intelligence activities—a spy, to put it more bluntly. And then some think I betrayed my congregation, generally speaking."

"Did you?"

"Yes, I did," he replied without hesitation. "Yes, I betrayed them. When a pastor begins to be suspicious of members of his congregation, even of his elders, well, he is betraying them. I couldn't take anyone into my confidence."

"Why couldn't you?"

"Fear, a simple fear."

"A justifiable one?"

"Unfortunately, yes. I spoke to you about the four men I had to abandon. One of them was an informer, and would you believe it, he was a son of one of my elders?" He paused and studied my face. "You don't have to believe me. As Colonel Chang told you, I was forced to go underground, to run away from my church. But I stayed in Pyongyang for two days before Colonel Chang's men could arrange our rendezvous with a motorboat on the west coast, near the port of Chinnampo. By that time, Colonel Chang, who was a major then, knew who the informer was. He didn't know his name, of course, because we used code names for our agents. I knew who it was because the code name was for one of my own men and I was the only one who knew them all personally. I contacted the three others to tell them to go underground. Actually, what I intended was to take them to South Korea with me. I had them meet me. A lieutenant, who was in charge of Colonel Chang's men, insisted that we liquidate the informer. I had no choice. We arranged for the four men to meet us and we were all set to go to the place of our rendezvous, when our double agent informed us that the Reds had been alerted. It was too late to warn the three men. We found out later that the Reds had arrested all four, but on their way to the police, they—our three men, that is— put up a fight and tried to escape. The Reds shot them, all four of them, on the spot, not knowing that one of them was their own informer."

I interrupted him. "Why are you telling me all this?"

He ignored my question and went on. "Now, the elder believes that his son died a hero's death in the cause. I saw the old man, you see. I went to the service at my church—I should say, my former church. Of course, I wasn't welcomed; it's a miracle they didn't turn me out. The old man didn't conceal his hatred and disdain toward me, nor did many others. Now, what would you do if you were in my place?"

I was startled by his abrupt and unexpected question. "Why do you ask me?"

"To be frank with you, I don't care what others think of me. I did what I had to do. I did what I felt was the right thing. I am not in sympathy with the notion of nonviolent resistance. I have no intention of turning the other cheek to be slapped twice. Heavens no! I am sorry but I don't admire those early

Christians who calmly—so the story goes—waited, praying, to be devoured by the howling beasts of Roman emperors. I am more inclined to worship the God of the Old Testament. I don't mind telling you that most of those twelve martyrs really don't deserve to be called martyrs at all. Why, they didn't lift a finger to resist the persecution, they didn't do anything to alleviate the suffering of the Christians in North Korea. They were afraid, you see, so afraid that they did not dare raise their voices. Their people could not hear them, did not feel that their pastors were waging a spiritual battle against the Reds, if not a physical battle. And what sort of sermons did they give? Pastoral, as though they were literally a bunch of shepherds tending sheep, as though that would convince the Reds that Christians were a harmless bunch of sweet angels. And what happened? Fourteen ministers are having a jolly good time at a dinner celebrating the birthday of one of them, in come the Reds to bag them all and shoot the twelve, all this for no good reason, and one comes back alive as a lunatic, and the other wishes he had been shot too so that he could be a martyr. Sheer nonsense! But I am glad that Mr. Shin survived because I still think of him as my best friend, no matter how he despises me."

"Does he despise you?"

"He used to," he said thoughtfully. "Yes, he used to."

"What do you mean?"

"As I said, I don't care what others think of me," he said. "But there is one opinion I care for. Mr. Shin's. I couldn't bear to think that he, too, despised me. So, when I saw him last night, I told him all about myself and about the elder, and asked for his advice.

"I told him the truth of the matter," the chaplain continued. "You see, I was getting tired of playing the role of a saint or a Judas, whichever way you look at it. I thought I had had enough of the conceited elder and the others. So I told him I was going to expose the entire situation. Not because I wanted to clear myself but because I couldn't take any more of the idiotic notion of meek suffering and false pride of these North

Korean Christians, who call me a coward, a renegade, and whatnot. They are sick, Captain; they are still paralyzed by the spiritual disease they caught from submitting obediently to persecution. And now that they are liberated, what do they do? Nothing but talk.

"Well, Mr. Shin was angry. I don't quite know why. Perhaps, he was angry at seeing me in uniform and meddling with what he calls the affairs of those who advocate violence in the name of justice. But I think he was more angry at my intention to strip the elder of his glorious illusion so that he should face the truth about his damnable son. So he says, 'Think of what might happen to the old man.' And I say, 'What do I care?' He says, 'He is an old man and he needs what you call the glorious illusion. How would you dare to make the old man suffer more! He lost his son, no matter for what reason, and that itself is an unbearable pain. But he has been able to overcome that pain because he believes that his son died as a hero and because others believe so too.' So I say, 'And what do you want me to do? Do you want me to go on conceding that his son was a real hero? Do you want me to go on telling a lie, because not speaking out the truth amounts to lying, a nice little lie so that the old man and all of you can keep on despising me?' He didn't know what to say to that. I pressed him hard."

"Did he say anything at all?"

"At last, he said I should leave him alone. I told him I was confused. I *am* confused. I'd like to know what to do. Do you know what Mr. Shin said? 'I am as confused as you are, perhaps, more,' he said. I asked him why. He wouldn't answer. He merely said that he was praying, praying for an answer to his confusion, whatever it is all about. 'You ought to pray more,' he said. What do you think of all this?"

"I don't understand," I admitted. "Does Colonel Chang know about the elder?"

He shook his head. "No, of course not. I wouldn't dare tell him."

"Why not? Don't you think he could make it all very simple for you?"

Chaplain Koh smiled. "My dear Captain Lee, I want you to remember that I don't let him operate in the domain of my private life."

"Then why are you revealing your private life to me?"

"Because you interest me."

"I don't think I have done anything to deserve your interest," I said. "I am getting as confused as you are, although for different reasons."

He stood up. "No, you haven't done anything. It's Mr. Shin."

I also stood up. "I don't follow you at all."

"As I said, I respect his judgment," he said. "I have known him for many years and I was once his best friend. I may disagree with him on certain principles but that does not mean I don't value his advice."

"Did he give you any advice?"

"He suggested that you might be interested in hearing about my personal problem and might even be of help to me."

He touched my arm. "I suppose I may tell you this. Mr. Shin said you must have been deeply hurt by the terrible injustice and despair that break the hearts of people.

"Well, good night, Captain," he said, when I failed to respond.

We shook hands at the door. Footsteps echoed in the dim hallway. Chaplain Koh said in a whisper, for the duty officer was coming up the stairway, "May I ask you again? What would you do if you were in my place?"

I met his eyes as bravely as I could. "Do you think that was what Mr. Shin might have had in mind, for you to put that question to me?"

He nodded.

"I would tell the truth, Chaplain," I declared. "Truth cannot be bribed."

"How I envy you!" he said. "How I envy your youth!"

12

Next morning, I attended the briefing at half-past nine, as usual, and was listening to the report concerning the encounters of our patrols with Chinese Communist soldiers on the western front, when I was wanted on the phone. I went to the desk of the duty officer at the entrance to headquarters.

"A call from K-10-9, Captain," said the lieutenant on duty. K-10-9 was an Air Force base across the river.

"Captain Lee speaking," I said.

"Can you come and pick me up, so I can report for temporary duty—to *you?*" It was Park.

I called the chief to inform him that I would not be in the office for some time, and told him of Park's arrival, of which, apparently, he had already been notified by Naval Intelligence.

"I understand he is assigned to you, is he not?" he said.

I replied that I was grateful for his kind consideration.

"Why thank me? You ought to thank the Navy," he said. "Anyway, tell your friend how sorry I am about his father. I was well briefed on him and I would like to meet him. Bring him up when you can, will you. And take good care of him while he's with us."

Putting the receiver down, I wished, for the first time since the war, that I was back at my university. Outside the window the gray morning hung low, blurring the city. In the sky, dirty clouds flew over the church. The bell clanged faintly.

Chaplain Koh walked in with a folded newspaper in his hand, and thrust it into my hand. He shook his head, muttering, "I simply don't understand."

I did not look at the paper. I wanted to be alone.

"I am talking about Mr. Shin," he said. "I don't understand him. I knew Colonel Chang was suspicious of him. But I trusted Mr. Shin. He told me he wasn't there. He told me he knew nothing about it."

"What are you talking about?"

"I am talking about the execution of the twelve ministers. Mr. Shin told me that he and Mr. Hann had been jailed separately from the others, so they didn't know anything about the execution. I know Colonel Chang believes differently. But I trusted Mr. Shin's words. Could he have lied to me? How could he, though?" He took the paper back from me, spread it open, and put it on the desk. "Here. Read this. It's all over the city."

On the front page of the *Freedom Press*, a local paper, appeared the following article—a public announcement by the preparation committee for the joint memorial service:

It was announced by the Army Counterintelligence Corps that the Army Intelligence Authority is in possession of sufficient evidence that twelve North Korean Christian ministers were murdered by the North Korean puppet regime's secret police, on the morning of June 25 at half-past twelve, only a few hours before the outbreak of the Korean War. Eight ministers from Pyongyang, including the Reverend Park, an eminent leader of the Christians in North Korea, and six ministers from the provinces had been arrested by the Reds on an alleged charge of "counterrevolutionary activities." It is believed that the murder was planned by the Internal Security Bureau of the puppet regime and was carried out by the Pyongyang secret police.

Of the fourteen ministers arrested only two ministers survived. The Reverends Shin and Hann of Pyongyang were present as the murder took place, and they witnessed the tragic last moments of the twelve martyrs.

We, on behalf of the Christian churches of all faiths of Pyongyang, now announce that preparations are under way for a joint memorial service to commemorate the twelve martyrs. It is to be held at the First Presbyterian Church at two in the afternoon on

Tuesday, the twenty-first of November. To honor the families of the martyrs, transportation and other facilities are being made available to them through the generous cooperation of the Army authorities, so that they will be able to be present at the memorial service.

It is sincerely hoped that the citizens of this city will attend the service, regardless of their religious affiliations, so that we can all share in the memory of our martyrs, who, for the cause of our everlasting freedom, shed their noble blood in glorious testimony of the suffering Christians and their eventual spiritual triumph over the Reds' persecution. Let us all remember the twelve martyrs.

A dozen or so names of the members of the committee followed the announcement. Among them were Chaplain Koh as the chairman of the committee, Park as the representative of the families of the martyrs, and myself as the liaison officer.

Chaplain Koh glared at me, as if the article were my doing. I put the paper in my pocket, walked out of my office, and drove off to the air base, confused and angry.

13

Parka-clad officers and men, shuffling to and fro and in and out, crowded the smoke-filled waiting room of the air base operations building. Loudspeakers bellowed, red and blue signal lights flashed, buzzers hummed, and the screech of jet fighters out on the runways cut through the murmuring voices. Park and I shook hands and examined each other briefly; then he plunged into the matter on hand with the flat declaration, "What is this all about?"

I produced the newspaper, suggesting that he read the announcement of the preparation committee for the memorial service.

He merely glanced at it. "I know, I know. I've read it in Seoul." The article seemed to have been publicized simultaneously in both South and North Korean papers. "I knew it wasn't your doing. I know you better than that." His left eye squinted slightly as he tried to smile. "I must admit, though, I nearly went back to Pusan when I read my name."

He had not changed much; he was as lean as ever, and as austere in his manner. His lips were closed tensely as I had always noted with a vague feeling of compassion; only the haughty sparkle of his eyes had given way to a brooding I had seldom observed before. For the first time I felt sorry for him.

He looked at me wearily and said, "Let's not talk about it yet, shall we? All I want now is to take a look at whatever is left of my hometown. It has been ten years since I saw it last."

We left the base; we did not speak much while we were driving into the city.

It was a little before noon when we arrived in my office. We took off our helmets, parkas, and pistols, then settled down in the chairs around the stove. Park lighted a cigarette; his left hand was visibly unsteady.

"How's your arm?" I said.

"Oh, all right," he said with a faint smile on his weather-beaten face. "How's your knee?"

"Fine," I said, looking at the stamped emblem of an anchor and the initials of the Korean Marine Corps—KMC—over the left pocket of his dark-green fatigue jacket. He stood up and went over to the window. I joined him. Outside, it was as gray as ever. At the moment, there was no traffic; no people were working in the ruins. It seemed hushed around the church.

"So, he is gone," he said quietly. "A martyr."

We stood there silently for some time, looking out. When we returned to our chairs, Park sat hunched, his clenched fists on his knees. "You know, of course," he said, "I refuse to have anything to do with the memorial service."

"Then why did you come?" I said. The harshness of my voice surprised me.

He did not flinch. "Why did I come?" he said reflectively. "I knew you would ask that question."

The telephone rang. Colonel Chang wanted to know if Park was there with me. "I would like to meet him," he said, "but I am occupied at the moment and I'll try to see him later on. Meanwhile, I suggest you take him to Mr. Shin. I am terribly sorry about his father and perhaps he is anxious to learn more about the tragic death. I can't think of anyone who could shed more light on it than Mr. Shin. Give my best regards to your friend, won't you? And by the way, do you know where Chaplain Koh is? No? Well, that is all."

I turned to Park. "It was the chief," I said. "Colonel Chang."

"I've heard about him," he said indifferently.

"He wants to see you."

"I couldn't care less. Do you want me to meet him?"

"Not for the time being. I'll take you to him when I think you should see him."

There was a knock on the door and my orderly came in. An old woman was waiting to deliver a letter to me personally. I excused myself and went downstairs. It was Mrs. Hann.

I took her into the duty officer's booth. She broke into tears as she handed me the letter, crying, "You must help him! You must help Mr. Shin!"

The short note said:

DEAR CAPTAIN LEE:

I should like to see you again. If you could come to me at the earliest opportunity, I shall be most grateful. I am hoping that you could help me in a certain matter that concerns your friend Park.

YOURS TRULY,
SHIN

"What does it say?" asked Mrs. Hann, drying her face.

"He wants me to come to the house."

"Then you must come at once," she burst out, "and do something about it." She was unable to control her agitation; she was nearly hysterical.

I asked her to try to compose herself and tell me what had happened.

"I don't know what's really happening," she said. "But I've never seen so many people coming to see Mr. Shin all at once. The house was full of people this morning. They are still there, I am sure—people from the church. Newspapermen, too, taking pictures of him and all that. It was maddening and he's coughing terribly but he saw everyone. You read the paper, didn't you?"

I nodded. "So you read it, too."

"Someone came to the house very early this morning. He brought the paper and after he'd gone, Mr. Shin wanted me to read it. It's true. Mr. Shin told me all about it."

"Did he?"

"He and my son were there and saw everything that happened," she said, searching my face. "Then people from the church started coming. That Army chaplain, too. They all wanted to know why Mr. Shin had told them before that he didn't know anything about what happened to the other ministers." She paused, looking at me meekly. "What do you think will happen? What do you think will happen to Mr. Shin and my son?"

"Did he tell you anything about your son?"

"He only said that it was too much for my son, and that's why . . ." She stopped and began to cry again.

I tried my best to comfort her. "Did Mr. Shin say anything to the people from the church?"

She shook her head. "No, nothing. He just let them talk."

"And he wasn't angry?"

"No. I wish he had been. He had nothing to say to them. That's what he said. One man even asked him why he'd been telling them a lie! Oh, I couldn't stand it!"

I told her that I would drive to the house with her. I had her take a chair and wait for me. I ran upstairs to my office, and found Park standing near the window, looking out. He turned to me.

"You asked me why I came," he said gravely. "I want to see Mr. Shin. That's why I came."

"Why do you want to see him?" I said. "What do you want from him?"

"Just one thing. I want to find out how he died," he said quickly. There was nothing in the tone of his voice that I might have called sentimental or pious; it was a flat statement uttered matter-of-factly.

"I thought you wanted nothing to do with your father," I said.

"I seem to surprise you," he said dryly. "I am surprised at myself. He was a fanatic, as you know. And I dislike fanatics. We had nothing in common. I seldom thought about him. But now that he's dead, I am obsessed with his death. I don't care whether he is a martyr or a hero. That is not my concern. I want to find out if he died as a fanatic, as faithful as ever to his image of himself as the most righteous servant of God on earth. I believe that is what he thought himself to be. And I want to know if he died with his image unshattered.

"Am I too harsh?" he added gloomily.

"He is a martyr now," I said. "You must remember that."

"No matter. I only want to know if there was anything in the last days of his life that I might share with him." He paused.

"Go on."

"If there is nothing, then we remain strangers to each other forever."

"But why such an obsession?"

His eyes were burning with intensity. "When we saw each other for the last time, I told him that he, too, was not infallible. The sooner he realized it, the better for the true salvation of his soul, since that's what he wanted. Yes, I told him that, and now the thought possesses me. Can you understand that?

"I am not interested in the ordinary, mundane sort of father-and-son relationship. I am not even interested in the fact that I am his disowned son. I am concerned with him as a fanatic, a God-drunk man. He never stopped to examine himself dispassionately, not even when he felt he had to disown me. He thought he was always right. He never doubted his faith in his god and never, for one moment, suspected that he and his god might not be in as harmonious a state as he always believed." He turned to point to the ruined church. "That was his world."

"Have you ever examined yourself," I said, "well . . . dispassionately?"

"Many times."

"Don't you think, then, that he might have before the end?"

He swung around impatiently. "That's what I want to see Mr. Shin about."

"Leave him alone!" I said. It shocked me to hear myself shouting. "Just leave him alone for a while."

He looked at me in surprise.

"I'm sorry," I said. "I want to tell you about Mr. Shin, but there's no time now. I have to go to see him."

"And you don't want me to come along, do you?" Park said.

"Not now," I said, ashamed of my outburst. "I will let you know when you can see him."

14

After thanking me for my prompt response to his note, Mr. Shin said, "I was a bit surprised to learn from Chaplain Koh that Park is here in the city." Trying not to cough, he cleared his throat, and forced a smile on his pale face.

I said that Park's arrival had taken me by surprise, too.

"Then you did not plan it," he said.

"No."

"I didn't think you would have arranged for him to come, shall we say, to play a role in the memorial service. How does he feel about it?"

"He won't have anything to do with it. It is absurd that he, of all people, should be asked to represent the families of the martyrs."

"But it did not seem absurd to your colonel."

"He is anxious for Park to see you."

"Isn't that why he brought him here?"

"That you might have something to tell him?"

"Perhaps. Chaplain Koh feels that his appearance at this particular time was arranged by your colonel to embarrass me."

"Are you," I said with some hesitation, "embarrassed?"

"No."

"Do you have something you would like to tell Park?"

He did not answer.

I pressed him. "Would you like to see him?"

"Do you think I ought to?" he said. "Or rather, Captain, is he prepared to see me?"

An uncomfortable silence fell between us. Through the dusty

window, I could see that the sky had not cleared. The snow-laden branches of the crooked pine trees, seen through the uneven windowpanes, swelled and shrank, wavering in the wind. Mrs. Hann tiptoed in, served us tea, and withdrew.

Putting his cup down on the small table next to his chair, he said, "What the newspaper said about me is quite true."

I remained silent.

"I was there at the execution of the ministers," he said firmly as though he wanted to make sure that I would not disbelieve his words. "Your colonel is not making it up."

"Meaning . . . ?" I said.

"Meaning I lied to you," he said quietly.

"You lied to everyone."

"Yes. I do not insist that my conscience is impeccable."

"I should be angry," I said.

"With me or with your colonel? Don't be. He is only doing what he has to do."

"You sound as if you felt grateful for what he is doing to you."

Without hesitation, he said, "I am thankful to him."

"He has exposed you as a liar."

"Yes, he has."

"Now, everyone knows that you have been lying."

"Yes."

"And that is what you want?" I said. "It's a serious matter, isn't it, Mr. Shin, for a man like you to admit he has lied?"

"Yes. Very serious."

"You have managed to shock people. When they recover from the shock and from the inevitable confusion, they will come to you to ask why you have lied to them."

"They already have."

"And you have nothing to say to them?"

"No."

"They ask you what it was that persuaded you to lie, and you have nothing to say to them."

"Nothing."

"So they can only think you must be guilty of something, isn't that right?"

He did not reply; he merely continued to sip his tea, his calm gaze fixed upon me.

"But, Mr. Shin," I said, "those who know you well may be convinced that you are not guilty of anything, speaking in human terms, of course. You know that. So they will come to the conclusion that there must be something you do not intend to tell."

He lowered his eyes as if pained.

"Yes, you may be innocent," I said, "innocent of the kind of guilt people like Colonel Chang can imagine. But those who knew you well may come to realize that what you do not intend to tell may be the truth about the execution." I stopped, disturbed by the tone of accusation in my voice, and above all by what I was about to say; but there was no way to retreat. "And that, Mr. Shin, is what you have been hoping for."

"Enough!" he whispered.

"Isn't it true," I insisted, "that you have been secretly wishing others might begin guessing the truth, which you yourself do not want to tell?"

A flash of anger shot from his eyes; then he looked away.

I could not restrain myself. "What are you trying to do?" I said. "Run away from the truth? Or, hide it from the others?"

"Neither," he said in a weary whisper.

"Are you sure?"

"I am guarding it."

"Who are you to act as the guardian of the truth?" Suddenly, I felt tired. "For whom are you guarding it? For whom, Mr. Shin?"

He looked out the window. It had begun snowing.

"For the Church? For the Army?" I demanded.

He remained impassive.

"Or, for your god?"

To my surprise and uneasiness, a sudden, quick convulsion seized him; his face and throat twitched; his eyes were closed. When, a moment later, he turned and gazed at me, I saw that his eyes were filled with tears. In a hoarse whisper, he said, "Captain, please do not force me to blaspheme."

A feeling of exasperation overwhelmed me. "Mr. Shin, they have asked for it. Why don't you tell them the truth?"

He stood up, clutching at the cup and the saucer, and in a voice that was at once stern and gentle he said, "My young friend, has it ever occurred to you that they may not want the truth?"

15

Park had not waited for my return from Mr. Shin's. The note he had left on my desk said he had borrowed a jeep from the Marine liaison officer and gone out to take a look around the city.

The snow was getting heavier, the sky darker. Through the window I saw columns of medium tanks, their guns prostrate, crawl past the ruins, trailed by another column of howitzers, northbound. The snow soon covered the tracks left by the heavy treads. Silence returned to the streets, and with it the brooding afternoon of a dreary northern city.

Hours went by monotonously. Alone in my office, I took care of the routine business of my section and administrative matters of headquarters. There were reports to draft, papers to sign; and then there was the meeting with the officers of my section, during which I had a telephone call from Colonel Chang. He wanted to know where Chaplain Koh was. I could not help him; I had not seen the chaplain all afternoon. He hung up without a word, only to call me back a few minutes later to say that he wanted to see me immediately.

In his cavernous room, silent behind the desk, Colonel Chang sat crouched, immobile; only the hissing of the stove and its flickering light that flitted about his glasses and his monkish head appeared to have noticed my entrance. He did not look up at me; I might just as well not have been there. Finally the telephone on his desk roused him. He took the call with a few grunting words of approval and disapproval, then slammed the receiver down. Rising briskly from his chair, he came around the desk toward me, exclaiming, "Well, we've got him!"

"Got whom, sir?"

"It was CIC," he said, shoveling more coal into the stove. "I've been waiting for this. They reported the capture of a Red major who had been with the Pyongyang secret police." He paused to wipe his hands with a handkerchief. "He confessed that he knew something about the murder of the ministers."

The colonel was unmistakably excited.

"Well, don't you have anything to say? Do you realize what it may mean to us?"

I congratulated him on the lucky turn of events.

"We shall soon find out more about your friend, Shin," he said, holding his hands over the stove. "What do you say to that?"

"I don't know what more we can learn about him, sir," I said.

"Ah, you will be surprised. I promise you that!"

"I presume you think this prisoner can produce information that will astonish us all . . . that is, in respect to Mr. Shin."

"You imply that you know enough about Shin."

"Don't you, sir?"

"No."

"I am afraid I fail to understand you, sir," I said. "After reading the announcement of the preparation committee, I assumed that you had already made up your mind about him."

"It's not as simple as that."

"I beg your pardon, sir, but I thought it was."

He ignored my remark.

"I saw Mr. Shin this afternoon," I said. "So did others, including many Christians in the city, of course."

"I know."

"He had no comment on the announcement except to say it was true."

"So I heard," he muttered, and repeated it in a voice that echoed weariness unusual for him. "So I heard."

"Doesn't that satisfy you?" I said. "He has admitted that he had been telling a lie. That's what it all comes to, isn't it, sir?"

He said quickly, "I knew that!"

"I didn't. It came to me as a surprise."

He glowered at me. "I am very sorry, Captain."

"Don't mention it, Colonel," I said. "After all, one can never be too sure of anything in our line of business."

"You are being rather humorous."

"Not at all, sir."

"Then I take it that you are dead serious."

"Yes, sir."

He looked away and stared at the stove. For a while, he was silent, hands clasped behind him. The red light, wriggling out of the stove, darted at his shadowy profile. He turned to me with a faint smile. "All right, Captain. If you are as dead serious as I am, then I assume that you are now ready to come out in the open and tell me what you think of Shin."

I said straight away, "Yes."

"Good! But before you tell me what you think of him, you may do well to speculate upon the possible causes for his silence."

"What would you expect him to say, sir? Or, should I say, what did you expect him to say?"

"I have never met him, but I know him well. I have heard enough about him; indeed, so much so that I am reasonably convinced he is a pious man, a good Christian, that is. I am also convinced he has always been a man who enjoyed the unconditional reputation of having an immaculate conscience. Now, a good Christian shouldn't tell a lie, should he? But he did. So we are now beholding a pious Christian with an immaculate conscience who publicly admits that he has been a liar. The curious thing is that he neither justifies himself nor indicates any sign of remorse. What we see about him is nothing but a glorious halo of supreme confidence, and I daresay I must give him some credit for that, although he gives me no other choice than to line up two possible explanations for his remarkable behavior. First, his conscience is as clear as it can be, despite his lying. Second, his conscience is as corrupt as it can be. Of course, I am not simpleminded enough to exclude any other possible explanations. For the moment, however, these two seem to provide me with enough to speculate upon. Now, you wouldn't accept the second explanation, would you?"

"No."

"Ah, it was stupid of me to ask you that," he said with a grin. "It may interest you, Captain, to know that neither would I accept it. Don't be surprised to hear that. It's a perfectly natural reaction on my part. It is difficult, after all, to believe that a Christian minister's conscience could be as stinking as a dead fish. Mind you, I don't mean to say that it could never be so. But let us assume, for the time being, that Shin's conscience is quite clear. Are you satisfied?"

"Quite."

"Good! So we carve out a crystal-clear conscience for him and, let us say, we intend to guarantee it for him. We then have this business of his lie, which may tarnish his beatific conscience, and we can't let that happen, now can we? We must insist that the fact—yes, the fact that he lied cannot spoil the purity of his conscience, and that his act of lying has nothing to do with the quality of conscience. But that may lead us to an intriguing question as to what sort of conscience we have just adorned him with. What do you say?" He looked at me as though he were waiting for my reply, but it was plain that he enjoyed his talk too much, savored every word of it too much to allow me to interrupt him. "How shall we justify the purity and admirable tranquility of his conscience when we have to admit, at the same time, that an act of lying is, in principle at least, no credit to any man's conscience?" He paused, then answered his own question. "His is the sort of conscience that is immune to this particular act of lying. Ah, there we are! That's what we'll have to say."

I said, "If I recall, sir, you were to appeal to his conscience. To which one did you mean to appeal, granting that there are several kinds of conscience as you seem to imply?"

"To the one that is not immune to this act of lying, naturally. There is something you must always remember about him. He is a minister, a shepherd, as Christians call him. He can't go around telling his flock that he is a poor shepherd, now can he? Or, should he? Of course not. Well, there you are. He must let his flock remain in its happy belief that he is not the sort of shepherd who will take to his heels in the face of a pack of wolves and leave the flock defenseless."

"Do you still insist that he gave in to the Communists and betrayed the other ministers?"

He did not answer.

"If you still do, sir, you have exposed the notion to his flock that he is a poor shepherd," I said. "At least from your point of view."

"I have indeed," he said.

"Are you disappointed that he does not, may I say, confess his alleged guilt?"

"Yes! But not the way you think!" He walked away from me to the window, where he stood looking out into the snow-filled late afternoon. "I am disappointed because he doesn't justify himself. Why doesn't he say something to clear himself?"

Why, indeed, I thought.

"I'll tell you why," he said. "The conscience he is relying on now tells him that he is guiltless and, therefore, he needs no defense for himself."

"In that case," I said, "you shouldn't be at all disappointed."

"One minister alive is better than twelve ministers dead! Is that what he thinks?"

I could not restrain myself. "Perhaps, he has something he doesn't want to say. Not for the sake of his own interest, as you seem to be convinced, but for the sake of others' interest, including yours, if I may say so."

"Nonsense! By what inscrutable magic could he have survived the lions' den!"

"Sir, I repeat, I believe Mr. Shin is innocent."

He swung around. "Of course, he is! Of course he is innocent! How can he be anything else?" He returned to the stove. "Are you surprised to hear me say that? Don't be. If he isn't, he would not have been able to enjoy the protection he now receives from his conscience. He believes that he has done something right by telling a lie and is still doing the right thing by not saying anything more. It's this notion of self-righteousness that gives him the halo of serenity, even of pride. Ah, that's what gets on my nerves! I am not accusing him, you understand. The real villain, Captain, in this whole business is neither he nor his act of lying. On the contrary, it is what forced him to lie and yet allows his conscience to remain as spotless as the soul of an angel—as Christians would say. Am I clear?"

The colonel was getting out beyond my depth.

"So you tell me Shin is innocent," he said. "And you are sure, absolutely sure about that?"

"He is, sir," I insisted, but I had to add, "from our point of view."

"Are you including mine?"

"Yes."

"Don't, because he is not from my point of view."

I reminded him that he himself had just declared a moment ago that Mr. Shin was innocent.

"Ah, I didn't say he was innocent from my point of view."

Perplexed, I burst out, "But you say you are not accusing him and yet you don't think he is innocent. You must be accusing somebody—the real villain, as you say."

He greeted me with a placid grin. "You are quite right, Captain."

"May I ask what it is?"

"Why, my dear Captain, I am surprised that you ask me what it is rather than who it is."

"Then, may I ask you who it is?"

"Don't you know?" he said, returning to his chair which squeaked under the weight of his body. "Who else but his god?" He chuckled. "Can't you picture him on his knees, telling his god what he has done? And his god, gently patting him on the back, says, 'It's all right, my dear boy. To err is human, to forgive divine.' Well, what do you think of that?"

I had to laugh in spite of myself.

16

When I left Colonel Chang's office, I hoped to find Park in my room, but he was not there. There was little I could do but stand in front of the window and watch the gray North Korean afternoon swiftly fade into a bleak night. It had become windy. The snow was turning into a blizzard, and I could hear the church bell clanging now faintly, now violently. Footsteps echoed in the hallway, down the stairs, perhaps toward the mess hall. My orderly came in; first, to clean the room, then with a bucketful of coal for the night. Park still had not come back. I felt helpless without him. I had decided, while listening to Colonel Chang, to take him to Mr. Shin; the sooner the better—I thought.

Colonel Chang telephoned me from his office to ask if I had seen Chaplain Koh. "Where on earth is he!" he shouted. "I haven't seen him since last night. And what about Park? Has he been to see Shin?"

I told him that, at my discretion, Park had not yet met the minister.

"Ah, hang your discretion!" he grunted.

About half an hour later he called again, this time from CIC. Again he asked after Chaplain Koh. He swore. "The trouble with that man is he's too damned sure of himself. Ah, I don't trust him."

There was nothing for me to say.

"I am waiting for a call from the Chief of Army Intelligence," he said. "Have it transferred to CIC if it comes through." After a pause he continued, "I promised you a surprise from our new prisoner, didn't I? I have something you might like to

know and I want you to think about it. The prisoner was quite
stubborn but we do have an efficient CIC, if you know what I
mean. From what he said, it appears that the commandant of
the Pyongyang secret police was liquidated, presumably by the
same firing squad that murdered the ministers. Not only the
commandant but three top aides of his. The most curious
angle is that they were shot the day after the ministers were
murdered. Why? The prisoner insists he doesn't really know,
except that they were arrested immediately after the murder
and were shot by an order from someone high up in their secret police. Now this is what astonishes me. The charges made
against them were counterrevolutionary activities in general
and insubordination in particular. How do you explain that?
But what interests me most is that it took place immediately
after the murder of the ministers. Try to figure that out. The
prisoner is reviving now and I am sure he has more to enlighten
us with. If you see Shin, and I expect you will, you might ask
him if he knew anything about this most significant event."
He hung up.

I felt bewildered. I could not see any possible connection
with the execution of the ministers, even though the colonel apparently did, or at least was trying to find such a connection.

By the time Park returned I was feeling pretty glum. His
face was haggard. I helped him out of his frozen parka, and he
slumped down on a chair. I poked the stove.

"He's gone," he said, unbuckling his gun belt.

Alarmed, I said, "Who is gone?"

"Mr. Shin. He and Chaplain Koh have vanished. Rather, the
chaplain kidnapped Mr. Shin and the young minister."

"Kidnapped?" It didn't make sense. I pulled up a chair near
the stove next to him.

"I just came back from Mr. Shin's house," Park said. "It was
too late. He had already gone."

"But where?"

"I don't know. After you left the office, our liaison officer
came in. He had been instructed to take care of me. He said I
could use his jeep while I was here. So I started driving around.
I thought I was feeling a bit nostalgic, you know, having

returned to my hometown after so many years of, let's say, exile. I was wrong. I wasn't nostalgic at all. The place depressed me. It was no use telling myself, 'Well, my dear, good old hometown, here I am. I am back.' I wasn't in a mood for that kind of nonsense. Instead, I began looking up the ministers I had known through my father. All I got from them was a pile of stock eulogies for my father, a great martyr, a hero—and some pious sympathy for me. I was visiting one of them—Mr. Sung—when I ran into Chaplain Koh. I used to be well acquainted with the chaplain. The three of us talked about Mr. Shin. Mr. Sung was worried about him because of the rumor that some hot-blooded members of the congregations of the murdered ministers were demanding justice. They were getting out of hand, threatening either to confront Mr. Shin or bring him to their churches and make him tell the truth, that is, make him repent or confess his sins. Ah, those Christians! While we were talking, a group of them came to see Mr. Sung. They were heading for Mr. Shin's house and they wanted him to come with them. He tried to talk them out of it, but they wouldn't listen, even though they were from his own congregation. They said others were joining them and they were all going together. Chaplain Koh was alarmed and wanted me to come with him to Mr. Shin's at once. I knew you had something on your mind when you asked me not to see him for a while, so I stayed behind."

The telephone rang. It was Colonel Chang again. He was still at CIC, and wanted to know if the chaplain had returned yet.

"No, sir," I replied. "I haven't the slightest idea where he is. I would appreciate it, Colonel, if you tell him that I would very much like to see him, that is, if you find him before I do, sir."

"You are getting more and more humorous," he grunted. "Never mind! I only wanted to have him gather the ministers on the committee for a meeting. Ah, hang him!"

"Can I do anything about that, sir? About the meeting, I mean, I am the liaison officer, after all."

"Forget it. I want you to go to see Shin. Tell him I want to see him. Either he could come down to headquarters or I could go to his house. You arrange it."

My silence irritated him.

"Did you hear what I said?"

"Yes, I did," I said. "Sir, have you been able to learn anything more from the prisoner?"

"Damn it, no! He's taking a long time off. Ah, we'll beat it out of him soon enough."

I decided to break the news. "I am afraid you are too late."

"What are you talking about?"

"You won't be able to see Mr. Shin," I told him. "He has left the city, Colonel."

There was no response from him for a few seconds. Then he shouted, "A damned fool! A coward!" With that outburst, he hung up.

"The colonel seems to be upset," I said, but Park merely shrugged.

"To go on with what I was telling you," he said, "after the chaplain left in a hurry, I got to worrying about Mr. Shin and decided to go anyway. I was too late. The mob was there, even if Mr. Shin wasn't, or the young minister, only the old woman. They demanded to see Mr. Shin and when they were told he wasn't there they broke into the house. Those good Christians searched the whole house. Then they got mad and began to smash the furniture, windows, everything they could lay hands on. I found the old woman outside in the snow, hysterical, while they were literally tearing down the house inside. I tried to talk them out of it, but nobody listened to me.

"Meanwhile more people, mostly women, were coming up the hill. They milled about the house chanting hymns and screaming, 'Judas! Judas!' It was uncanny. There they were, imagine, in the blizzard, chanting crazily and screaming, 'Judas,' beating their bodies, their poor ragged bodies—pouring out all their sorrows, all that had been simmering in their darkened souls during the years of persecution. What passion! What self-lacerating passion! I tell you—I didn't know whether to despise them—or love them. Ah, the lambs disfigured into a wailing mob!

"I tried again to send them back to wherever they came from but they wouldn't listen to me. Finally I fired a few shots in the air. That broke the spell. I told them who I was. Well, who was I? The son of my father, of course. Ah, my father's name—it was a magic word. Suddenly everything was hushed. They listened to me, they literally adored me, the son of the great martyr, who was one of them, one of the persecuted. What did I tell them? I don't know. I just talked, and after a while they went back down the hill, still chanting, in the slashing snow and the wind.

"I was left alone with the old woman. She looked nearly insane. She insisted she didn't know where Mr. Shin was. At last, she told me the chaplain had come to the house shortly before the Christians came and had a big argument with Mr. Shin, about what, the poor woman didn't know. Mr. Shin then told her he was taking the young minister to a place where he could be well taken care of. He told her he would come back for her. Then the three of them got into the chaplain's jeep and drove away. I think she knows where they went. She might tell you. You seem to be in her confidence. She pleaded with me that I bring you to her."

I called my orderly and told him to get a box of rations from the kitchen and come to my office, armed, with his bedding; he was going to stay with the old woman. We were ready to leave when Colonel Chang burst in. It was the first time he had ever come down to my office to see me.

17

"I am dumbfounded, I must confess," exclaimed Colonel Chang. "You are Captain Park, aren't you? I am happy to see you here, especially so because I have always admired your father." He paused to wipe his wet face and his glasses. "The prisoner testified that he was one of those who had interrogated—I mean tortured—the ministers. He swore that they all conducted themselves like heroes." He turned to me. "Have you told Captain Park about the execution of the commandant and his three aides of the Pyongyang secret police?"

When I said I had not, he explained to Park, "Do you realize that they were shot just because they had murdered the ministers? Apparently, the Reds had arrested the ministers for possible future use as hostages. They were not supposed to be murdered—not without a special order from the chief of the secret police."

"Then, why?" said Park.

"Ah, it's all beyond me," said the colonel. "The commandant and his aides have a party one night and get drunk. They come down to the jail, order some prisoners out into the torture chamber, and beat them up. They are not satisfied with that. They remember they have Christians in the jail. They order the ministers out of their cells, beat them and herd them out into a truck and off they go and murder them. Of course, we can't really trust every single word the prisoner said. For all I know, he might be trying to win our favor. But that's what happened, according to him. Next day, the chief of the secret police is scandalized. He gets abused by his superiors. He gets furious. He orders that the commandant and his aides be shot—by the same firing squad that murdered the ministers the night before. Ah, it's all damned bloody. And do you realize how they murdered the ministers? One after another!"

He continued. "And how did Mr. Shin and the young minister get out of it alive? I still don't understand. The prisoner insists he telephoned the chief of the secret police when he realized what the commandant was up to. He says he never liked the commandant. I asked him why. He just didn't like him, he says. Anyway, he gets the order from his chief to stop the commandant and if he resists the order, well, either arrest him or shoot him on the spot. The prisoner goes after the commandant with a squad of Red guards, but he is a bit late. By the time he got around to arresting the bloody butcher, only two ministers were still alive."

"Divine intervention," I said.

Colonel Chang turned his tired face to me. "Captain Lee, I must see Mr. Shin immediately. You realize how important it is for me to see him at once."

"He is not here, Colonel," I said. "I have told you that."

"I know, I know," he said in agitation. "But—why?"

Park briefed him on what had happened at Mr. Shin's house.

"But why?" Colonel Chang asked again, frowning. "Why would he disappear like that? Why should he run away?"

"I don't think he ran away, Colonel," I said.

Colonel Chang scrutinized me narrowly. "What do you mean, Captain Lee, you don't think he ran away? All right, what would you call it? Or maybe you know something that I don't know?"

"I doubt that, Colonel. You already know I talked with Mr. Shin today shortly before he left the city. He didn't tell me he was going to leave; he hadn't even thought of it, as a matter of fact; I'm sure of that. He had nothing to say about why he had lied. I asked him to tell the truth, which I suspected, with your permission, Colonel, concerned the circumstances involving the execution." I paused and took a chair. "I presume that the truth about the execution is what everyone wants to know, including you, Colonel."

"Of course," Colonel Chang said. "So does Captain Park, I am sure."

Park paid no heed to his remarks.

"And so do I, sir," I said. "But, Colonel, are you so sure that you want to know the truth about the execution?"

"Now, come, come!" he said. "What are you talking about? We already know the truth. So it doesn't matter whether we want it or not, does it? We already have it. I have just told you how magnificently all the ministers conducted themselves in their most difficult time. That's the truth, and I am sure anyone would be proud to know it, except the Reds, of course."

I could not restrain myself from bursting out, "Sir, are you saying Mr. Shin is a Red?"

He laughed. "Certainly not! What makes you think that?"

"If the truth about the execution is as you described, Colonel, if we should be proud of the executed ministers, then why did Mr. Shin tell me that we may not want the truth? I assume that 'we' includes everyone concerned, you and Park and the Christians. Why, Colonel, should a man like him believe that such a glorious truth about the ministers as you have pictured may not be welcomed?"

Colonel Chang responded impatiently, "Did he say that?"

"I am surprised, sir, that you still seem to suspect Mr. Shin even when you insist that the truth about the ministers is so magnificent. Or, are you excluding Mr. Shin from their company?"

Tilting his head he stared at me.

Park said, "What I want to know is why everyone should assume that the twelve were all such martyrs. Is there any evidence that they were all good and saintly, while the survivors were not? All we have is your word, Colonel."

Colonel Chang retorted in a deliberately calm voice, "Yes, you have my word. The martyrs were all good and saintly."

"What about the survivors, sir?" I said.

"They were good and saintly, too," he said. Then he suddenly exclaimed, "What you don't understand is that there should be no doubt about the glory of the martyrs. They were good and saintly. Why? Because they *are* martyrs. Because they were murdered by the Reds. It is as simple as that. Now, what about the survivors? Well, they are good and saintly, too. Why?

Because they too have been imprisoned by the Reds. Because they too have been tortured by the Reds, and above all, because they are Christian ministers. Don't you see? That is how everything ought to be. They all deserve to be praised. They must all be good and saintly, do you understand?"

"Even if someone was guilty?"

"Naturally. But you must understand this clearly. No one was guilty of anything. Every single minister was as heroic and saintly as any heroes and saints we know of. Every minister in this case is and must be as immune to any charges of impurity as fresh snow. And that's that!"

"I do not understand you, Colonel," I said. "May I then assume that you no longer suspect Mr. Shin?"

"Yes, you may," he said and added placidly, "I have never suspected him of anything."

I looked at him, amazed.

"But what about his words?" said Park. "What are we to make of what he said—that we may not want the truth?"

Colonel Chang ignored the question.

Park turned to me. "What do you think?" he said. "Is the truth about the martyrs so ugly that he thinks we would rather not hear it?"

"Captain Park! I implore you to refrain from uttering such an impious statement," said Colonel Chang.

"Sir, I wish to know the truth," retorted Park. He turned to me. "Why do you think Mr. Shin left the city?"

I remained silent; I did not know what to say.

Colonel Chang said, "Now that I have the truth about the execution of the martyrs, and how all the ministers carried themselves, I do not feel it is important for us to know the reason that he left the city."

His statement vexed me. "Colonel, I am confused," I said. "You were anxious to find out why he had disappeared from the city. In fact, you accused him of running away. And now . . ."

"You completely misunderstand me. What I meant was that, in view of the truth about the entire situation, I could not comprehend why he should vanish as he did, only to increase and intensify suspicions and misgivings directed against him by a certain segment of the Christians. He is not guilty of any-thing. Why should he, then, leave without a trace, especially when the Christians want to see him? I am extremely un-happy about his act, which as I said, may inadvertently prompt some hot-blooded Christians to form a hasty and misguided conclusion. Do you understand me now?"

Park said gloomily, "I think he has a certain secret which he believes may be harmful to the Christians."

"What secret?" said the colonel, frowning.

"That not all the twelve ministers were martyrs."

"Do you share the same opinion, Captain Lee?" The colonel turned to me.

"I only know that Mr. Shin believes that we may not want the truth," I said.

"And that means," said the colonel, raising his voice, "that you don't accept my words as the truth."

"I must admit, with your permission, sir, that your truth may very well be only a part of the whole truth. I cannot evaluate the entire situation until I know what Mr. Shin has in mind."

"And what does he have in mind?" Colonel Chang said, now pacing about the room.

"I don't know, sir. He has not told me. All I know, because he told me so, is that he is guarding the truth."

"Guarding it? Well, for whom?" Colonel Chang said, visibly annoyed.

"For us, sir. For the Christians, for the Church, for the Army."

With an immense frown, Colonel Chang cluck-clucked.

"And for his god, too?" said Park.

"Ah, no use bringing God down into this," said Colonel Chang. "If what you say is true, Captain Lee, I am afraid Mr. Shin is trying to be too humble. We should understand him, of course. We understand that a man like him is not willing to publicize his sufferings and his triumph. It is very like him that he should want to efface himself. But I think he is going too far in not letting the others share the glory of the martyrs. The living should not deny the dead their suffering and their ulti-mate victory."

Park and I stared at him in silence.

Unperturbed, Colonel Chang continued: "The martyrdom of the twelve ministers is an established fact, which does not need to be questioned but needs only to be made public to render full justice to their heroism and saintliness. And there is no one better qualified than Mr. Shin for testifying to the glory of the martyrs. And that's that."

I looked at him, and when his eyes challenged mine, I said, "Colonel, what do you know about the execution of the ministers that I don't know?"

But he simply turned away and stalked out of my office.

18

The next morning, the *Freedom Press* carried an article, head-lined "Christian Intrepidity," about Chaplain Koh. There was a picture of the chaplain, dressed in combat fatigues and wearing a steel helmet on which was painted a white cross, leaning out of an Army jeep against the background of an artillery battery. The article quoted extensively from the testimony of Colonel Chang, who extolled the chaplain's "heroic virtues" in his reminiscences of how significant and valuable Chaplain Koh's contributions had been to the cause of the Army, how courageous a Christian hero he was on the front line in the grim days of the early battles, and so on. The testimony was augmented with recollections proffered by several Christian ministers in the city in praise of the chaplain.

At Colonel Chang's request, I drove with Park to see the ministers on the committee; the colonel planned to have a meeting in his office that afternoon.

The blizzard of the night before had quietly left the city, leaving behind it a thick layer of fresh snow over the battle-scarred earth. It was cold. In the blue sky streaks of white vapors from combat planes stretched beyond the northern mountains; on the ground, convoys of supply trucks from the southern side of the river plowed through the streets. The news from the front was gloomy. We had been receiving more and more intelligence reports concerning the increasing activities of the Chinese Communists. Some units on the western front had even captured some of their soldiers; it was beginning to look as if we might expect an extensive operation on the part of the Chinese on North Korean soil.

We reached the colonel's office shortly before two o'clock.

Five ministers had already arrived, and were sitting around the stove, listening to Colonel Chang, who was narrating the history of the intelligence operations in which Chaplain Koh had been involved. Park and I stood by the window. The ministers were old men, some with thin, white hair, some with gray hair; they were uniformly dressed in ash-colored, cotton-padded winter robes, on the left sleeves of which they wore black bands. They sat rigidly on olive-green metal chairs, nodding politely to the high-pitched voice of the colonel. After a while I left the room to tell my orderly to serve tea to the ministers.

When I came back Colonel Chang was saying, "Well, now, what's the use of reviving the past? The war is going to be over soon, and we have more than enough to do now and in the future."

His guests nodded pensively in agreement.

Another minister arrived. He, too, wore an ash-colored robe and a black armband. He was much younger than the others, perhaps in his mid-forties. After muttering an apology for being late, he said to no one in particular, "I am afraid there isn't much we can do about them."

Someone said, "Yes, I know."

"Are you talking about your people?" asked the colonel.

The younger minister said, "I have to admit that they are becoming rather unruly and uncontrollable."

Someone sighed and cleared his throat.

"I have said this already but I feel obliged to emphasize it again," said Colonel Chang, "that what happened yesterday at Mr. Shin's must never happen again. I may be forced to take certain measures which may be embarrassing to everyone concerned. I don't mean to say that I don't understand how they feel, but we can't afford to allow them to be swept away by their emotions. Besides, I assure you that you will soon discover how utterly disgraceful it would be for you or for your people to do anything rash, as far as Mr. Shin and Mr. Hann are concerned. Any doubt you might have felt about the two ministers, about Mr. Shin especially, is, I assure you, completely groundless."

Park and I exchanged a quick glance. The ministers stirred uneasily.

The younger minister came to the window, nodded to Park and me, and motioned us to look outside.

"There they are," he said for everyone to hear.

The others joined us.

The sky was still bright and clear but down below, the uneven shadows of the buildings had already darkened nearly half of the street, reaching out for the glittering whiteness of the ruins across the street and the church over the slope. About half a block to the left of our headquarters was an empty square, not yet touched by the shadows, illumined by the sun that glistened upon mounds of snow here and there; and out of the square filed a silent procession of people, coming slowly toward our building; then it turned to the left and went up the slope to the battered church. The snow atop the belfry reflected the sunshine brilliantly.

"They have been out since morning, going to the churches of the martyrs," someone behind me said. "It's a kind of pilgrimage, I suppose."

"Poor souls," another muttered.

The crowd of about three hundred had by now gathered in front of the church; some men were standing on the steps, facing the people.

"What are they up to now?" said the colonel.

I opened the window.

One of the men on the steps was gesticulating. The congregation kneeled on the snow. The face of the man speaking to them was cast heavenward, his arms upraised. Then, he, too, knelt down. Presently, we began to hear the murmur of voices, now rising high and loud, now subsiding and tremulous in the wind. Gradually, the voices ebbed. The man stood up. His hands cut the cold air several times. The congregation, now standing, began to sing a hymn—*"till we meet again beyond the River Jordan . . ."*

The black shadow of our building had already crept across

the street, and now was spreading unevenly upward on the slope over the ruins. A cold wind blew in through the open window.

Colonel Chang closed the window. "Well, well," he said.

The ministers returned to their chairs.

Colonel Chang stood by the stove. "I must say they seem indeed inspired."

"I have never seen anything quite like it," said one of the old men. "In all my life as their pastor, I have never been able to move them like this."

"I have seen many revivals. I myself have conducted them many times," said another. "But this is the greatest of all. I am deeply touched by it as you all must be, I am sure."

"The most miraculous thing about it is," said a third old minister with a gray beard, "they are doing it entirely on their own. I am certain that none of us here started it or even suggested it."

"It puts us all to shame," said the younger man.

"Ah, but it is a heaven-sent opportunity for them and for us," said another. "They have received the blessing. I dare say it is ordained by our Lord. We have needed it, let us admit. We needed an event mighty and divine enough to awaken us and free us from years of bad dreams."

"Inscrutable shall ever be the holy will of our Lord," someone said.

"Amen," echoed the others.

"We must not let the martyrs down," Colonel Chang said. "I have been saying it all along."

"Yes, our people know the martyrs died for us and saved us from the sins of our meek suffering and submission to the forces of evil," said a minister who appeared to be the oldest of the company. "Yes, we know it and they know it. We have sinned much, Colonel Chang, and we are ashamed that we have allowed our spirits to suffer from despair. It shall never happen again. I fear the Church needed the sacrifice offered by our martyrs, God bless their souls." He paused and looked about him. "I would like to ask everyone here to join me in a prayer. Would you mind, Colonel Chang?"

"Certainly not!"

My orderly came in, followed by a private; they proceeded to serve tea. The proposed prayer was delayed until they withdrew.

The cups and saucers clattered as the ministers put them down on the wooden floor. They bowed their heads. Colonel Chang, sitting hunched on a chair, gazed down into his cup. Park looked out of the window. I watched the ministers in their devotional posture.

"Lord, we ask Thee to forgive our many sins. We have just witnessed the spiritual agonies of Thy children. They cried out from the bottom of their penitent hearts, offering Thee their sinful souls, their spirits aflame with renewed zeal and vigor, through the inspiration of our holy martyrs. Lord, forgive us our many sins and show us the way, show us, Thy sinful children who have suffered much from the evil forces of Satan, show us the way to reach Thy light and Thy blessing. Hear us, Lord. We were weak, but we know we have not sinned beyond all hope. Lord, forgive our many sins and receive us into Thy everlasting kingdom. Amen."

"Amen," came the murmured response.

Colonel Chang broke the silence. "Now gentlemen, I asked you to join me here today because I want you to meet someone who was close to our martyrs during the last few days of their lives. Needless to say, I take great pride in what he wants to tell you about them. I won't talk about it now. You shall hear it directly from him. It is only a small service I can render you in my limited capacity as the officer in charge of this establishment. He will be here presently." He pressed a buzzer on his desk.

Polite nods and murmurs responded to his remark.

Suddenly Park stepped forward. "I am sure you all know who I am," he said. "I am glad you are all here, because I wanted to tell you that I do not wish to be included on this committee. I do not wish to have anything to do with the memorial service."

Colonel Chang interrupted, "Captain Park, I must ask you to restrain yourself from being overwhelmed by your grief. We all understand how unhappy you must be!"

Unperturbed, Park went on, "I am leaving the city as soon as I can. I am sorry that I cannot represent the families of your martyrs, but I have never asked for the honor. That is all I wanted to say."

Indifferent to the frowning and bewildered faces of the ministers, Park was about to stalk out of the room when there was a knock on the door. Two officers came in with a white-robed man between them. I recognized the lieutenants; they were from CIC.

The prisoner's head was shaven; his swollen, bloodshot eyes set above high cheekbones glanced about the room. His hands were heavily bandaged.

Colonel Chang held his arm. "Gentlemen, I would like you to meet Major Jung, formerly in the service of the Pyongyang secret police of the People's Republic of Korea. Major Jung, I want you to meet these gentlemen, distinguished ministers of the Christian church of this city, and, of course, dear colleagues of the martyrs. It was very thoughtful of you to agree to come here and personally tell my friends about the martyrs. My friends, Major Jung saw much of our martyrs and he was one of the few who witnessed their unforgettable last moments. Now, Major Jung, will you kindly tell these gentlemen what you have told me about them." He released his grip on the prisoner and stepped aside.

Major Jung's eyes lingered over the faces of the ministers. He was thin and tall. He moistened his lips; his cheeks twitched; his Adam's apple jerked up and down his long throat. His hoarse voice said quietly, "So you are ministers."

Colonel Chang said, "Incidentally, gentlemen, although we must admit that he has committed many sins in the past, Major Jung has given us invaluable help and has fully repented his ignoble past. And that means he shall be a free man—after certain administrative measures have been taken, that is."

Major Jung turned to the colonel. "You're a liar," he said.

The lieutenants seized his arms.

"I know your kind," the prisoner went on calmly. "We knew enough about you. You and I are in the same trade. Don't think you can fool me. I know what you are up to. You don't have to hide from these gentlemen the fact that you are going to shoot me. When? Tonight? Tomorrow morning?"

"What is this!" shouted the colonel.

The lieutenants tried to drag the prisoner out.

"Let him stay!" the colonel ordered; then to the prisoner, "Look here, you must be out of your mind. I warn you to behave yourself. I may indeed be inclined to shoot you, you understand!"

"Have mercy on him, Colonel," someone whispered.

Major Jung faced the ministers. He shook his bald head and grinned. "Yes, have mercy on me. Have mercy on me? But you make me laugh. You are too forgetful. It was I who had mercy on you, don't you remember? I had a chance to shoot all of you but I didn't because I foolishly thought you weren't worthy of our bullets. Ah, but I should have shot you all. I realize it only too late."

"Take him away!" Colonel Chang shouted.

I saw the door open behind the lieutenants; Chaplain Koh entered.

Major Jung said, "You don't have to send me away before I can tell these friends of yours about your great martyrs. Isn't that what you wanted me to do? I must say you have a sense of humor, though. Gentlemen, you wish to know how your great martyrs died. It gives me great pleasure to tell you that your great heroes and martyrs died like dogs. Like dogs, whimpering, whining, wailing. It pleased me to hear them beg for mercy, to hear them denounce their god and one another. They died like dogs. Like dogs, do you hear! Ah, I should have shot them all!"

"Why didn't you!" the sharp voice of Park cut in.

"Why? You ask me why?" The prisoner whirled about to face Park. "Because one went crazy. Crazy, like a mad dog. I am not a brute. I don't shoot mad men."

"And why didn't you shoot the other one!" boomed the voice of Chaplain Koh. He strode toward us.

"What is this!" shouted the colonel.

"He was the only one who put up a fight. I like a good fight.

He had guts. He was the only one who had enough guts to spit in my face. I admire anyone who can spit in my face. That's why I didn't shoot him. I should have shot him, though. I should have shot you, too, when I had a chance. I know you, a phony pastor."

Chaplain Koh stood facing the prisoner, then swiftly knocked him to the floor with his fist. He spat out, "Monster!"

The CIC lieutenants dragged the prisoner out of the room.

"What is this?" said the colonel to the chaplain.

"Indeed, what is this?" Chaplain Koh looked at the ministers. "What are you all doing here?"

"Where is he?" said the colonel. "Where is Mr. Shin?"

"Where is he now?" asked the oldest minister. "You must tell us if you know where he is. We must know the truth. He is the only one who can now tell us the truth about all this."

Chaplain Koh did not speak.

"What are you up to?" Colonel Chang said angrily; he glared at the chaplain.

"I won't allow you to disturb Mr. Shin," said the chaplain. He spoke to the ministers. "Now that you are all here, to whom shall I have the honor of delivering the message from Mr. Shin?"

"I feel obliged to warn you, Chaplain," said the colonel, "you are under my authority, you understand."

"Ah, hang your authority! Is that all you can think of? Speaking of authority, I have already talked with the Secretary of Defense, who is a very good friend of mine, my cousin, to be exact, as you know. Perhaps, you didn't know. It doesn't matter. I have been given a certain authority, the nature of which I shan't bother to explain. You can call him, if you like."

I stepped forward. "Chaplain, you said you have a message from Mr. Shin."

He nodded. "But I frankly don't know to whom I should deliver it." He glanced at the ministers.

"Please speak to us all," said the oldest. "Our leaders are gone but we shall try our best to be worthy of our duty as the interim representatives of our churches."

"Very well," the chaplain said. "Mr. Shin has already notified his congregation that he wishes to be relieved of his duty as their pastor, and a similar notice has been sent to the congregation of Mr. Hann."

No one spoke; no one stirred.

"Mr. Shin," the chaplain said, "wishes to resign from the ministry."

"Fool!" Colonel Chang exclaimed, "Bloody fool!"

19

For some time after the ministers had left in an atmosphere of confusion and uneasiness, a heavy silence prevailed among the four of us. Park and I stood by the window; Chaplain Koh sat quietly near the stove; while Colonel Chang leaned back in his swivel chair behind the desk, gazing at the ceiling. It was getting dark outside. The wind blew hard. A streetcar clanged by, spattering pale sparks in its wake.

Colonel Chang at last broke the silence by sitting up abruptly in his chair. "Captain Lee," he said, "you asked me what it was that I knew and you didn't about the execution of the twelve ministers. Do you remember?"

Park and the chaplain looked at the colonel, who now sat with his hands clasped on the desk.

"It's true, I do know something that all of you here do not know. I had hoped that I would never have to tell you what I know, but now I feel I have no other choice. The prisoner was telling you the truth about the ministers, although he exaggerated and understandably so. Among the twelve there were some who betrayed their fellows; they were unable to resist the Reds and allowed themselves to be manipulated into denouncing the others. I needn't say anything about Mr. Shin or about the young minister. You have heard the prisoner's words."

"Colonel, how long have you known all this?" I asked.

"Ever since I was assigned to the case. Of course I didn't know everything in detail. But that there were betrayers I knew for certain prior to the capture of Major Jung. Under the circumstances I had no other choice than to suspect Mr. Shin and Mr. Hann. I now know they are innocent. We have Major

Jung's word for the fantastic and complicated but true circumstances regarding the last moments of the execution. It was only when I got his confession that I was able to understand why Mr. Shin at first denied any knowledge of the execution. He decided to tell a small lie rather than a big lie about the martyrdom of the twelve, rather than reveal the truth about the shameful frailty and infidelity of some of them."

Colonel Chang's thin lips curled with disdain.

"Now," he continued after a pause, "Mr. Shin has vanished in the face of angry Christians who accuse him of an alleged betrayal. He wants to resign from the ministry and from his church. What are we to make of this? Consider for a moment that you are in his position, that you are falsely accused of a shameful act which you did not commit; consider also that you are subjected to unspeakable humiliation—such as having your house smashed by those for whose sake you are keeping silent. Captain Lee, I accept what you said—that Mr. Shin is guarding the truth, that the others may not want the truth. But I am afraid of what he might do, of what he may be thinking of doing."

Chaplain Koh said, "Mr. Shin did not say anything about his intention of resigning until this morning. He hasn't explained why he wants to resign, or what he plans to do afterward."

"That is why I am disturbed," Colonel Chang said.

"Are you afraid that he might speak the truth?" I said.

"The truth which you don't want?" said Park bitterly.

Colonel Chang scowled at Park.

"Colonel, are you sure," the chaplain said, "that what you have just told us is beyond question?"

"Yes, I am sorry to say I have all the details—the names of the ministers, what they did and said, what confessions they gave to the Reds. I regret to say that I have the evidence."

"Colonel, may I . . . ?" said Park.

Colonel Chang interrupted him. "I know what you would like to know, Captain Park," he said gravely. "You can be proud, as we all are, that your father was the bravest man of them all. He was magnificent, Captain. Even Major Jung admitted that your father could inspire a certain kind of awe and respect among the Red torturers. Rest assured, Captain, he is a great martyr."

Park, with eyes closed, remained silent.

Colonel Chang said, "Chaplain, where is Mr. Shin?" And when there was no response, "It doesn't matter whether you tell me or not. I shan't disturb him. But tell me, do you have any idea what he is thinking of doing?"

The chaplain shook his head. "No."

"Does he know what happened to his house?"

"He knows what they did."

"How did he take it? Was he angry?"

"Yes!" shouted the chaplain, jumping up from his chair. "Yes, he was angry. What did you expect? I've never seen him so angry. He didn't want to go away. I forced him to go. I admit that it was my way of revenge. I hated those petty Christians who behaved like mice yesterday and today are howling like hungry beasts!" He stopped for breath. "All right, he is at the service headquarters of my brigade in Chinnampo. I thought I could keep him over there for a while, at least until the memorial service is over. But is there going to be a memorial service?" Chaplain Koh glanced furiously about him. "For whom? To commemorate whom?"

Colonel Chang brought his fist down on the desk. "Yes! There is going to be a memorial service. To commemorate whom? The twelve martyrs, of course, the twelve glorious martyrs! What do you think! Never mind what I told you. You've heard it, and now forget what you know. I told you only because I wanted you to help me, to help the Christians."

"To help your propaganda, too?" said the chaplain.

"Yes! To help the Army's propaganda, too. Why not, after all! I am not going to let anyone defile our cause. I am not going to let anyone give the Reds an upper hand. Understand that. I don't care who betrayed whom. All I care is that the betrayers and the betrayed alike were murdered by the Reds. That is what you must remember. That is what we must emphasize. And that is the most important thing to tell the whole nation. Army Intelligence has been compiling the data about the inhuman practices of the Reds; we are especially interested in collecting evidence on how the Reds treat Christians. The murder of the twelve ministers cannot be dismissed lightly just because there were a few weak human beings among them. What counts is they were murdered by the Reds, and don't forget it!"

"Aren't you overlooking something?" cried the chaplain. "We are dealing with martyrs, religious martyrs! If you wanted a hundred heroes out of a hundred Army deserters, very well, you should have them. But, by God, you are not going to man-ufacture religious martyrs. It would be the most despicable blasphemy. Martyrs serve the will of God, not the ephemeral needs of men!"

"Leave your god out of this, Chaplain," the colonel said. "You know I don't give a damn for your god."

"You are unnecessarily blasphemous, Colonel," the chap-lain said indignantly.

"Am I? How do you know that what I am going to do—manufacture martyrs as you say—well, how do you know it is what your god may not want? How do you know that I may not be doing a greater service to your Christianity by present-ing twelve martyrs than by exposing all the dirty linen under the holy garments of those miserable ministers?"

For a moment Chaplain Koh was too furious to reply. Then he said, "Something must be said to explain Mr. Shin's act, to explain that he has nothing to be ashamed of. You must tell the truth, Colonel, or I shall!"

"Well, Captain Lee," said the colonel, "you have been quiet. What is your opinion? Do you also insist that I tell the truth?"

There was in the tone of his voice an unmistakable challenge. Feeling upon me the silent gaze of the chaplain and Park, I said, "With your permission, sir, let me say I don't understand why you are all so disturbed. What I would like to remind you is that we are talking about *your* truth, Colonel. We have *your* truth before us and we are arguing what to do with it. But it seems to me you have forgotten about Mr. Shin. What about him? What is he going to do? What is *Mr. Shin's* truth? That is the heart of the matter."

"I don't understand you," said the colonel.

"Sir, the Christians will be more willing to believe what he tells them than what you tell them," I said.

"Hm, don't be too sure of that. But I am glad you brought Mr. Shin up. Why does he want to resign? I'll tell you why. I am afraid he has become rather emotional about the whole damned affair. I fear he has come to a decision to speak out the truth, all the filthy truth about the betrayers. Otherwise, why resign from his calling? It is not a simple thing for a minister to accuse and expose the crimes and failings of fellow ministers. So he quits to make a clear way for his conscience."

"And if he states the fact," Park said, "that there were betrayers, what do you propose to do about it?"

"He won't say that," Colonel Chang said angrily.

"But suppose he does."

"I will do my best to deny it."

"And claim that he says so because he wants to hide his own guilt?" said Chaplain Koh.

Colonel Chang glared at him. "We must persuade him not to lose his head and do anything rash. That's why I said I need your help. We must do our best to stop him from resigning, first of all, and then persuade him to tell the Christians that no minister was guilty, including himself and Mr. Hann, of course. And I will back him up."

"With enough evidence, I hope, sir," I said.

"I don't want to hear any more nonsense from any of you," he shouted. "And I remind you that you are not to divulge any part of this confidential information, you understand."

"You assume," Park said quietly, "that he will either speak the truth or distort it for your benefit, or even maybe his own. But why not assume that he just might say nothing, as he has not so far? Suppose he continues to keep an absolute silence? What then?"

"Nonsense! Sooner or later, he has to clear himself. Otherwise, everyone will be convinced that he is really guilty of something terrible, as many have already begun to think."

"It is imperative that Mr. Shin's innocence be established," said the chaplain.

"How would you accomplish that, Chaplain?" the colonel asked.

"Tell the truth," the chaplain said in anger. "How else? I am a Christian and a chaplain and I was once a pastor myself, but that does not mean I should compromise the truth, however painful it might be to the cause and interest of Christians. Truth cannot be hidden away. Perhaps, it was God's will that such a painful truth as this should have come to Christians."

"And you, Captain Park? What do you say to that?" said the colonel.

Brooding, Park did not reply.

"And you, Captain Lee?"

"I cannot agree with you, sir," I said. "I cannot twist the truth to suit it to the purpose of our propaganda. Besides, sir, as Chaplain Koh has pointed out, the truth has to do with the religious nature of martyrdom, a matter which must be dealt with by religious authorities."

"You then refuse to understand my position," said the colonel.

"Colonel, my only argument is that truth must be told for the sake of its simply being the truth. I must make it clear that I have no other motives. If Mr. Shin were to be found guilty of betrayal, I would insist that he be brought to account for his crime. That's all, Colonel."

"Why must truth be told?" Exasperated, the colonel sprang up from his chair and began pacing the room. "Truth can be buried and still be the truth. It doesn't have to be told."

"The problem in our case, sir, is that you are obliged to say something about the execution of the ministers," I said. "You have created the situation as it stands now, and I am afraid there is no way out of it for you, no way other than either to tell the truth or, as you insist, to distort it. It is your choice, Colonel."

"And what is your choice, Captain? Suppose you were in my position, what would you do?"

"I would tell the truth," I replied.

"And make the damn Reds happy and bring all the disgrace to us, eh?"

"I would have no other choice."

"Enough!" Colonel Chang cried impatiently. "We must persuade Shin to cooperate with us."

"You mean, cooperate with you," said the chaplain.

"Suppose he refuses to be persuaded or to cooperate with you?" I said.

"Then I won't have any other choice. I will have to force him, no matter how much I may be disinclined to do so."

"Do you really think he is the kind of man you can force to do something against his principles?" the chaplain said.

"Ah, that we shall see."

"How would you force him, may I ask?" retorted the chaplain.

"I would rather not say anything about it at this stage."

A long moment of silence followed. At last the chaplain turned to me. "Captain Lee, do you remember, some time ago I told you of a certain problem which is exclusively my own?"

"Yes, I remember," I said. "Why do you ask?"

"You remember I asked you what you would do if you were in my place?"

I nodded.

"What are you talking about?" said the colonel, darting a vexed look at me and at the chaplain.

"I am merely trying to pose a question," the chaplain said. "You asked Captain Lee what he would do in your position. What would you do, Colonel, if you were in Mr. Shin's place?"

"What would *you* do?" said the colonel, frowning.

"I confess," Chaplain Koh sighed, "I wouldn't know what to do."

"I would tell the truth," I said.

"Enough!" cried Colonel Chang once again. "Enough of this nonsense."

20

Chaplain Koh, Park, and I withdrew to my office when Colonel Chang left headquarters to attend a meeting at the Pyongyang Area Command. I had my orderly bring us a pot of tea, and we sat quietly around the stove and sipped the tea, relieved not to be arguing and shouting anymore.

It was Park who spoke first. "Chaplain, tell me," he said with his head bowed, "has Mr. Shin said anything to you about my father?"

"No, he hasn't, only that he has something to tell you. I know he wants very much to see you." The chaplain turned to me. "Captain, did you see those Christians out there in front of the church—Park's father's church?"

"Of course I saw them," I said. "Why do you ask?"

"I wonder if you understand them," he said, glancing at Park. "Do you?" I said.

"I don't have to," he said softly. "After all, I am one of them. Perhaps what I felt as I watched them was something deeper than what we call understanding."

"Maybe," I shrugged. "I'm not much for mysteries. Incidentally, Chaplain, what you told Colonel Chang about your talk with the Secretary of Defense—was that true?"

He laughed. "I've been too busy to call him. He is my cousin, that's a fact, and Colonel Chang knows it. So you see, I wasn't exactly telling a fib." He got up from his chair. "Well, I think I should be on my way. Don't worry about Mr. Shin and Mr. Hann. They are comfortable. I'll tell Mr. Shin about our discussion with the colonel."

Park did not look up to bid the chaplain good night. He

seemed to be intensely preoccupied with his own thoughts. After a while he said softly, almost as if he were speaking to himself, "I said I suspected I was the very source of my horror. I don't suspect it anymore. I know it. I don't know any other way to explain all the misery in this world, generation after generation."

Suddenly he exclaimed with surprising bitterness, "So my father is a great martyr. The colonel says so. Even the Red major said so. He won as he always has. And I lost as I always have. I can't hide it any longer. I must tell you what I have been secretly hoping for, so you will know how base and wretched a man can be. Do you know I wished my father hadn't been a martyr? I wanted him to have failed at the last moment. I hoped he had been defeated, yes, crushed, so he would know what it was like to be weak in spirit. What it was like to doubt—to doubt his god, his faith, everything—to taste the horrible injustice and suffering of this life. But he didn't fail. He was a great martyr. How like him! I can see that proud face of a fanatic, possessed by his conviction that he was right, so that nothing could defeat him. How he must have said to himself, 'Well, you hoped I would fail, but I was right and just and I won!' I can see his blazing eyes and triumphant smile, hear his roaring voice, that magnificent voice thundering down from his pulpit, 'You—apostate!'"

Park brought his clenched fists down on his knees. "I can't—I can't weep for him. I could have if he had failed. I could have wept for him if he had experienced at least a moment of human weakness. That's why I sometimes weep for Christ."

"You shouldn't torment yourself so," I muttered.

"How would you judge Christ?" he cried. "'My God, my God, why hast Thou forsaken me!' How would you listen to that cry of anguish! That cry from the dying Christ—a pathetic figure of a pale, death-stricken yet divinely mad young man, nailed to a cross, jeered at and hated, riddled by bloody Roman spears, helpless in the face of his enemies—the pitiful body of the alleged son of God, gasping, panting, sweating, bleeding, without a miracle to save him. Who knows what terrifying doubts he might have felt at that last moment that all his life and work had been an utter waste! Even the son of God, even Christ, had a moment of doubt."

I got up to shovel some more coal into the stove. "I have no use for fairy tales," I said.

"You may not, but are you so sure that others, perhaps including myself, have no use for a fairy tale, as you call it? And don't look so surprised to hear me say it!"

Park came over to me and gripped my arm. "Those wailing, chanting Christians at Mr. Shin's yesterday, and today at my father's bombed-out church. What do you think it was they wanted, that they need so desperately? Tell me, would you despise them? Or would you perhaps love them?"

I felt too disturbed to reply immediately. I could only stand there staring into his flaming eyes. At last I said, "I do understand them. That's all I can say. Yes, I understand their suffering and their despair."

He let go of my arm and cried out impatiently, "Ah, your kind of understanding is not enough. That's what Chaplain Koh was trying to tell you. You only say you understand them. You view their suffering and their despair in a detached, intellectual way precisely because you are merely a sympathetic observer."

His passionate words struck me with relentless force, piercing deep into my heart.

Park strode over to the window and looked out into the dark, cold world. "I love them," he said quietly. "It's as the chaplain said: 'After all, I am one of them.'" He turned to face me again. "That's why I wouldn't know what to do if I were in Mr. Shin's place."

Late in the evening, Chaplain Koh called me from Chinnampo. Upon arriving at the service quarters of his brigade he had found neither Mr. Shin nor Mr. Hann. He was worried about them. I promised him that I would come down to Chinnampo at the earliest opportunity. Meanwhile he would do his best to find the two ministers.

21

Nothing could change Park's determination to leave Pyong-yang immediately. Shortly after eight o'clock the next morn-ing, I instructed our transportation officer to secure him a seat on a flight to Hamhung on the east coast. Park and I did not have much time to speak to each other; I had to prepare for a meeting at headquarters of the U.S. forces. But first, Colonel Chang wanted to see me.

When I entered his office, I found him seated behind his desk, drinking tea. He had just finished eating; a small tray with an empty plate was pushed to one side. His orderly came in to re-move the tray and Colonel Chang asked me if I would like to join him in a cup of tea. When the orderly brought in a cup and a pot of fresh tea, the colonel asked me to pull up a chair.

I informed him that Park was leaving the city.

"So he meant what he said," he said indifferently.

I then told him that Chaplain Koh had called to say he had been unable to find the ministers at Chinnampo on his return.

To my surprise, he took the news calmly. "Now, that's going too far, don't you think?" he said offhandedly. "What do you think should be done?"

I told him that I would like to drive down to Chinnampo as soon as I could.

He nodded. "Of course, you should go and find them," he said. "But I am afraid I shall have to detain you here for a while. Well, shall we get down to our business?"

"As you wish, sir."

"I had a call from the Chief of Intelligence last night. I had talked with him some time ago, in fact; I asked for a transfer.

He is at last convinced that I have had enough of political intelligence, which isn't my specialty anyway. I asked for a job in a field intelligence operation, in which I am sort of an expert, if you'll allow me to say so. So I am going to be transferred. I have asked that a replacement be sent here immediately, but it will take some time and, besides, according to the chief, there isn't anyone available at the moment. Meanwhile you are to run this outfit. I have no doubt that you can do it—better than I have, I am sure. I am glad I am going back to my old kind of job. It is beyond my power to deal with another man's conscience. You must have guessed that."

I was touched by his confiding in me; I was seeing another side of Colonel Chang.

"There is something else I want to tell you but, of course, it will have to be kept confidential," he said. He then described to me the nature of his new assignment and his plans for carrying out the project that went with it. He had received instructions from the Army's Chief of Intelligence to go underground in order to establish an intelligence network in the Pyongyang area. He was to be aided by agents personally selected by the Chief of Intelligence.

"I shall have to disappear," Colonel Chang said. "We'll be setting up a secret base from which we will be operating later on."

"But why are you telling me about this, Colonel?"

"You know what my assignment means, don't you?"

"Yes. I know what you are supposed to do. But I don't understand why it is necessary."

"Neither do I understand it," he said, "nor does the chief. All we know at this stage is that it has been decided at some very high quarters that if the Chinese strike us, we won't fight. We'll pull out. Ah, it's all very disgusting."

"We aren't even going to hold onto Pyongyang, I suppose, sir," I said, "since they made it clear you are going to be left behind here."

"I am not the only one. I stay because I want to and because I am ordered to. But think of all those people." He shook his head.

Gazing toward the window at the gray world outside, Colonel Chang said quietly, "If there really is a god who can observe from high up in heaven what we down here are doing, it surely must look rather childish." He paused for a long moment. "Do you know that I am a baptized Christian? Accidentally, that is. My grandfather was an incorrigible believer in magic, any kind of magic. He had a friend who was a Baptist or Methodist—I forget which. One day my grandfather took me along to a church with this friend of his who had a baby in his arms. Well, there was a ceremony of baptism going on that day and my grandfather got curious about it. You see, the minister was sprinkling drops of water on babies, and that interested the old man. But what interested him most was the invocation of the Holy Ghost. He didn't understand the Father and the Son, but the idea of the Holy Ghost certainly fascinated him. You must remember that he was devoted to magic and ghosts and all that. So he had me baptized right then and there, firmly believing that any ghost was better than none. That's how I became a baptized Christian. The most amazing part of this ghost business was that my grandfather thought I would never be thirsty because the ghost blessed me with water."

I told him that I, too, was a baptized Christian, a Presbyterian, to be exact.

"Are you really?" he said. "Not an accidental one like me, I suppose."

"An involuntary one, if you like, sir. My parents were Christians."

"They died in this war, I understand."

"It was a bomb."

"Mine starved to death in Manchuria. You are the only one left in your family, aren't you? So am I. I had two brothers, but they both were killed by the Japanese. So we are both orphans," he said, "and baptized Christians."

"Apostates, if you like."

"I would say sinners."

Colonel Chang dismissed me. As I got up from my chair he said angrily, "The prisoner, Major Jung, was shot last night."

———

When I returned to my office my orderly told me that Park had gone to see the Marine liaison officer. I called the transportation officer, and was told that there was no flight to Hamhung in the morning but one might be available late in the afternoon. After a brief meeting with the officers of my section, my orderly brought in a batch of mail, in which I found a bulky envelope from Chaplain Koh. Inside the envelope was another one to which was attached a note scribbled by the chaplain:

I discovered the enclosed in my quarters soon after I called you last night. I have learned from several persons here that Mr. Shin and Mr. Hann were seen heading for a village about six miles from where we are. I then recalled that Mr. Shin had an old friend of his who was pastor of the church in that village. I don't know if the pastor is still there. Anyhow, I can't lose any time and I am going to the village myself. I will call you if and when I find them there.

The enclosed envelope was addressed to me by Mr. Shin, and within it I found this letter:

DEAR CAPTAIN LEE:

Though I have always been a family friend and have always regarded his father as my closest friend and mentor, I do not know the young Park too well, and it has been nearly a decade since I saw him last. You have been close to him and you are his best friend, so I entrust my letter to him with you, hoping that you will pardon my reliance on your best judgment and discretion. I beg you to read what I wrote to Park and if you believe that he is prepared to read it, then give it to him, but if not, then please destroy it. I am taking the liberty of assuming that you will do me this favor. From what I have learned through you and Chaplain Koh I must tell Park what you are about to read. I would like to have talked with him in person, but the situation I now find myself in prevents me from seeing the son of my dear departed friend and venerable teacher.

TRULY YOURS,
SHIN

Mr. Shin's letter to Park read:

> From out of the city the dying groan,
> and the soul of the wounded cries for help;
> yet God pays no attention to their prayer.
>   JOB 24:12

On the fourth night of our imprisonment, your father, who had been separated from the rest of us, was brought into our cell by one of the interrogators. There were five of us in that small cell and we were grieved to see him; he had been tortured much; his swollen face was smeared with blood, he had lost most of his hair, his nails were broken, and he had difficulty opening his eyes. He was nearly unconscious when he was thrown into our cell. We tried our best to cleanse him but he was in pain and we did not know what to do. Gradually his breathing relaxed and we thought he was falling into a deep sleep. In that dark, malodorous cell, with the stifling heat benumbing our senses, we knelt around him and prayed. Presently one of us began to recite a passage from Job. It was then that your father stirred and made an effort to raise himself. In the dim light that projected the iron bars against the concrete wall, his face, with his eyes closed, pained our hearts. For a while he listened to the hushed voice that spoke the words of Job. And then suddenly, when the voice came to the passage I have quoted at the beginning of this letter, your father, to our bewilderment, cried: "Stop! No more!" I say "to our bewilderment" because we did not understand him at the time. But I understood him later. I wonder if you can. So it was that we passed the night in silence, to be disturbed only when they came during the night to take away and return the five of us, one by one.

I still remember the night when you came to see me before you went away from Pyongyang. Do you remember? You had just left your father. You were quite young then. I remember your angry face, your harsh voice, and your defiance. You accused your father, saying that he was a self-righteous fanatic. You told me you had told your father that he, too, was not infallible. Strange, now that I recall your words, how they have come to mean so much to me.

Should you still maintain your accusation of your father, I say you are partly wrong and partly right. You are wrong when you say he was a self-righteous man; he never was, as you surely must know. But you are right; he was a fanatic to the very end of his life, one way or the other. You may insist that a fanatic *is* a self-righteous man, but with your father you must remember and understand that he had never said that *he* was right, but that *his God* was right, that his God was just. Do you understand this about him? You must, for he understood you.

It is true that he had never mentioned your name, as far as I know, until a few days before our imprisonment. But I knew he was well aware of what you were doing, where you were. I recall our conversation, in which he said that he was glad to hear you had become a historian. I asked him why. "If one is a good historian, he must transcend the particulars in human history to discover the general and once he does that he will inevitably come to the large question of whether or not history must have an end one day. Thus he will have to face another, larger question—not as a historian but simply as a man. If he does that some day, then I shall have to admit that we are not so far apart from each other as it might appear." I remember saying to him that, perhaps, he had some sort of teleological question in mind. No, he said, it was an eschatological question. I do not know whether or not I was right in conjecturing that this was his way of saying he felt reconciled with you.

I am not sure what you really wish to know about him, about his last days on earth. I confess that I was surprised to learn of your particular wish. How did he die? I understand that you do not want to hear any more about his heroism and his martyrdom. I would have liked to talk with you but I can hardly expect to see you at the moment. I can give you what you wish to know, but I must make it clear to you that what I am about to tell you came to your father through the terrible agonies of a wounded soul.

That night, which became the last night for those twelve, we were taken to the bank of an upstream branch of the Taedong River. We knew we were going to be shot. We were given one minute to say whatever we wished: to pray. "I cannot pray!"

These were your father's last words, and now I pass them on to you in his name, in his memory. Your father did not pray; he died in utter solitude.

YOURS TRULY IN CHRIST,
SHIN

I called the transportation officer and told him not to bother with arranging a flight for Park. I then rang up the Marine liaison officer, asked for Park, and was told that he had gone out. It was getting late for the meeting. I had to go. I left Mr. Shin's letter with my orderly to give to Park and left my office.

When I returned at noon I found Park in my room, waiting for me. I greeted him and suggested that he join me for lunch.

"I have decided to stay here for a while," he said.

"You have read the letter from Mr. Shin," I said.

He nodded. He walked over to the window and stood there, looking out. It was windy; the windowpanes rattled; the bell across the street clanged faintly.

He muttered, "Why don't they do something about that bell?"

"It's too dangerous to get up to the belfry," I said.

Abruptly he swung around and came back to me. "I can't bear to look at that church!" he cried out. "It's as if . . . as if . . ."

Under the gray sky the skeletal remains of the battered church stood lonely over the snow-covered slope littered with ruins. I turned to Park and for the first time since I had come to know him I saw his eyes glisten with tears.

"Come," I said, holding his arm. "Don't speak. I understand."

22

Matters concerning the transfer of Colonel Chang and my new duties as acting commanding officer of the detachment prevented me from leaving headquarters for Chinnampo. I had not received another call from Chaplain Koh nor had I been able to reach him at the service headquarters of his brigade. Meanwhile, the local papers had been carrying various articles of a grandiloquent nature about the heroism and martyrdom of the twelve ministers. The articles were often sensational in their headlines and melodramatic in their tone, so much so that I went to Colonel Chang and asked him if he was the source of inspiration.

He did not hesitate to admit that indeed he was.

"But why?" I protested.

"I gave the papers what they wanted," he said calmly.

"But you did not give them the truth," I insisted.

He did not respond to my charge, but launched directly into the business of the transfer of our duties.

I interrupted him and reminded him that he had not yet replied to my protest.

With a weary look, he stared at me. "Captain Lee, when you finally take over my job, do you know what you will be asked to do? Or forced to do, if that suits your taste better? My dear professor—lectures, speeches, and all sorts of moral talks. Propaganda, if you insist. Do you think you can do it? Can you tell all sorts of people we are fighting this war for the glorious cause of our independence, our liberty, and, to make the matter more complicated, for the interest and preservation of our democratic system of government? Can you tell a bevy of sweet old ladies and housewives or a flock of young students here who are dying to know what is going on in the South—well, can you tell them all their sufferings are worthwhile because this is a noble war we are fighting, that people, many, many people will have to be sacrificed in order to make sure that the cause of individual liberty, the duty of man and free social, political, and economic life will survive and be maintained for us and for our posterity? Well, what do you say?"

I was dismayed at the prospect.

Colonel Chang went on. "Or, would you rather tell them this war is just like any other bloody war in the stinking history of idiotic mankind, that it is nothing but the sickening result of a blind struggle for power among the beastly states, among the rotten politicians and so on, that thousands of people have died and more will die in this stupid war, for nothing, for absolutely nothing, because they are just innocent victims, helpless pawns in the arena of cold-blooded, calculating international power politics? Well, now?"

He paused to examine me. "Let me tell you what I think. I don't give a damn what you believe in. Is that clear? It is none of my business whether you are an out-and-out patriot or a noncommittal intellectual. The important thing, as far as I am concerned and as far as this job goes, is to tell them what is necessary for them to know, and what is demanded of them by this collective body called the state. As I said, I don't care what you believe in deep down in your guts, but when you say something in that uniform of yours to the people, heaven help you if you go around making those miserable people more miserable by going against the stand taken by your country, telling them what they already know but don't want to think they know. Do you understand that?"

Though I tried to control myself, I could not help speaking out. "Sir, I think I know what I am doing and what I will do; I will hang onto my truth and will not compromise it. As the acting commanding officer of this unit, I shall do my best to stop immediately any more manufacturing and dissemination of false information."

Colonel Chang gazed silently at me for some time, then he

shook his head. "I envy you, Captain Lee," he said wearily. "So stubborn, aren't you? At least you are committed to that stubbornness. I am glad to see that. After all, it's better than nothing. Truth. What is truth? Well, you are right. I am turning my duties over to you and you will do what you think is best. I am sure you know what you will have to do."

"Yes," I said, preparing to go.

Suddenly he raised his voice and shouted in fury, "Well, are you so sure, so damned sure? Are you so sure of your conscience in this bloody war? You have licked the sweat and sucked the blood of this war, haven't you? Well, haven't you?"

I retorted, "Yes, I have killed plenty, enough and more than enough."

"Then what makes you think you are so righteous!" he cried. His forefinger shot out of his clenched fist and pointed at me. "You have killed, I have killed! We are all murderers! Don't you ever forget that! We are all up to our necks in our bloody doings. I am guilty, and you, professor, you too are guilty!" He stopped, then said resignedly, "We only do what we have to do for our country, don't you understand!"

That evening when I was alone in my office, Chaplain Koh came to see me unexpectedly.

"I did not have time to call you to tell you that we were returning to Pyongyang," he said. "We just came back. I left them at the house and came straight here." He had found the two ministers in a small village near Chinnampo, where they had stayed at the house of the local pastor. "The pastor was an old friend of Mr. Shin's, as I might have told you. We were there, all three of us. It's unbelievable the way things are in that village. People are literally starving, and sick. Almost half of the village is gone, not just the houses but the people. And what despair! People there are tired, so tired of war and life. The poor pastor! He doesn't know what to do. He is worn out himself, with so many of his people starving and sick and then he has to lead services practically every evening. Ah!

"Yesterday afternoon I left Mr. Shin and Mr. Hann and went back to our headquarters to collect alms, you might say; and when I went back to the village, Mr. Shin insisted that we return to the city. Why? I don't know. Of course I have told him everything that happened here—what Colonel Chang confessed."

I informed him of the colonel's transfer.

He shook his head. "I don't envy your position."

"Why not, Chaplain?" I said. "I know exactly what I am going to do. But tell me. What can I do for you?"

"I came to see you because Mr. Shin wants to have a few words with you. Can you come?"

"Is he still determined to resign?"

"Yes."

"Do you think he is going to tell the truth?"

"God only knows," sighed the chaplain as we left the office.

When I stood face to face with Mr. Shin I did not know what to say. His pale face was shaven and his hair trimmed; he stood erect and serene in his black robe in the bare room chilled by a cold draft.

"How are you, Captain Lee?" he said quietly, smiling.

"Quite well, thank you. And you?" I had not seen him smile before; his tranquility disturbed me.

"Oh, fair, though I wish I could say I felt splendid. I have taken a short trip down to Chinnampo, as you know. The driving was rough and the chaplain is a reckless driver, I am afraid. But it was well worth the trouble. I had a good bath and the chaplain found me a barber who shaved me and cut my hair and then there was an old friend of mine to visit with and chat. I haven't had that much luxury for a long time."

I stood there in front of him with Chaplain Koh, like an idiot, speechless at his matter-of-fact attitude.

Slightly raising his voice he said, "Captain, I was going to ask you to take me to Colonel Chang but now you are in command. So I ask you to do me a favor. Would you mind making arrangements so that the Christian ministers in the city can come to your headquarters? I have given the names of the ministers to the chaplain."

"Why would you like to gather them? And why at headquarters?"

"I would like it all to be official," he said quietly. "Tomorrow afternoon?"

"If you wish," I said. "Mr. Shin, I know everything that you know."

He nodded.

"What are you going to tell them?"

"I have returned, Captain Lee," he said, "because I know I can no longer guard the truth."

"Then you are going to tell them," I said.

"Are you?" exclaimed Chaplain Koh almost joyfully. "I knew you would, I knew you would!"

"Captain Lee, did you also know that I would tell the truth?"

"I don't know, Mr. Shin," I said. "All I know is that the truth must be told."

He gazed at me. "Is it your official wish, Captain?"

"I have only one wish," I said. "My wish."

"And you want me to tell the truth," he said.

"Yes. But it is your choice and not mine."

"Would you tell the truth," he said, "if you were in my place?"

"Yes," I declared. "There is no other way."

"What if I didn't?" he said. "Would you despise me?"

I did not reply.

"Good night, Captain," he said gently. "I will see you tomorrow." He took my hand. "I shall tell them the truth."

I searched his face, only to be met by his smile and calmness. I bowed to him and withdrew.

His serene voice followed me. "Yes, I will tell them the truth of my faith."

I challenged him. "The truth does not belong to you alone or to Colonel Chang, Mr. Shin."

23

At four in the afternoon the next day, I had assembled the ministers in one of our conference rooms, including those who were on the preparation committee for the memorial service. Colonel Chang and Park were also present. Before long, Mr. Shin arrived, accompanied by Chaplain Koh. Everyone stood up hurriedly.

I went to meet Mr. Shin. When we were alone together for a moment, I said, "Whatever you are going to do, please don't do it for the sake of someone other than yourself."

He looked at me intensely.

"Not for this establishment," I said. "Not for our propaganda, Mr. Shin . . ."

Impulsively he seized my hand. "Captain, Captain!" he whispered.

". . . or for your god."

Almost violently, his hands gripped mine, trembling; he gazed into my eyes feverishly, and whispered, "For my faith, Captain! For my new faith!"

With a bow I left him.

Standing in front of the assembled ministers, tranquil and somber in his black robe, Mr. Shin greeted everyone in silence; then he began to speak slowly:

"Gentlemen, I am guilty. It was I who betrayed our martyrs."

Suddenly, taking everyone by surprise, a minister, a young man of about thirty, leaped forward, pushing the older ministers aside. "I knew it was you!" he shouted. "I knew it!" He glared furiously at Mr. Shin, as though he were about to pounce upon him and tear him apart.

Chaplain Koh rushed to Mr. Shin's side and so did Colonel Chang.

The young minister hissed. "Judas!" He then stalked out of the room, quickly followed by a few of the younger men.

Then it happened; I might have spoken out to contradict Mr. Shin, to defend him in spite of what he had decided to do and to declare the ugly truth, had I not been too astonished by what took place immediately after the outrageous performance of the young accuser. All the remaining ministers hurried over to Mr. Shin, embracing him, touching him, begging him to speak no more for he had said enough; they prayed then and there; they blessed him; they confessed and repented their past complacency and meek submission to the enemies of their god; and they took him into their hearts as one of them, as their sacrifice. Nothing more was said by Mr. Shin, who stood dazed—so it seemed to me—silently shedding his tears; and they all left together, Chaplain Koh and Park with them, leaving Colonel Chang and me alone and speechless.

24

Later in the evening Colonel Chang invited me to his room for tea.

"Well, here we are," he said with a slight shrug of his hunched shoulders. "You and I."

Yes, here we are indeed, I thought.

"I suppose you would rather I talked," he said. "More tea?" He replenished my cup. "I have been thinking what I would have done, how I would have behaved, if Mr. Shin had not said what he said this afternoon. When Chaplain Koh reported that Mr. Shin was going to resign from his ministry I felt the whole affair was outrageous. Ah, but I am a simpleminded idiot! As if a man like him could turn into a coward."

"I don't understand what you mean," I said.

"I thought he was going to tell the truth to defend himself. That would have been cowardly in my book. I was quite sure that was what he intended to do."

"What would your reactions have been if he had defended himself?"

"I would have denied his words. You knew I was determined to do that. But he didn't defend himself, he didn't justify himself. If he had, at the expense of his colleagues, I would have lost all my respect for him. I don't have anything to say, really, about what he should have or shouldn't have done. He did what he had to do this afternoon, and that's that. When I had the sorry facts about the twelve ministers, my attitude toward him changed, naturally. So when the chaplain announced that he wanted to resign, I thought he was going to do something utterly foolish that would completely upset my plans. I thought he was going to claim his innocence. You remember that I had once hoped he would clear himself? Well, I didn't want that any longer because I had found out there were betrayers among the ministers. Instead, I made up my mind to defend him. I wanted him to keep silent, then I would get the others to accept him as a man as heroic and saintly as all the twelve ministers were supposed to have been. I confess I underestimated Mr. Shin."

"No doubt," I said, but Colonel Chang was impervious to my sarcasm.

He continued, "I saw the other ministers here this afternoon, those guilty men, and now I realize why they embraced him. Do you understand why? I am sure you do. I thought I would help him to be a hero. Instead, he appeared here as a Judas, and lo and behold, they accepted him. It was not for me to help him or them. They did not need the kind of help I thought I could offer. I understand what he did and I dare say I understand why he felt he had to do it." He stood up. "Now that it is all over, I must say I shouldn't have worried about Mr. Shin, you know, about what he was going to do, what he should or shouldn't do. I should have known better. He had his church and its reputation to protect and I had my state and its cause to guard. What I failed to realize was that he and I had a legitimate common interest to look after in this little affair, whose happy ending we are now celebrating. I think you and I can congratulate ourselves that it all turned out to be the way we wanted, don't you?"

I thanked him for the tea and started toward the door.

"Do me a favor, will you?" Colonel Chang called after me. "When you see Mr. Shin, will you tell him that it was my honor to have met him?"

I turned to face him. "With your permission, sir, may I suggest you do that personally?"

He stared at me, then he shook his head wearily and turned away.

About an hour or so later, when I was getting ready for the night, Park burst into my room, panting.

"I need your help," he gasped. "The Christians stormed up to Mr. Shin's house and demanded to see him. He wanted to meet them, but we didn't let him go out for fear he might get hurt. They were throwing stones, shouting, threatening to break into the house. They are still there. I went out with a few ministers and we did our best to send them away, but it was no use. I think they are led by the young minister who was here this afternoon. There is the curfew and I don't know how they got there at this time of night. Look! Can you round up some of your guards here, or call the Military Police? The mob is getting out of hand."

I lost no time calling up a detail of guards. We drove to Mr. Shin's house and stopped at the foot of the hill, when we heard the burst of a submachine gun in the midst of eerie chanting in the darkness—"Judas! Judas! Judas! Judas!" A squad of Military Police had arrived before us and was trying to disperse the crowd. Our guards joined them, lining up in front of the house, facing the mob. Flashlights crisscrossed. Park and I urged them to go away, but their shouting, wailing voices drowned ours. Young voices kept on screeching, "Judas! Judas! Judas! Judas!" A roaring voice boomed, "Come out, Judas! Repent, Judas!" I could not tell how many of them were there in the dark—perhaps forty or fifty. Suddenly I heard Park's voice commanding, "Who is your leader! Who is responsible for this mob!" I saw him snatch a submachine gun from a guard and fire into the black sky. The crowd grew silent briefly, but Park lost his chance to speak as several voices screamed out, "There he goes! Catch him!" "Kill him! Kill him!" Some men were running toward the left wing of the house into a thicket bleakly laden with snow. Feet crunched on gravel, hysterical voices shouted—and then there was a wailing, piercing cry like that of a terrified beast. Part of the mob broke away to join the chase, crying, "There he is, down the hill! Get him!"

Suddenly the front door opened wide and I saw Mr. Shin standing there framed by the dim light behind him. Then a woman shrieked, "Judas!" and an answering roar of "Judas! Judas!" went up from the crowd. I ran over to Mr. Shin and tried to push him back into the house.

"Please, Captain Lee," he said in desperation. "Let me go. It's Mr. Hann. He is out there! I must find him!"

"Go back into the house," I said. "I'll go and find him. Please go back inside!" Park approached, brandishing a carbine now. I told him that I had to go after Mr. Hann. "Stay here," I said. A sergeant in charge of the Military Police came up to us. "Captain, what's going on here anyway? Any gathering of a crowd like this at this time of night is against martial law, sir. I'll have to arrest all or shoot at them if they don't go away." I told him to be patient and do his best to disperse them. "I sent for more men and trucks," he said. "Then we can handle the idiots!" Stones flew out of the dark, smashing against the wall and the windowpanes. Glass broke. Park fired his carbine into the air. "Get inside!" I cried to Mr. Shin and closed the door after him. Then I ran down the hill to where I had left my jeep. Two men ran past me. "Where is the man? What did you do to him?" I shouted after them. "We beat him up!" one of them flung back. "But he got away," the other cried. I searched the hill for Mr. Hann but in vain. Trucks were roaring up the hill, lighting up the darkness with their searchlights. A platoon of MPs joined the others and our guards. The mob broke up; many tried to run away but were checked by the cordon of soldiers.

Within ten minutes or so all was quiet.

I had not been able to find Mr. Hann.

Park and I searched the area once more. We drove down the hill slowly, stopping here and there to listen for footsteps or to explore the hushed lanes between the silent houses; we inquired of nearly half a dozen patrols; nothing. We were already on the dark, deserted main street.

Park suggested, "We should go back to the house."

I shook my head. "Come. Let's go," I said. "Let's try your father's church."

"Why? Why there? How could he have gone there?"

"I'll explain later," I said.

I could not tell how he had managed to run all that way so quickly and without having been stopped by the patrols. We found the young minister at the devastated church, his face cut and bruised, his mouth swollen and bloody, as he lay unconscious, sprawled over the stone steps outside the silent, desolated church.

By the time Park had brought Mr. Shin and Chaplain Koh to our headquarters, I had had Mr. Hann moved to the office of the dispensary, where he lay covered with a blanket on a cot. I had called an ambulance to take him to a field hospital across the river. Mr. Shin, flanked by the chaplain and Park, gazed in grief at the grotesquely battered face of the young minister, who was hardly breathing.

"The shouting of the mob frightened him," whispered the chaplain. "It is my fault. He could not control himself and I had to hold onto him to quiet him down. A stone broke the window upstairs where we were and I let go of him for a moment to open the door to take him down to the basement. Then he ran off and . . ."

"Enough, Chaplain," said Mr. Shin.

A few minutes later, Mr. Hann began gasping for breath. His eyes suddenly opened wide and his whole body trembled under the dark-brown blanket.

"I am here!" Mr. Shin said softly. "Can you see me? Can you hear me?"

The bloodshot eyes stared into empty space; the lips quivered.

Mr. Shin held the young man's bony hand. "I am here with you. Can you hear me? I am here with you."

The young man's eyes rested on Mr. Shin for a second; then his head rolled to the right; his mouth twitched.

A second later, we heard the faint, broken voice: "No . . . God . . . no . . . God . . ." A series of convulsions seized his body, then suddenly stopped. The body lay still under the raw light of a naked light bulb, shrouded in the silent gaze of those present.

A moment later, Park said quietly, "He is dead."

Mr. Shin, his face pale, with a strange faraway look, stood motionless, as though paralyzed in the presence of death. "I have killed him," he muttered. "I have killed him."

25

Mrs. Hann was determined to bring the body of her son back to her village, where she wanted to bury him, near the graves of his ancestors. Mr. Shin, Chaplain Koh, and Park accompanied her and the body to the village a few miles west of Pyongyang. I was unable to join them; I could only provide transportation for the journey, from which they returned a day later. Mrs. Hann, however, did not return.

The day after they were back, Chaplain Koh came to headquarters early in the afternoon to inform me there was to be a special service that evening at Mr. Shin's church; he said he hoped he would see me there. The announcement had been sent out to other churches and the chaplain expected many from their congregations would attend. Of course, Mr. Shin would be present.

"Very much present," the chaplain added.

"After what happened the other night?" I said. "I should think he'd be afraid to risk it."

"He's not easily frightened," Chaplain Koh said.

I remained in my office for an hour or so before I attended a staff meeting. Around five o'clock, as I prepared to go out, Colonel Chang telephoned me to say that he had been told by Chaplain Koh about the special service, which he wanted to attend; he invited me to join him. However, he was unable to leave for some time as he was working on a report concerning his transfer. I told him that I would wait for him in my office.

When we were at last ready to leave, the howling Siberian winds were blasting the city with gusts of slashing snow.

The service had already begun; even before we had struggled to the top of the steps we could hear the singing of the congregation mingled with the wind and the snow. When we passed through the small gate Colonel Chang said, "Do you remember what I said about this church when we were here last time?"

"About how it was saved from our bombing?"

"Yes. You know, I am beginning to wonder if it would have made any difference whether this building was destroyed or not. Do you understand me?"

"I suppose the only thing that could have mattered was how long it would have taken the Christians to rebuild it, either here or somewhere else."

"Precisely. In the meantime, they would be meeting someplace. It doesn't matter where."

"That's how Christianity in this country has managed to survive."

"Do you realize that ever since Christianity came to this land, these people have never had a peaceful day? After all the persecution by Chinese, Koreans, Japanese, and now Communists, they are still here. Where do they get this ability, even liking, for suffering? Listen to them singing!"

"With the promise of heaven and eternity, perhaps," I said.

"Is that all? Anyone can promise that," he said, "one way or the other. Buddhist, Shintoist, Communist, Hindu, you name them."

"There is one thing peculiar to Christianity, Colonel," I said. "Someone died for their sins, for their salvation, and this someone happens to be the son of their god."

"A very strange notion," he said. "Sacrifice, martyrdom."

We opened the door and entered the church, where we were met by Chaplain Koh, who was acting as an usher.

"I have been expecting you," he said. "I am glad you came. Follow me."

Colonel Chang said that we would stay in the back.

"Oh, no. You two are our guests of honor. Captain Park is up there with Mr. Shin already. So come along."

"I suppose I am in your house," said the colonel. "Well, coming, Captain?"

We followed the chaplain up the aisle, flanked by the congregation that still sang, standing. Only a few of the chandeliers were lighted. A cold draft chilled my bare head, though I felt the warmth of human bodies surrounding me. Halfway up the aisle, I looked up toward the altar, behind which stood the elders, Park and a few others, and Mr. Shin. Soon Colonel Chang and I were with them, facing the congregation. Mr. Shin stepped forward. The candles on the lectern flickered. The congregation sat, hushed.

"Dear brethren," he began quietly. "You all know who I am, and I know you. I know you, yes, I know you so well that I do not hesitate to say that I belong to you and you belong to me. I am you, you are me, and we are one. And I stand here in the shadow of my inglorious past, and say to you, welcome to the house of our Lord. This house of our Lord is filled tonight, and I am out there with you and you are up here with me. We are here together as one to worship our God and praise Him. Amen."

Scattered voices in the congregation said, "Amen."

"I know you well, so well that I know you did not come tonight to this house of our Lord to worship Him. You came to hear me. And I shall speak to you and you shall hear me. I am you and you are me. But who am I?" He paused. "I am a sinner."

He paused again for a long moment; then, suddenly, his powerful voice boomed. "You came to hear me, a sinner, and you shall hear me, a sinner! Open your eyes! Bare your hearts! And hear! It was I who betrayed our martyrs!" He stopped, his hands clutching the lectern, his body bent slightly forward. He had stressed "I" so strongly that the high-ceilinged interior of the church rang with a vibrating "I" in a tremulous echoing that pervaded the dim, cold air—". . . I . . . I . . ." Not a soul stirred.

He said quietly, "On the eighteenth day of June, as you all know, the Communists imprisoned fourteen ministers, and I was one of them. On the twenty-fifth day, twelve ministers were murdered. For seven days and nights, they tortured our martyrs. My dear brethren, I say to you that they tormented the flesh of your martyrs for seven days and nights. I say, 'flesh of your martyrs,' for they could not harm their spirits. But how did they torture your martyrs?"

To my surprise—and uneasiness—Mr. Shin, for the next twenty minutes or so, described to the congregation in the minutest detail how each minister was tortured, one after another, all twelve of them. Mr. Hann, said Mr. Shin, collapsed after three days and nights of torture and became ill. At first it seemed that the silent congregation was spellbound by the blood-smeared description, but gradually it began to bestir itself; the rustling of clothes, coughing, and concentrated heavy breathing disturbed the cold air.

Suddenly a woman shrieked. Cries went up. The entire congregation stirred with agitation. Some of the elders rose to their feet. Chaplain Koh hurried over to Mr. Shin, who stood unmoved, rigidly facing the crowd.

A voice in the back shouted, "Away with you!" and another voice, "We don't want to hear from you!"

Then a woman hissed, "You—a sinner! How dare you defile our martyrs!"

Colonel Chang jumped up from his chair, as did I. There was a murmur of voices. Here and there women were sobbing. The two candles on the lectern flared up. A woman was being carried down the aisle toward the door. Many were standing. Several men came up the aisle. I stepped forward, followed by Colonel Chang, and we stood at the edge of the platform facing the congregation. "Do you think we should get him out of here?" the colonel whispered. I was about to say yes, when Mr. Shin, taking everyone by surprise, struck the lectern fiercely with both palms. He lifted his face toward the ceiling, his eyes closed; his fingers gripped the front edge of the lectern. Then he lowered his dark, angry face, opened his eyes, and gazed sternly at the congregation.

He spoke in a hushed voice. "My brethren, what is the matter with you?" He paused, looking about him at the congregation as if he wanted to distinguish each individual. Then he shouted, "Sinners! Weaklings! Can you not share with your martyrs their suffering! Do you not want to share their suffering! Do you not want to taste the blood they shed, hear the agonies of their voices, hear the breaking of their bones! Can you not, do you not want, to hear the voices of your martyrs, their last prayers! Can you not share the heavy load of their sacrifice, their sacrifice for you!"

The congregation had grown deathly silent.

He continued, now quietly, "I—do you hear me?—I could not. I was a sinner. I was a weakling. I was defeated. I submitted to the forces of evil. And I let myself be paralyzed by the withering breath of despair!" He paused, then his voice rang out, "Blessed be the names of your martyrs! For they forgave me. And they died in the name of our Lord, for His glory and in His glory. They died, and I lived. Glory to your martyrs! Blessed be their memories in your souls. Hallelujah! Amen!"

"Amen!" responded the congregation.

Colonel Chang and I returned to our chairs. The long, dark shadow of Mr. Shin stretched in front of me. Robed in black, he stood erect and firm.

He told the hushed congregation how the martyrs resisted their captors. The Communists wanted them to issue a public statement that the Christians in North Korea supported the Communist regime, that they upheld the "liberation" of South Korea by the North Korean Communist regime and urged everyone to join and help the "Army of Liberation." The ministers were offered, in turn, a promise that a post in the government cabinet would be given to a representative of the Christians, that those Christians held by the Communists as political prisoners would be freed unconditionally, and the property of the churches would not be confiscated by the regime. They refused everything, and they were tortured. Their captors then demanded that the ministers sign a petition to the Communist Party that they be admitted to its membership. This, too, they refused to do, and were tortured. Then the Communists commanded them to sign a proclamation which stated that they "wholeheartedly obeyed and cooperated with the government," and urged fellow Christians to do the same. The ministers refused to sign and were tortured again.

"And they laughed at us," said Mr. Shin. "They said it did not really matter whether or not we signed. They laughed at us, my brethren, saying it did not really matter, because the Christians in the North did obey and did cooperate whole-heartedly with the Communist regime. They said they did not hear any complaints from the Christians, did not hear any voices of protest. Christians must be contented and happy, they said. Christian children joyfully sang hymns of praise for the Communist heroes, they said. Christian young men happily donned the uniform of the Red Army, willing to die for the Communist paradise, they said. Look at your churches and count how many of your Christians are still there, they said. Your churches are becoming emptier and emptier. Christianity was dying out in the North, they said. But your martyrs were not defeated; they defied the torturers. But, my brethren, I could not, I did not!"

After a long moment of silence, he said, "When I succumbed to my torturers, they brought me to your martyrs and said to them, 'Look, here is a man who is sensible, practical, and able to live by the wisdom of this earth. This is the man who truly represents your Christians. Look, we shall let him live and be free, but you shall die unless you follow his wisdom.' My brethren, what did your martyrs do?" He stretched his arms upward and raised his voice. "Blessed be your martyrs! Hallowed be their names! They forgave me. I was forgiven, do you hear! I was forgiven. And they embraced me and shed tears and said to me, 'Do not be discouraged. We will pray for your soul. Do not despair, do not despair, for the Kingdom of God is near and we shall triumph. Do not despair, do not despair!' Do you hear me, my brethren? Do not despair! These were the words with which your martyrs forgave me. And they died . . . for me . . . and for you.

"And on their last night on earth, as they were standing by the dark water of the Taedong River, waiting to be martyred, they offered their last prayer to the Lord. They prayed for me—and for you; they loved me and they loved you till their last moment. And they turned to me, and your martyrs said to me, 'We pray for you and you shall pray for us. Tell your brethren when you return to them that we love them and care for them, that we shall soon relate to our Lord the agonies of their sufferings, the heavy burden of despair. Tell them we do not die in vain, that we die in the name of our Lord, in the glory of our Lord, we die gladly for our brethren, for their sufferings and for their sins. Tell them that we shall meet again soon in the glorious, everlasting Kingdom of God, the paradise of our Lord. Go and tell them that we shall watch over them.' Then the enemies came and took me by the arms and made me stand there and watch the murder of your martyrs." He lowered his arms, and spread them wide; he lifted his face, and said, "And, my brethren, our enemies murdered your martyrs one after another and as volley after volley of murderous bullets shattered the dark night, a mighty hymn rose high into the dark heaven from the souls of your martyrs, and behold, the black clouds were suddenly shaken asunder by the moon and in the silvery light I saw, yes, I saw the heavenly smiles on the faces of your martyrs and I heard, yes, I heard, a thundering voice from the heavens, 'You are my children in whom I am well pleased. Do not despair, do not despair, for you have won the battle!' And I stood there like a stone, and I stretched my arms toward the majestic voice of our Almighty Lord, tears rolling down my cheeks, and I cried out from the bottom of my soul, 'Father, forgive me!' And I heard the mighty voice say, 'Repent! Repent and enter ye into my Kingdom. Repent!' And I fell down on my knees and cried out, 'Father, I repent. Forgive this sinner, for I shall not, I shall never, never again despair!' And my soul was suddenly light and clear, and I stood on my feet, I opened my eyes, and I blessed your martyrs, yes, I blessed—*I* blessed them for you. Glory to your martyrs! Glory to our Lord! Hallelujah! Amen!"

"Hallelujah! Amen!" echoed the voices of the congregation.

Mr. Shin cried out, "You! Sinners! Down, down on your knees and repent! I say unto you in the name of your martyrs, repent, ye sinners, for my sins and for your sins. Repent!" He stopped for breath, and whispered in a strange, tremulous voice, "In the name of the Father, the Son and the Holy Ghost, amen."

I woke as from a spell and looked about me. Everyone—everyone but Mr. Shin, who stood with his head lowered—everyone but Colonel Chang, who had risen from his chair, and Park, who still sat staring into the shadowy space above him—everyone was on his knees. The surge of their voices engulfed my senses. I looked at Park; our eyes met, and he looked away. Colonel Chang drew near to Mr. Shin.

"Mr. Shin, I must leave now," he said, "but I wanted to tell you before I go that it is an honor to know you."

The minister's face, expressionless, turned to the colonel; he bowed.

I asked Colonel Chang to wait for me, and went up to Mr. Shin. His dark eyes looked deeply into mine. I had to say it; I could not help saying it. "Mr. Shin, is your god truly aware of their sufferings?"

He closed his eyes for a second. He held my arm with one hand and, with the other, he pointed to the kneeling congregation. His face was bathed with tears; but he did not speak.

26

The next morning, Colonel Chang left Pyongyang for Seoul to work out with the Chief of Intelligence the details of his future operation. Before he left headquarters, he called me to his office, where I found him stuffing a brown briefcase with papers. It was cold in his room; the stove had not been kindled.

As soon as I closed the door and approached him, he said, "Well, let's have it. What is your estimation of the situation last night? What do you think of it?"

I did not know what to say. I had parted with him the night before when I had driven him to his quarters; we had not mentioned Mr. Shin on our way back from the church.

"Well, how do you estimate Mr. Shin's conduct?" he said. "He gave them what they wanted, don't you think?

"Yes, he did what I hoped he would," he said, when I remained silent. "Only in a different way from the one I had in mind, that is, not as a man with an impeccable conscience but as a sinner." He closed the briefcase with a faint click, then locked it. "It's a strange notion beyond my comprehension that somebody dies for your sins and for your salvation. I don't believe in their god and their doctrines; the notion that those twelve martyrs—well, they *are* martyrs now, aren't they?— that they died for me is meaningless; actually, the notion would never occur to me. But that seems to be the only way these Christians could accept and worship the ministers as their martyrs." He studied my face for a moment. "Captain, I hope you don't think I am too curious, but you asked Mr. Shin a question last night, didn't you? Something about his god. Do you mind my asking about it?"

"I asked him if his god was aware of the people's sufferings."

"I could have asked the same question," the colonel said. "I suppose it's because we are outsiders."

"Outsiders?"

"Nonbelievers, that is. If you believe in a god, you wouldn't ask that question. You would rather ask what you have done wrong against him to deserve your suffering. Well, I think I'd better be going. Good luck, Captain, and I hope it won't be long before you can return to your university. I don't think I'll be back in the building again. When I return from Seoul, I will be underground."

"Will I see you again, sir?"

"Oh, yes," he said, smiling. "I will be at the memorial service. Of course, I shall have to be incognito. What's the matter, Captain? You look dubious. You don't think there is going to be a memorial service. Is that it?"

He smiled as we shook hands. I saluted him and left his office.

So, at last, "this little affair" was over. With bitterness, I reflected on the recent events and realized that I had been tricked into a sort of nice little game, in which both the pursuer and the pursued skillfully staged a clever play of intrigues, of plots and counterplots, all this only to reveal that they were fellow conspirators, after all. I felt cheated. In a moment of fury, I promised myself that I would have nothing further to do with them. And yet I could not help thinking of Mr. Shin. I could not forget his sorrowful face or that he had not uttered a word in reply to my question.

For the next few days I did not see him, nor much of Park or Chaplain Koh either, not because I was too busy to see them, but because they were always together as they moved from one church to another. Mr. Shin was conducting a series of revival meetings, which the local papers reported fulsomely. They told of the zeal and magnitude of those meetings; each day the number of people who were converted to Christianity was printed together with a substantial excerpt from Mr. Shin's sermon. Urged by the chaplain, I attended one meeting and found that it was merely an extension of the service I had attended at Mr. Shin's own church; I left the meeting just as I had left the one before, seeing his face everywhere, stern and imperious, as he gazed at the prostrated congregation while he stood erect behind the lectern. He had not resigned from his ministry; the Christians would not hear of it; and he delivered his words from every pulpit in the city, constantly surrounded by a troop of ministers, who sat demurely in his shadow during those meetings.

Meanwhile, preparations for the memorial service were in progress. Following the departure of Colonel Chang, Chaplain Koh had assumed sole responsibility of overseeing the arrangements. I had reached an understanding with him that the Army, or rather its Political Intelligence section, should not underwrite the memorial service. I had no difficulty in getting him to agree with me, explaining that we should not commit the error of giving the public an impression that the propaganda machinery of Army Intelligence was masterminding the service. I might have added that I did not wish to be an accomplice in placing haloes on false martyrs, had I not seen plainly that the chaplain was anxious not to touch upon that subject. Everything was going according to plan, he said; Park had consented to represent the families of the twelve ministers at the service, at which he was to be one of the speakers; Mr. Shin, of course, would be the main speaker.

Left alone, I devoted my time to operations. Soon after Colonel Chang left for Seoul, we received instructions from headquarters to prepare ourselves secretly for a probable evacuation from Pyongyang. We were also instructed to devise and carry out later certain measures against possible alarm and panic on the part of the civilian population when the withdrawal should become apparent. The massive Chinese intervention in the war had definitely been established by higher headquarters. We anticipated that the people would be shocked and fearful to learn that we did not intend to defend them; and higher headquarters did not allow us to give out any intimation of the impending general retreat not only from Pyongyang but from all of North Korea.

The weather had been unusually severe; the snow storms continued day after day and on the bleak northern streets that had not seen the sun for days few people walked in the knee-deep snow past the shattered windows and nailed doors. Our morale was low; a damp, conspiratorial hush pervaded the rooms and halls, where we who knew what the others did not spent those gray days and cold nights waiting for the order to pack our things and run. The officers were asked to contribute to a fund, which the local YMCA and YWCA were raising, to enable orphanages to celebrate Christmas; they gave what they could, knowing full well that there would doubtless be no merry Christmas for those who would be left behind. I felt sick to find myself forced into taking part in this grand deception, as it were; and I was ashamed.

It was, then, in such a mood that I saw Chaplain Koh in my office a few days before the memorial service. He stood with his back pressed against the window, his large body framed in the frosty windowpanes. Outside, snow flurries bleached the gray sky.

After briefing me on the progress of preparations for the service, he asked me if I had seen Mr. Shin lately.

"No, I haven't. You know that."

"He has asked me about you on several occasions."

"I've been busy," I said.

He scrutinized me. "I suppose you have been."

"You will be leaving Pyongyang after the service, I assume?" I asked him.

"Yes. I'll have to join my brigade, if I am not permitted to have my way."

"What do you mean?"

"I have sent in my resignation to the Army," he said.

"Then you intend to stay here?"

"Of course, I'll have to wait and see what the Army is going to do with me."

I could not tell him about the Army's plan for general retreat nor about the instructions we had received. He was not allowed access to classified information.

"I have been asked to return to my old church here," he said. "Remember the old man I told you about, one of the elders? He came to see me the other day and we had a pleasant chat. Can you believe it?"

"Did you tell him the truth about his son?" I said.

"Of course not."

"I thought you were determined to tell the truth."

He looked hard at me. "I couldn't do that."

"So you told him a lie," I said, "a nice little lie."

He came over to me and confronted me. "Why? Why are you so bitter, Captain? Don't you understand what Mr. Shin has done? Don't you realize what he has done for the Christians?"

When I did not respond he said gravely, "I owe him so much. I have learned so much from him. My own faith has been strengthened through him, through his acts, and through his words of faith, an incomparable faith! He has helped me to examine the condition of my faith and my relationship with my God and, above all, with my fellow Christians." He gripped my arm. "Captain, is it possible that you despise Mr. Shin?" He added quietly, "And me?" He shook his head. "I am sorry." After a moment of silence he said, "The elders of my old church were happy to have me back. I tell you I was grateful that they wanted me to come back to them. My Lord, they are even proud of me . . . me, someone who deserted them once!" He let my arm go. "Perhaps it was what I secretly wished for when I came to Pyongyang."

"To forgive the old man?" I said. "To forgive them?"

He shook his head, smiling. "No. To be forgiven."

I turned away from him. "Good-bye, Chaplain," I said.

He held onto my hand. "Captain, Captain!"

Slowly shaking his head, he said in a voice unmistakably tinged with pity, "You do despise us, don't you?"

That evening, Park, who had been staying at Mr. Shin's, came to see me. He was in a hurry and apologized that he could not stay long, for he was on his way to the house of an elder of his father's congregation.

Declining the chair I offered him, he said, "It seems that the elders got together and talked about me. They thought I should come and stay with them. I will stay at this elder's I am going to tonight, then at another's tomorrow."

"I am glad to hear about that," I said.

"It was strange to see all those familiar faces," he said. "I had thought they had forgotten about me. I must admit that I was not too sure whether they would want to see me, after all. Frankly I was surprised when they invited me. You know—the elders gathered quite a few people and gave a feast, you might say, in my honor. Can you believe it? Have you noticed the tent in the back of the church?"

"No, I haven't."

"They have a tent there," he said, "and that's where they meet for service. Mr. Shin has spoken to them there, and—"

I interrupted him. "When do you plan to leave Pyongyang?"

He looked at me as though startled by the question. "I haven't really thought about it," he said. "Why do you ask?"

"I want to make arrangements for your transportation," I said. "I have to know your plans."

He remained silent.

"I understand you agreed to represent the families of the twelve at the service," I said.

Still silent, he gazed at me, nodding only slightly.

"Are you going through with it?" I said.

His gaze became intense. "Yes," he declared. "I am. I had a talk with Chaplain Koh. He has been to see you today, hasn't he? It seems to me that you are deliberately refusing to understand what we are doing."

"I am sending you back as soon as the service is over," I said. "To Pusan. You will report to the Marine Corps headquarters there."

"Why to Pusan? Our liaison officer told me the same thing," he said, unmistakably agitated. "I have to join my unit."

I had already arranged with the Marine liaison officer to

have Park return to headquarters in Pusan; I had also asked him not to mention the general retreat, since Park was not an intelligence officer. I said, "It may be difficult for you to locate your company by the time you are ready to leave Pyongyang. Even now, we can't locate it. You must have been told about that."

"Yes."

"There you are. I will arrange it so that you can leave the day after the service. After all, you came here to fulfill a certain function at the service, which you will be doing. After that, I have to send you back as soon as I can."

"Yes, I understand," he said quietly. "But I would like to stay here a few more days, well, as long as possible. The elders are talking about raising funds to rebuild the church. I would like to do something for them before I leave."

"I am sorry."

Suddenly he strode over to me and glared at me. "What is the matter with you? What is it? Do you despise me, too?"

I was agitated beyond control. "No! I don't despise you or anyone," I almost shouted. "It is what you all are doing that I despise!" Then trying to moderate my voice, I went on, "You say you give them what they want, what they need. But why deceive them? Why deceive the people who have been cheated countless times already? Why add more lies to their miserable lives? You say you give them what they want? How do you know that a pack of lies is what they want? Are you sure that is what they need? They need truth. It may be painful but truth is what they need and what you must give them. You say you do all this for them, for their happiness. But no! You do it because you want your propaganda. You do it because you want to save your church from being scandalized. You do it because you want to deceive the people into believing that everything is all right, everything is going to be all right, that a god in heaven takes good care of them, that a state sincerely worries about their lot, and all this in the name of the people. I am tired, I am sick of all this pretension, all these noble lies, all in the name of people, for the people. And meanwhile the people continue to suffer, continue to die, deceived from birth to death."

"Listen to me!" Park cried out. "Would you like to know what really happened to my father?"

"I know," I said. "I've read the letter Mr. Shin wrote you."

"I know that. But that isn't all," he said impatiently. "Let me tell you about it, instead of arguing about what you just said. When the ministers were taken to the riverbank to be shot, the Communists gave them two minutes to say whatever they wanted for the last time. My father was their leader, as everybody knows. The ministers gathered around him. They asked him to pray for them."

"Including the betrayers?"

"No. Ah, it infuriates me to think of what they did. Mr. Shin wouldn't tell me at first but I forced him to tell me. Those betrayers were wailing, they were begging the Communists for mercy, crying out to remind the Reds what they had done in their service, reminding them of the bargain. That's when the other ministers knew about the betrayers for the first time. So they asked my father to pray, to pray for their souls and for their salvation, for their courage, to pray for the last time on earth. And my father, that blazing fanatic—he didn't pray, do you understand? He didn't pray. 'I can't pray for you,' he said. 'I can't even pray for myself.' Then he cried out, 'I do not want to pray to an unjust God!' So he died, as Mr. Shin said, in utter solitude.

"That's when the young minister broke down. Did you know that he had been my father's protégé? He had believed in my father, believed in everything the old fanatic said to him about his God, and his faith. And what he had been taught, molded into, and made to believe in—all by my father—that was what sustained him in those terrible days and nights in captivity. His body broke down but his spirit survived the ordeal because of his faith in God, because of the brave resistance the old fanatic offered his enemies. And then, at the last moment . . ."

He stopped abruptly and turned away, then quietly said, "Good night. I must be going now."

I saw him out of the room. "Do you pray?" I said. "Can you pray?"

"I can't," he whispered. "Do you understand me? I can't!"

"Do you want to pray?"

"Yes. Yes, I do," he said. "I wish I could."

I held his arm. "Are you returning—or have you already returned to the Christian God?"

With an intensity that disturbed me, he said, "It seems that I have never really left Him. He has been my God ever since I was born. How can I explain it to you? He has been always with me. Otherwise how could I have been fighting against Him all these years?"

"Are you still fighting Him?"

He cast me a defiant look but he did not speak.

"Good night," I said.

"Listen! I must tell you," he said. "I am not going to this elder's house or any elder's because *I want* to. Do you understand that? I am not fulfilling a certain function, as you said, because *I want* to."

"I don't understand you," I said.

"It is Mr. Shin, don't you see?" he said. "He persuaded me to go to the elders of my father's congregation. 'Go to them,' he said, 'and let them welcome you—the return of a prodigal son. Go to them and tell them that you have returned, you have returned to your father to be forgiven, returned to the faith of your father, their faith. Go and comfort them, because they have suffered much, and you can give them what they want to see—the return of a repentant son.' He also persuaded me to be of use to the memorial service. Many will think that my return to my father, to my father's faith, is a miracle, as it were, born of the sacrifice of my father and the ministers."

"Why didn't you tell him you couldn't do it? How can you, when you don't believe in what you are doing?"

"'Then, pretend,' he said to me," Park whispered. "Pretend!"

"But why! Why!"

"For the people, don't you see?" he said passionately. "For the poor, suffering, tortured people, can't you see?"

We parted in silence.

27

In due course, headquarters sent us detailed instructions to evacuate the detachment from Pyongyang and return to Seoul. Colonel Chang's replacement would join us there; until then I was to supervise the evacuation, and upon its completion I was ordered to report for a new assignment at Army headquarters. According to the instructions, we were to leave Pyongyang four days after the memorial service: November 25, 1950.

Meanwhile the enraged and frightened populace took to the streets of the tense city for a series of mass demonstrations. The people were protesting against the Chinese intervention; they were reminding us of the hope and promise we had brought to them at the time of their liberation; and they were demanding that we counter the Chinese invaders with a full-scale offensive. In the bombed-out square and in the snow-covered stadium massive rallies went on; loudspeakers set up at various street corners carried angry voices, impassioned calls to arms, invoking the spirit of liberty. Under the gray sky in the interminable snow, column after column marched through the streets; the wet snow shrouded the banners hoisted on bamboo poles, blotted out the inked messages on the cardboard placards.

We disposed of our possessions, burning stacks of documents and papers and crating office equipment and propaganda material. By noon on November 21, we were ready to dispatch an advance party by rail to Seoul.

At 11 A.M., I went to the station to supervise the departure of the advance party, but the train could not leave on time; it was delayed by emergency trains—two southbound, laden with tanks, trucks, and field guns, and one empty hospital train bound north. By two o'clock I was able to leave the station and return to headquarters, where I had to preside over a staff meeting. According to intelligence reports, the battle situation was becoming tense; our forces were preparing for an offensive along the entire front. A little before three, I managed at last to leave for the memorial service.

I was not too late; an usher who greeted me at the door told me the service had begun only a short time before. He gave me a copy of the program, whispering that the short, stocky man in the black suit who was addressing the congregation was the mayor of the city. Mr. Shin had already spoken briefly, as had the commanding general of the Korean troops in the city, who represented the President of the Republic, and a representative from the U. S. Army Command in Pyongyang. After the mayor would come the delegate from the Federation of Christian Churches in South Korea; the representative of the foreign missions; the chairman of the Anti-Communist Youth Association; Chaplain Koh, representing the Christians in North Korea; and then Park as the representative of the martyrs' families. The eulogies were to be followed by the posthumous presentation of Freedom Medals to the martyrs, hymns by a mixed choir from the YMCA and YWCA, and a benediction by Mr. Shin.

On the wall above the platform hung twelve large black-ribboned portraits of the martyrs, dimly lit by twinkling candles on the altar. On both sides of the platform sat dignitaries, families of the martyrs, and others. The mayor left the lectern; the next speaker came forward. The delegate from the Federation of Christian Churches in the South bowed to the portraits, to the martyrs' families, to the honored guests, then to the congregation, and began, "My dear fellow Christians, my dear brethren in the north . . ."

It was during the impassioned oratory of the young chairman of the Anti-Communist Youth Association that I heard someone whisper to me: "I say, you missed hearing Mr. Shin." I turned my head and saw on my right a gray-haired old man in a cotton-padded dirty white robe. I did not recognize him until he whispered, "How are you, young man?" It was Colonel Chang. He had shed his glasses and was leaning on a cane.

"He did a marvelous job," he whispered. "No one, I am sure, could glorify the martyrs as well as he did."

"Indeed."

"Yes, sir, he made a lot of us weep."

The young chairman concluded his speech.

"There comes the Reverend Koh now," he said. "He is going back to his old church, you know."

"Is he going to stay here?" I said. "Only his god knows."

". . . and sons against fathers, brothers against brothers," Chaplain Koh was saying, ". . . reveling in their senseless murder . . . forever thirsty for the blood of vengeance . . . eternal captives of their mortal hatred . . ."

"Ah," Colonel Chang sighed. "Now I've lost him."

The door squeaked open and one of my officers slipped in. I edged along the wall toward him. We went outside.

"It's the train, Captain," he said. "I thought I should let you know."

The train carrying the advance party of my detachment had been blown up, presumably by mines, sixty miles south of Pyongyang.

"Guerrillas?" I asked.

"Yes, sir. Our choppers spotted them in the nearby hills. We are tracking them down."

"Any casualties?"

"Two killed; seven wounded; four, seriously. The rest of the party is all right. The lieutenant in charge has called for your instructions."

"Tell him to proceed to Seoul according to the original instructions. And you get hold of a truck and drive down there. The road is safe, I suppose."

"It's heavily patrolled."

"All right. Do what you think is best. I'll be back at headquarters as soon as I can. Any further news from the front lines?"

"A couple of regiments have been attacked by the Chinese on the west. Much infiltration there. Nothing from the east."

He left and I went back into the church.

Chaplain Koh was reading from the Bible: ". . . though we

live in the world we are not carrying on a worldly war, for the weapons of our warfare are not worldly but have divine power to destroy strongholds. . . ."

"Anything bad?" Colonel Chang whispered.

"Sabotage by the guerrillas. Blew up our train."

He swore.

"Rather hectic on the front," I said.

". . . that in due time he may exalt you. Cast all your anxieties on him, for he cares about you. Be sober, be watchful. Your adversary, the Devil, prowls around like a roaring lion, seeking someone to devour. Resist him, firm in your faith, knowing that the same experience of suffering is required of your brotherhood throughout the world. And after you have suffered a little while, the God of all grace, who has called you to his eternal glory in Christ, will himself restore, establish, and strengthen you. To him be the dominion forever and ever. Amen."

Chaplain Koh finished reading from the Bible and withdrew.

I glanced at Colonel Chang.

"No one seems to be content with speaking eulogies today," he said. "Everyone has been preaching."

Park came forward and stood stiffly in his dark-green Marine uniform, his hands gripping the lectern tensely. "As one speaking in behalf of the families of our martyrs," he began, "I don't know how best to express my gratitude for this opportunity. The gratitude of all of us for your sharing with us our sorrow and our loss. I stand before you, penitent and reconciled, but I cannot speak as well to you as my heart desires." He paused and reached into his breast pocket and took out a small book. "This is the Bible my father gave me when I was old enough to read, and I would like to read from this Bible, to which I have now returned once again after many years of exile. . . ."

Colonel Chang and I exchanged a quick glance.

Park began to read: "Why are not times of judgment kept by the Almighty, and why do those who know him never see his days? Men remove landmarks; they seize flocks and pasture them. They drive away the ass of the fatherless; they take the widow's ox for a pledge. They thrust the poor off the road; the poor of the earth all hide themselves. Behold, like wild asses in the desert they go forth to their toil, seeking prey in the wilderness as food for their children. They gather their fodder in the field and glean the vineyard of the wicked man. They lie all night naked, without clothing, and have no covering in the cold. They are wet with the rain of the mountains, and cling to the rock for want of shelter. . . ."

Colonel Chang whispered, "What is he reading?"

"Job."

". . . among the olive rows of the wicked they make oil; they tread the wine presses, but they thirst. From out of the city the dying groan and the soul of the wounded cries for help; yet God pays no attention to their prayer." Park stopped and put down his Bible; then, looking out at the people, he recited from memory, "From out of the city the dying groan, and the soul of the wounded cries for help; yet God pays no attention to their prayer."

Mr. Shin came over to Park and put his hand on his shoulder. Park looked gratefully at the friend of his father's, then continued to recite:

". . . and the Lord said to Job: 'Shall a faultfinder contend with the Almighty? He who argues with God, let him answer it.' Then Job answered the Lord: 'Behold, I am of small account; what shall I answer thee? I lay my hand on my mouth. I have spoken once, and I will not answer; twice, but I will proceed no further.' Then the Lord answered Job out of the whirlwind: 'Gird up your loins like a man; I will question you and you declare to me. Will you even put me in the wrong? Will you condemn me that you may be justified? Have you an arm like God, and can you thunder with a voice like His?' Then Job answered the Lord: 'I know that thou canst do all things, and that no purpose of thine can be thwarted . . . therefore I have uttered what I did not understand, things too wonderful for me, which I did not know.' 'Hear and I will speak; I will question you, and you declare to me.' 'I had heard of thee by the hearing of the ear, but now my eyes see thee; therefore, I despise myself, and repent in dust and ashes.'" Park was silent and stood with bowed head in the sea of silence around him.

Then he stepped down and returned to his chair, followed by Mr. Shin.

Colonel Chang touched my elbow. "I am afraid I must leave now."

I held his arm and led him out of the church. It had begun snowing again; the soft, thick snow fluffed down over the gray city. We stood by a pillar.

"Well, here we are," he said; and looking back toward the door, "and there they are. How does it feel to be an outsider, Captain?"

I did not know how to reply.

He touched my arm. "Good-bye, Captain."

"Take care of yourself, Colonel. I hope to see you in Seoul some day," I said, taking his hand.

"Yes, let's hope so."

I watched his stooped figure slowly receding as he limped away from me, leaning on his cane. When he disappeared through the small gate I turned to go back inside the church. But I stopped, turned around, and returned to where I had just parted with Colonel Chang. Alone, I stood there for a while, looking down at the sorrowful city, listening vaguely to the hymns of praise sung within by those who had their god. Soon I left and trudged down the hill in the wet snow.

28

The day after the memorial service, at 1 P.M., I was ready to drive Park to the air base. We were standing outside headquarters, waiting for my jeep to be brought from the motor pool. For the first time in several days the sun shone through patches of white clouds. There was no wind. The snow-covered city glistened in thin, tremulous mirages. The special transport plane of the Intelligence Service, which was to carry Park to Pusan, was not leaving until 2 P.M., so when the jeep came, I told him he did not have to hurry. "You have about half an hour to spare," I said. "Would you like to drive around the city for a last look? It will be a long time before you get a chance to come back here."

He shook his head. "I would rather take a walk," he said, "if you don't mind. Would you like to come along?"

As we walked down the street, he said, "I didn't see you yesterday at the service. Were you there?"

"I left before it was over. But I stayed long enough to hear what you had to say."

He looked at me. "I didn't plan to read from the Bible. I had many things in my mind that I wanted to say, but when I got up there and faced the congregation I forgot all about them."

"Aren't you glad you read those passages?"

"I am not," he said sharply, stopping his walk. "You know I don't, I can't believe in what I read yesterday. I can't affirm as Job did.

"Do me a favor," he said suddenly. "Would you come with me to my father's church?"

We crossed the street and walked up the slope.

"When I read Mr. Shin's letter," he said, "I couldn't fail to understand what must have been in my father's mind at that last horrible moment. Perhaps it was the same thing that had made me leave the church and him. It has been my obsession ever since. Why must we have so much injustice and misery in the world? Why must we suffer?" We paused to stand now in front of the church. "It seemed to me, when I was younger, that it was too easy and too simple to say that we suffer because of our original sin or because we have to suffer to prove our faith in God." Gazing at the battered building, he added, "I am not so sure any more."

"You are then coming around to Job's affirmation."

"I don't know. I can't yet. I resist it. Do you understand me? I resist it consciously. Then why did I read Job's words? As I stood there facing the people, looking into those thousands of human eyes that have seen horror and injustice, hunger and sickness, and sudden, meaningless death, all waiting for me to utter the next word, I felt Mr. Shin's hand on my shoulder as if to say, 'Go on, go on. They are waiting for your words. Don't stop here. Go on, and say it!' The next thing I knew—I was giving in to God. No! I wasn't. It was Job!"

"I understand," I said.

"I grew up here and lived here for twenty years," he said, looking at the ruins about him. "And now it is no more."

The bell overhead clanged once, faintly.

"Come along," I said. "We'd better go."

Later when we were driving out to the air base he said, "I have been thinking of what we said the other night about a fairy tale. Do you understand that a fairy tale can be an integral part of our lives? Then it ceases to be a fairy tale. It becomes real. It becomes something that is meant to be. What those Christians wanted and needed was not merely a nice little story that would give them comfort and confidence but something that would make their lives meaningful, something that would make their sufferings worthwhile. Do you recall this, I forget from where? 'Deeper truth lies in the fact that the world is not meaningless and absurd but is in a meaningless state.'

Never before have those words meant more to me than they have during the last few days. Yes, those Christians have something that sustains their lives in a world that is in a meaningless state. But we don't. Why should we call what they have a fairy tale?"

"Because we can understand it but we can't believe it," I said.

"The wall between our fairy tale and their reality, if you know what I mean, sometimes seems very thin."

"But the wall is there, isn't it?"

He shook his head. "You are a stubborn man," he said.

We arrived at the air base ten minutes before two. When Park had checked in and was about to board the plane I told him about the plans for the general retreat. "We are not going to defend Pyongyang when it comes to that," I said.

"Why didn't you tell me about it before?"

"I am sorry. This is an official secret."

With an impatient gesture he said, "And here I am, flying out!" He added, frowning, "What about those people? What about Mr. Shin? What about the chaplain? Are you going to tell them about it?"

He held my arm. "Will you look after Mr. Shin? Will you do that for me? He has no money, nothing much to eat left in the house. Yesterday I did my best to collect supplies for him but they won't last long. He has been selling clothes and whatnot for some time. He wouldn't take anything from his congregation. I tried to stop him from selling things but I know he has been to the market several times."

"Why didn't you tell me about it before?" I said.

"I didn't think you would be interested in hearing about it. You despise him, don't you?"

Park had to go. "Listen!" he said. "It doesn't matter what you think of him but do this for me. Will you see to it that he gets to Seoul before it is too late? Once he gets there, I will look after him."

I shook his hand. "Good-bye and good luck," I said. "I will look after Mr. Shin."

"Thanks. Go and see him. Talk with him."

"I will," I promised. "Take care of yourself."

The plane left five minutes after two, and I drove back to the city.

When I reached headquarters I was told by my orderly, who met me at the entrance, that Mr. Shin was waiting for me in my office.

As soon as he saw me he said, "I thought it was about time I came to see you. I haven't seen you for some time."

"I was at the service yesterday, Mr. Shin," I said. "I arrived too late to hear you, but I understand you did a marvelous job of glorifying the twelve martyrs."

His serene gaze did not waver. "I hope so," he said.

"You satisfied everyone."

"You too, Captain?"

"I have nothing to be satisfied or dissatisfied with, Mr. Shin," I said. "It was your decision to glorify all the twelve ministers and save your church from shameful scandal. It was your decision. Not mine."

When he did not reply I told him that I had been to the air base to see Park off to Pusan.

His continued silence made me uneasy. "Was there anything special you had in mind?" I asked. "I mean . . ."

He stood up. "I must have had something in mind to come to see you, but I seem to have forgotten what it was." He paused. "I would rather not remember it now. Good-bye, Captain. It was nice to have seen you again. I am sorry I troubled you."

I tried to detain him but he rushed past me to the door and disappeared.

I knew I had hurt him, and I hated myself for it.

That evening we had the first air raid in Pyongyang.

29

The next morning, while the feeble sun filtered through the sky plastered with gray clouds, jeeps with loudspeakers prowled through the streets, grinding out martial music and a young woman's hysterical, shrill voice that appealed to the populace to be calm and steadfast in their trust in the United Nations Forces; it was only a matter of a few days before the Chinese invaders would be beaten back across the Yalu River. Armored cars were patrolling the city and for the first time since the liberation, antiaircraft guns were taking up positions here and there; heavy machine guns were set up on rooftops and street corners; and from the air base across the river sortie after sortie raced toward the northern sky.

While I was still in my office, around eleven o'clock, our communications officer sent up a special cable message he had just received from Army headquarters. It was addressed to Chaplain Koh and I was to deliver it to him.

The message, sent by the Office of Chaplains, stated that there had been an administrative error and that Chaplain Koh was to report to the Chief of Chaplains immediately; it also requested my cooperation in the speedy departure of the chaplain from Pyongyang.

At half-past eleven I went to Mr. Shin's church, where I knew I would find him. When I went inside, the scanty congregation was singing a hymn. I took a seat in the back. Between where I was and the congregation there were nearly forty or so empty pews; the grand interior of the church looked hollow with so many seats unoccupied. The congregation sang without the accompaniment of the pipe organ or the choir; their voices were subdued, as if smothered by the cold air and the empty space. When they had finished singing and sat down, Mr. Shin emerged from the shadows on the platform and mounted the lectern. The sun shone through the stained glass, making a slanted path of dusty air and hazily illuminating Mr. Shin's right cheek. He closed his eyes for a moment, and when he opened them he said quietly, "My dear brethren, I have nothing to say to you today. What I would like to say and what I feel deep in my heart are beyond the power of my words." He paused. "Come. Let us offer our silent prayers."

I tiptoed out of the church and waited for the service to be over. I heard nothing from within for some minutes, then the congregation sang a hymn, followed by a silent pause, presumably for Mr. Shin's benediction. Presently people began to come out and quietly drift away. The bells started clanging overhead. Mr. Shin appeared, accompanied by three elders. They stood at the threshold and talked to one another for a few minutes. One of the elders glanced at me occasionally, perhaps at my uniform, my pistol, and my steel helmet. Then Mr. Shin was left alone. He came to me. "Come, let us take a walk," he said. We went down the steps and walked over to the cliff that overlooked the city.

Resting his hands on the iron fence, he gazed into space.

"Mr. Shin, I would like to get you out of Pyongyang," I said. "I would like to take you with me to Seoul."

"I do not understand you, Captain." He folded his arms, frowning. "Why should you take me to Seoul? You surprise me. Is this official?"

"No, Mr. Shin. Please don't think the Army has anything to do with it. It is my idea, more precisely Park's wish, that you should leave Pyongyang. The sooner you leave the better." Then I told him about the impending general retreat of U.N. Forces from North Korea.

"Do you mean to say that you are going to abandon us?" he said.

"We are not going to make a stand in North Korea. We may even give up Seoul if necessary, temporarily, of course. But I doubt we will try to come up this far north again." I explained to him the overall situation on the battlefront, adding that I had already dispatched one third of my detachment to Seoul.

He listened to my words but his thoughts seemed to be elsewhere.

"We are an intelligence detachment, an administrative one, more or less. So we are evacuating now ahead of time. But it won't be long before combat troops will pull out of Pyongyang. The withdrawal will be sudden, I assure you; it has already been planned."

"That doesn't leave one much of a choice does it?"

"Then will you agree to come with us?"

"I shall have to think about it," he said, "although from what you have told me there seems to be no alternative."

"I have a small house in Seoul, Mr. Shin. It has survived the war so far, fortunately. I will be glad if you will use it, since I won't be using it anyway."

"That's very considerate of you, Captain. I have a few friends in Seoul and also in Pusan. I suppose I won't be without something to do."

We then talked about people we knew in the South. I told him what it was like in Seoul and in the South in general and what had gone on there since the end of the war in the Pacific. He told me of his acquaintances, most of them ministers who had studied with him at a seminary in Japan years before. He had a sister who was married to a man who owned an orchard on a small island off Pusan. She had been asking him to come and live with her family ever since he had lost his wife several years ago. "I am ready to accept her offer," he said, "and retire. I am looking forward to a quiet life."

"We are leaving Pyongyang on the twenty-fifth. I am sorry we will have to hurry," I said. I told him about the sabotage by the Communist guerrillas. "We are planning to leave by truck, armed, of course. It may take longer to get to Seoul by truck but it will be safer, I think."

He was quiet. I felt he was hardly listening.

"There is one thing I would like you to promise me," I said. "I would like you not to tell anyone about it."

"I understand," he said. "Of course, no one should know what the Army is going to do."

I told him I would come to his house on the morning of the twenty-fifth.

"Captain, I haven't really made up my mind yet about leaving," he said. "I will have to think about it."

"Don't think about it," I said a little impatiently. "There is no time to think, no time to lose. When the combat troops from the North and from this area begin to pull out it will be chaotic. Unless you are escorted by our troops you won't be able to get too far."

We stood there, side by side, listening to the distant chiming of church bells. The sky was becoming cloudy. A cold wind began to blow. We walked back to the church and stood at the bottom of the steps.

"Good-bye, Captain," he said, offering his hand.

I took his cold bony hand. "Mr. Shin, what was it that you wanted to tell me yesterday?" I asked.

He did not answer, but turned away and walked up the steps and disappeared into the empty church. I heard the hollow interior of the church resound with his harsh coughing. The door closed with a metallic click.

At 10 P.M., I had the following telephone conversation with Colonel Chang:

COLONEL: Now, don't ask me where I am calling from. Have you seen the chaplain yet?

I: Colonel—I have sent word to him that I would like to see him tomorrow morning. The cable message from the Office of Chaplains—did you arrange it? I think it was very thoughtful of you.

COLONEL: Kind of you to say so, Captain. You do understand why I did it, don't you? Excessive humility can often turn into excessive pride.

I: I think it came just in time.

COLONEL: I didn't want to see him taking a chance of becoming a martyr. I think we have had enough martyrs for a while, don't you agree? What about Mr. Shin?

I: I can't say anything definite yet. I saw him today.

COLONEL: Get both of them out of here. Do what you can but get them out before it is too late. Well, I wish you a safe journey, Captain.

I: Thank you. Good luck to you sir. Take care of yourself.

COLONEL: You too. Give Mr. Shin and the chaplain my best regards.

I: I will, sir. How is your project coming along?

COLONEL: Excellent! It couldn't be better. We've got every corner covered. All we have to do now is to wait. I've been polishing up my Chinese, ha, ha, ha! Good-bye, Captain.

I: See you in Seoul.

COLONEL: We will see.

30

The next morning Pyongyang Area Command notified me that, following the evacuation of my detachment, the building would be turned over to the Field Hospital Command; I was to meet an officer from the Hospital Command to work out the details of the transfer. A little after two that afternoon, he came to see me. Major Minn, a tall man of about fifty, graying at the temples, had been a general practitioner in Seoul before the war. I showed him around the building, accompanied by my supply officer, who explained what we could and what we could not leave behind.

When the three of us returned to my office, Major Minn said, "Splendid, splendid! Just leave every single bed and whatever bedding you can spare. That will be luxury enough for us for the time being. I tell you, I couldn't do a damn thing on the line. We kept our patients in those miserable tents all night. Why, they died before you could get around to taking care of their wounds. It was too damn cold. Ah, this will be splendid! The patients will be coming in by the hundreds but they will be lucky. We will find places to receive them. But what are we going to do with those refugees who are pouring down this way? I hate to think about it. God, where will they all go in this cold? What will they eat?" He paused and I could see the pain in his eyes. "They keep following us but we are pulling out too fast for them to catch up with us. What a mess we are in!"

He got ready to go. "I keep telling myself to shut my big mouth and just do whatever I can to save as many lives as possible. But I can't forget the morning in June I woke up to find that the Army had simply vanished from Seoul overnight, blowing up the only bridge, without even saying a word to the people about it. I couldn't believe it! Now how do you like that, eh? You go to bed feeling secure because the Army told you it would never give up your city, and you wake up the next morning and see thousands of Red soldiers and Russian tanks milling about in the streets. And where is your trustworthy army? Way down in the South, having sneaked out like a thief in the night. I tell you I didn't know what to do. So now I am in the Army myself, a major and all that, and I am supposed to understand the hush-hush ways of the Army—strategic, tactical, and so on. But, my God, why shouldn't we do something at least for those poor people who are determined to follow us, starving in this cold? I just hope it won't happen here as it did in Seoul."

I wanted to warn him that it was exactly what was going to happen, but I had to keep silent.

"On my way down here, I noticed our troops were digging in. I don't know a damn thing about how to fight a war but it was reassuring to see them in position. Lots of guns are out there. I guess we will make a stand. Even I can guess that."

My supply officer looked at me, excused himself, and walked out.

"Maybe I shouldn't be talking like this with you intelligence people," Major Minn said. "I guess I am still not used to the strange ways of the Army. You don't know how pleased I am that this building is being turned over to us. I say that as a doctor, you know. I will be able to relax and do a better job on our men once we settle in here. So, you are leaving tomorrow?"

"Tomorrow morning," I said.

"Back to Seoul?"

"Yes."

"Glad to hear that," he said, nodding. "You've had your share. I can see that. I can tell you have a bad knee or something there. You limp, though not too noticeably. Wounded, I suppose?"

"Mortar," I said. "Shrapnel."

"Damn! When are we going to stop this idiotic soldier game?"

"It has been going on since the time of creation, hasn't it?"

He shook his head. "I tell you—there is something wicked in mankind. Ah, well."

We shook hands.

"When this war is over and if I am still alive," he said, smiling, "maybe we will run into each other in Seoul."

"Who knows? Perhaps we will."

"And if you get sick or something, come around to my place. I will give you good treatment." He scribbled his address on a piece of paper he tore from his notebook and gave it to me. "Free of charge."

"I'll be in Seoul in a few days," I said. "Can I do anything for you? I could look up your family if you would like me to."

"No, thank you anyway," he said matter-of-factly. "My wife got bombed out. We didn't have children, fortunately."

I had expected to see Chaplain Koh in the morning but it was only in the late afternoon, a few hours after Major Minn had left, that he came to see me. It was strange to see him out of uniform; he was wearing a double-breasted dark suit.

He was in a cheerful mood. "I take it that you know my resignation has been accepted," he said. "Ah, I can see you are not interested in my new status."

"I regret to say I am not, Chaplain," I said.

"You'll get used to seeing me like this soon enough," he said with a grin. "Let me first give you the message from Mr. Shin, then you can tell me why you wanted to see me."

"When did you see him?"

"An hour or so ago," he said. "I told him I was going to see you and he said I could tell you that you didn't have to—you shouldn't, rather—bother to come for him tomorrow morning. I am glad you saw him, for whatever reasons, and I don't want to pry into your business. But what is the matter with both of you? Did you have a quarrel?"

"No, of course not."

"Then why does he refuse to see you now? And what is the significance of this date tomorrow morning?"

"Chaplain, we are leaving Pyongyang. Will you come with us? To Seoul."

"Why? Why are you leaving? I can't leave my church now. But why?"

"I am going to tell you an official secret, and you know what you are expected to do with it," I said. I explained to him about the general retreat and about the evacuation of my detachment. "So I am escorting you back to Seoul. You will join us, of course."

He did not hesitate at all. "I have no intention of leaving Pyongyang with you. Not because I don't welcome your company. But you understand. I have my church and my congregation to look after."

"Are you sure, Chaplain? Are you determined to stay here? You realize what that means, I hope."

I handed him the cable message. "This is for you. Forgive me for keeping it with me so long."

He read it, looked up at me, read it again, then handed it back to me. "When are you leaving, Captain?" he said quietly.

"You will come with us then," I said. "Tomorrow morning."

"Tomorrow morning," he said. "So that is why Mr. Shin doesn't want to see you. You asked him to come with you?"

"That's right."

"He is not leaving," he said, "and I am not leaving either, Captain."

I gave the cable back to him. "This is your order, Captain. You are not going to ignore it."

He tore it up. "There!" he said. "You can say you couldn't find me."

Then, "Good-bye, Captain," he said. "I must hurry to my church. We are having a special service to baptize children born since the war. And this evening . . ." He stopped, glared at me with his enormous eyes, and suddenly shouted, "So we are going to abandon the people! My people! What did you think I would do? Run away? Again? Betray them again? Don't you understand I couldn't do that?" He put his hand on my shoulder and made an obvious effort to control himself.

"Captain, Captain," he said, "there is a loud voice in the dark corner of my heart that says, 'Go! Why let yourself suffer here? Go! You will be more useful elsewhere, in the Army, on the battlefield. So—go!' But I have seen, I have learned how much my people suffered while I was away from them. Yes, I suffered too, but mine was easier to bear because it had the halo of glory, hope, and promise. But theirs—it's a silent, hopeless, ugly suffering, weary and despairing." He left me and went over to the window. "Undoubtedly, when it comes to the worst, there will be many from my congregation who will leave, but I know there will be more who will not be able to leave. Where will they go, those old people and starving people? How far, without food, without money, and without hope or promise they will be cared for? The whole country is at war. . . . This is where I must be. This is my place, at the side of my people."

The telephone rang; it was from the commanding officer of CIC. He had put in a special request to the Chief of Army Intelligence that an officer from my unit be attached to him temporarily, and the request had been granted.

"It appears I am not leaving tomorrow morning after all," I said to Chaplain Koh when I hung up. "I have been ordered to stay here as long as I can."

He looked at me searchingly.

"I understand you, Chaplain," I said. "Perhaps, more than you think I do. Come. I am on my way to see Mr. Shin. If you are going that way, I will give you a ride."

"No, thank you," he said. "I don't think you can see him anyway now. He is out of town. He had to go to a wedding. An elder's daughter is getting married. You see, life goes on. He will be back tonight."

He made as if to go, yet seemed hesitant. "I'm puzzled, Captain. You seem to have a certain kind of influence over Mr. Shin and he over you. What is it? I have followed him to all those revival meetings and, you know, at each meeting he always asks me if you were there. You weren't except at one. Why should he have to know if you were there or not? When I told him you weren't, I couldn't help noticing that he seemed relieved. Why? I dared ask him one day. Do you know what he said? He said there is something, a question, you asked him when you first met him, and whenever he sees you he is reminded of it and that he has not answered yet, so much so that it makes him uneasy. 'Pray for me,' he said, 'pray for my soul, and pray for him, too. His question has been terrifying me.' That's all he said. What is it? What is it, Captain?"

I did not, I dared not, reply.

"I pray for him, I pray for his soul, though it is he who should pray for me," Chaplain Koh said. "I pray for you too, Captain."

At ten past five, the commanding officer at CIC called to tell me that he and I had been requested by G-2 of the Area Command to attend a special intelligence meeting in his office at seven.

Before going there I stopped by CIC to be briefed on the latest intelligence reports, particularly on those concerning the guerrilla activities south of Pyongyang. As of 6 P.M., my detachment had officially ceased to operate and our communications facilities had stopped functioning.

The commanding officer, a red-faced, short, squat lieutenant colonel, briefed me personally. After that he said, "I am grateful that you are going to be with us for a while, Captain. As you know, we used to depend greatly on your detachment for information analysis and interpretation, but now you are leaving. The point is that there has been increased infiltration in this area and we've been capturing quite a few enemy agents and propaganda material.

"Your new instructions are," he went on, "to dispatch your detachment as planned under the supervision of an officer you designate and to stay with my detachment until we evacuate. Everybody else is getting out. CIC will be the only unit remaining here that is directly controlled by Army Intelligence. We are supposed to stick it out until the last minute, then get out. I want you to read and analyze every single intelligence report and whatever information we can squeeze out of enemy agents."

I drove him to the meeting and on the way, we decided that I would continue to stay in my office, if the Hospital Command agreed.

"I am glad you don't mind staying where you are now," he said. "You wouldn't particularly enjoy staying at CIC. There are a few things going on which you might not want to hear or see."

Early the next morning, I drove to Mr. Shin's house. The detachment was to leave the city shortly, and I wanted to try once more to persuade him to leave with them. Armored cars patrolled the hushed streets; a man pushed a cart across the empty, wide avenue; a Military Police jeep, blinking red lights, its radio antenna swinging, screeched around a corner. A cold wind whipped about, fluttering torn pieces of war posters on the shop windows.

Mr. Shin was not home. An old man, who introduced himself as the janitor of the church, seemed to recognize me.

"I am sorry, officer," he said, "but he said I am not to show you in. Anyway, he isn't here. He has been out since four in the morning."

I asked him if he could tell me where Mr. Shin might be found.

"I don't know," he said. "All I can say is somebody is dying and the pastor had to be with him."

At 8 A.M., my detachment left Pyongyang under the command of my executive officer. From my office window I watched the trucks and jeeps leaving the once-liberated city. The wind blew relentlessly, lashing at the men and at the vehicles, and from across the street I could hear the clanging of the bell. The silence in our deserted headquarters seemed ominous. I felt depressed beyond all hope.

31

I tried to shake off my mood of depression by busying myself at rearranging my temporary quarters. My supply officer had left half a dozen boxes of field rations, a cot, and sufficient bedding, and my orderly, who had left with the detachment, had stored several cans of fresh water, a pile of coal in a large wooden box, and a few odds and ends—candles, boxes of matches, cooking utensils, and the like, all neatly arranged on my desk. It was strange to find myself in the midst of all these things, as though I were about to start on a long, solitary journey. Yet I was not totally alone; I had a telephone directly connected with the CIC detachment and a field-radio set. By nine o'clock I was ready to drive over to CIC, where I spent the rest of the morning perusing a stack of reports, preparing an intelligence analysis and estimates.

Around noon, as I did not feel well and since there was no more work to be done, I left; I felt I had a slight fever. I returned to my room and found that a contingent from the Hospital Command had already begun to convert the building into a transient field hospital. Several trucks were still unloading beds and bedding. I went up to my room, took a few pills, lay down on the cot, and immediately fell asleep.

When I woke, I found myself covered with blankets. I turned my head toward the stove and saw the dim figure of a man, sitting quietly in the warm, dusky room. It was Mr. Shin.

"Go back to sleep," he said. "Don't get up."

Though I felt a bit weak I got out of the cot. "Have you been here long?" I said. My watch told me that it was half-past five. "I slept all afternoon."

He said he had been told by Chaplain Koh that I was staying in the city; he had thought he would stop by to see me on his way to a church where he was to conduct a special service that evening. "I was surprised to find that you now have a hospital in here," he said. "But I asked for you anyway. An officer came out to meet me and took me up to your room. He told me that you were running a fever. He had found you here, alone and in a deep sleep. He took your temperature and gave you a shot but with all that going on you didn't stir a bit. Do you remember anything?"

I shook my head. "No, I don't. That was very kind of him."

"You must have been exhausted, Captain. You seem to be in need of a good, long rest. How are you feeling now?"

I confessed that I felt slightly dizzy.

"Then you must go back to bed and be still," he said.

"It could be that I am hungry."

"Have you eaten anything since morning?"

"No."

"Well, then, you must have something," he said. "Shall I call someone for you?"

I told him not to; I had canned food and I could make some tea. I invited him to join me, if he did not mind tasting canned American food. "What time do you have to be at the church?"

"Half-past six," he said. "I am to have dinner with the minister after the service, but I will be delighted to join you for a cup of tea."

Later, we sat quietly by the stove in the candlelight, sipping tea. It was dark outside and the wind was howling. I drew the curtains over the window.

"As you may know, I have to stay here as long as I can," I said, "but I will be ordered to leave before our combat troops begin their withdrawal. Mr. Shin, when I leave, please plan to come with me."

He did not reply.

"I have promised Park that I will look after you," I said. "Do you have anyone to help you in the house?"

"Yes. I am well taken care of," he said. "The janitor of my

church and his wife are staying with me. Yes, I am quite comfortable."

"Give them my name and address, just so that if you need me for anything or if they need me they will know where to find me."

"That's very kind of you, but I am sure we won't have to trouble you."

I poured more tea into his cup. "Mr. Shin, why did you come to see me?" I said.

But he had again withdrawn into himself. His silence disturbed me. "Why did you come, Mr. Shin?" I asked again.

He stood up. "I must leave you now, Captain. Thank you for the tea. I think you should go back to bed and get some rest."

I detained him, holding his arm. "What is it that you want to tell me? Why do you hide it from me?"

He looked away, then looked into my eyes. "Help me!" he whispered. "Help me!"

"Help you? Why? How!"

"Help me!"

I let his arm go. "You haven't been able to answer my question, Mr. Shin. Why? Why!" I cried out. "Your god doesn't care how you suffer, does he!"

Feverishly his eyes remained fixed on mine. "Go on!" he said. "Go on!"

"Your god, any god, all the gods in the world—what do they care for us? Your god—he does not understand our sufferings, he doesn't want to have anything to do with our miseries, murders, starving people, wars, wars, and all the horrors!"

"Go on!" he said, now nearly delirious. "Go on!"

"All right," I cried. "I'll tell you. I despise what you have done, what you are doing to your people! Lies, lies! Why? Why do you do it! Your twelve ministers—they were butchered for no good reason. They didn't die for the glory of your god. They were murdered by men and your god couldn't care less. Tell me, then, why glorify your god! Why glorify him while men are murdered by men! And why betray your people?"

We both fell silent.

"Mr. Shin, Mr. Shin! Why all that?" I said in desperation. "Why all that, why deceive your people, when our sufferings here and now have no justice to seek for beyond this life?"

He clutched my arms and whispered compassionately, "How you must have suffered! How you must be suffering. I, too, Captain! I, too, suffer!"

Hardly knowing what to say, I looked at him in wonder. "Then you, too," I said at last, "you too, don't believe . . . ?"

He interrupted me with an agonized gesture. "Don't! Don't say it!" Tears filled his eyes.

"Then . . . why!"

"All my life I have searched for God, Captain," he whispered, "but I found only man with all his sufferings . . . and death, inexorable death!"

"And after death?"

"Nothing!" he whispered. "Nothing!"

The searing anguish in his pale face was overwhelming.

"Help me! Help me love my people, my poor, suffering people, tortured by wars, hungry, cold, sick and weary of life!" he cried. "Help me! Sufferings seize their hope and faith and toss them adrift into a sea of despair! We must show them light, tell them there will be a glorious welcome waiting for them, assure them they will triumph in the eternal Kingdom of God!"

"To give them the illusion of hope? The illusion of life beyond the grave?"

"Yes, yes! Because they are men. Despair is the disease of those weary of life, life here and now full of meaningless sufferings. We must fight despair, we must destroy it and not let the sickness of despair corrupt the life of man and reduce him to a mere scarecrow."

"And you? What about you? What about your despair?"

"That is my cross!" he said. "I must bear that alone."

I took his trembling hands. "Forgive me!" I cried out. "Forgive me! I have been unjust to you!"

"There is nothing to forgive," he said. "You, too, you, too, because you know, bear your own cross!"

"And others?"

"Many will not be able to bear it," he said, suddenly tender.

"Those are the ones who need Christ. We will give them their Christ and their Judas."

"And the resurrection of the flesh?"

"Yes, the resurrection of the flesh!"

"And the eternal Kingdom of God?"

"Yes, the eternal Kingdom of God!"

"And justice?"

"Yes, justice—oh, how one craves for justice! Yes, justice! The ultimate justice in the name of God!"

"And you?"

"I must continue to suffer. There is no other way."

"How long! How long must you suffer!"

"Till we die and never meet again!" he whispered.

And for the first time since the war, I abandoned myself to uncontrollable tears, my tears, my contrition—for my parents, for my countrymen, and for those many unknown souls I had destroyed.

"Courage," he said gently, laying his hands on my shoulders. "Courage, Captain. We must hope against hopelessness. We must dare to hope against despair because we are men."

Soon after Mr. Shin had left, someone knocked on the door and Major Minn entered. I was in bed; I tried to get up. He drew a chair near the cot, motioning for me not to rise.

"I saw him leave," he said, "so I thought I would come in and take a look at you. How are you feeling?"

I told him I felt a bit tired but otherwise fine.

"I told your relative you will be all right by tomorrow," he said.

"My relative?"

"Isn't he someone in your family?"

"No."

"Oh, I thought he was," he said, shrugging his shoulders. "I asked him if he was related to you and he said, 'Well, in a way.' Anyway, I was surprised to find you were still in town."

I explained the circumstances.

"I was told that an officer attached to CIC was going to be staying in the building," he said, "but it never occurred to me that it could be you. Glad to have you with us. I am a man of foresight, am I not? Do you remember my promise to treat you free of charge?"

I thanked him for what he had done for me.

"Don't mention it. You were exhausted. Nothing too serious. I think you should rest for a while. You are fortunate, you know, being right in the middle of my hospital. We aren't quite settled in here yet; we will be by tomorrow."

I asked him when he was expecting patients.

He frowned. "Tomorrow evening. It's getting worse on the front. We don't even seem to have a front and troops are pouring down this way. I am supposed to receive nearly two hundred patients tomorrow evening and God knows how many more the next day."

"Are you keeping them here or are you sending them south?"

"We are sending them off as fast as we can but there are just too many," he said, shaking his head. "What a mess!" He took my temperature, checked my pulse, and said I would be feeling well soon.

"I am sleeping in the next room. If you need me, just call. I told my orderly to look after you, so don't be surprised to see someone come in during the night and tinker with the stove."

I thanked him.

"You are most welcome," he said; then, pausing on his way toward the door, "By the way, and I hope you don't mind my being nosy, but are you a Christian?"

"Why do you ask?"

"Just being curious. My wife was one, a very devout one, too. You know . . . it's a strange thing. When she was alive, I sort of tolerated her religiosity, if you know what I mean, but I never understood her sense of commitment to her god. Now I am beginning to understand it in some vague way."

"Could it be because you have seen so many men die?"

"In my profession I have seen many men die. As a doctor I can explain why or how my patients die. But God knows I can't explain the reason for all these men dying in war. There is no rational explanation when you get down to the bottom of it. It doesn't make sense. Yet somehow it must make sense."

"So you begin to understand your wife," I said.

"To be more precise—her need, her desperate need for her religion, for her god. Well, I didn't mean to keep you up. He was a minister, was he not?"

I explained to him briefly about Mr. Shin.

"He came here around two o'clock," he said. "He asked me if it was all right for him to stay, so I left him alone with you. I came back about two hours later and of course, by that time I had forgotten about him. Then I heard a low voice coming from this room. I thought you were up. I opened the door and saw that you were still asleep."

"Was there anyone else here besides him?"

"No. He was praying. I left as quietly as I could. Well, good night, Captain. Get some sleep now." He shook his head again, smiling. "You must be a terrible sinner," he said. "I think he was praying for your soul."

32

My temperature was erratic. It rose slightly during the night but was down again in the morning. The major ordered me to stay in bed. The commanding officer at CIC was kind enough to telephone me to say that he would send a lieutenant with my work so that I would not have to leave my bed. I did not think I was that ill but I was content to stay indoors.

The day began with another dreary morning, cold and windy, and with reports from the front which were anything but cheerful. The lieutenant, who had come with a briefcase full of captured enemy documents and propaganda material for me to study, stayed with me for an hour or so. At noon the major's orderly brought me a lunch tray and later the major himself came in, took my temperature, and assured me that I was getting better.

Alone once more, I drew up a chair near the window, and spent some time looking out. Several army trucks, their canvas tops crusted with snow, were plowing their way toward the bridge across the Taedong River. Here and there I saw people hurrying through the street, alone and in groups, some empty-handed, some carrying bundles. An ambulance sped by, its siren shrieking. The church over the slope became more and more indistinct in the waning afternoon. A plane, seen above the dim belfry, flew in a circle, blinking red and green lights. It quickly became darker outside.

After a while Mr. Shin came in. He could not stay. He had been to a funeral and then to a meeting with the ministers of the city. "I was just passing by and thought I would stop by and see how you are doing," he said. "I am glad to hear that you are feeling better."

I put the teakettle on the stove and persuaded him to have a cup of tea with me. "You shouldn't be walking around in the cold," I said. "How is your cough?"

"I feel fine these days. I don't think I have ever felt better since before the war."

"You ought to see a doctor, though, Mr. Shin," I said. "Are you sleeping well?"

"Oh, yes. I sleep too much, in fact," he said, smiling. Steam rose from his wet shoes and damp overcoat. "You don't suppose your detachment has reached Seoul yet, do you?"

I told him they had stayed overnight at Sariwon and that they should arrive in Seoul by the next morning.

"The city is becoming crowded with refugees from the North," he said. "The ministers met today to find out what we could do for them. We are offering them our churches for shelter. But I don't know how we can feed them. My church already has five, six hundred. Many of them came all the way from the border. What will happen to them?"

"Do you find many Christians among them?"

"Yes. Where will they go from here?" he said. "Where can they go?"

The tea was ready; I poured him a cup.

He gazed thoughtfully into the steaming cup. "We buried a boy, twelve years old," he said. "His father had been taken away by the Communists shortly before we were liberated, and we have heard that he died on the way to the North—one of those death marches. The boy was dying; I stayed with him all night. Before he lost his strength the boy asked me if, when he died, he would see his father in heaven. I said, Yes, he would see his father. Would there be any of those Communist policemen in heaven who would take his father away from him again? Of course not, I said. And his mother? Would he see her there someday? Yes, I said to him, Yes, he would, of course, he would. And you know the boy looked at his weeping mother with eyes so full of longing and love, I, too, wept. And today the white coffin, the snow, and the black, wet dirt—no more, no more. All these years as a pastor I have prepared many men to die peacefully. Yes, I prepared that boy to die in peace. But I failed twice, Captain; I betrayed twice."

Again the terrible anguish in his eyes. I have never seen such anguish. "I married late in life," he said, "only to bury my first child, a boy, and my wife within the same year. My wife died a few weeks after the boy. She became ill. She blamed the loss of our child on herself, on her sins, and she spent all her time praying, fasting. And I—I was sick with my grief but I had my life to live here and she had hers and I resented her slavish devotion to her god, her pitiful prayers. And I dared—I dared to tell her that when we were gone from this life we would never meet again, we would never see our children again, that there was no afterlife. My unhappy wife, my terrified wife—she could not bear the thought, she was not strong enough to live with my terrible truth. She could not live without her hope and promise that in the life hereafter she would meet her lost child. She became a living corpse and she died in despair." Mr. Shin groaned like a soul in torment. "I promised," he went on painfully, "I promised myself that I would never, never again reveal my truth, my secret truth—a maddening truth coming from a servant of God. But I failed again with Mr. Hann. The last moment of Park's father had already wrecked the soul of that poor young man, and I, overcome by temptation, revealed to him the secret of my life, and despair seized his young body and soul and tore them up into shreds." Too agitated to remain seated, Mr. Shin jumped up from his chair and began to pace the room.

"And then you came and at one fatal stroke you pierced the core of my secret truth."

I was too moved by Mr. Shin's confession to say anything.

"I must go now," he said after a while. "I have to be at the church and do what I can. Do you have any idea when the city is going to be abandoned?"

"No, I don't, but I'll find out soon."

"What is it like on the front?"

I explained the battle situation.

"Then it won't be too long," he said.

"No," I said. "A matter of a few more days, perhaps."

The teakettle hummed softly, occasionally oozing out sizzling drops of water on the stove. Footsteps and voices mingled in the hall. The floor squeaked under my feet. Major Minn came in and told me that he and his men were going to the railway station to receive patients. When I stepped out of my room, no one was in sight; the building was deserted. Somewhere downstairs a telephone rang, unanswered. I left the building on foot for Mr. Shin's church, drawn there as if by a magnet, to be in his presence.

Within the freezing church there hardly was room to move. Pews were piled on top of each other and were stacked against the walls. Refugees were crowded on the bare, wooden floor, some sitting up, hunched over their bundles, many lying curled up. The church smelled of bodies and food; the odor of vegetable soup hovered in the damp, cold air. Here and there a baby cried. Children ran about, the high-ceilinged interior echoing their shouts and laughter. An old man, waving his hand for attention, was shouting the name of a woman. Hazy dust hung low above the multitude of shadowy bodies in the dim light of the chandeliers. I edged toward the altar, where Mr. Shin was busy doling out food to a line of refugees. A little girl, bundled up in a torn piece of quilt and chewing on a dried fish, gazed at me, then moved to the side of a woman who was suckling a baby. The child hid behind the woman's back, then buried her stained face in the woman's skirt and began crying. The woman lifted her weary eyes and stared at my uniformed figure.

I stayed there for an hour or so, long enough to hear Mr. Shin speak to the refugees, but not long enough to hear the end of the service. It was when he was reading from Psalms that I suddenly felt a shiver and began to tremble; my fever had returned. Mr. Shin, framed in the quavering light of two candles on the lectern, was saying:

. . . The Lord is my rock, and my fortress, and my deliverer,
my God, my rock, in whom I take refuge, my shield, and the
horn of my salvation, my stronghold. I call upon the Lord, who
is worthy to be praised, and I am saved from my enemies. The
cord of death encompassed me. . . .

I felt dizzy, and I left the church. When I returned to the
hospital I saw that it had been filled with wounded soldiers.
Ambulances came and went. Voices echoed in the halls; doors
banged; telephones rang; stretcher-bearers carried men up and
down the corridors. I managed to drag myself up the stairs to
my room.

"Oh, you fool!" Major Minn exclaimed when he came to
my room later. "To go out in weather like this. Now stay quiet
and get some sleep. You may hear lots of noises tonight. We
are operating on them as fast as we can. Don't let it bother
you. I'll send my orderly with some pills."

I thanked him.

"You can't afford to get sick now," he said.

The telephone rang when the major was about to go to his
room next door. He brought me the telephone.

The call was from CIC. When I hung up, Major Minn re-
placed the telephone on the desk. "Anything new?" he asked.

"The Chinese have just smashed our entire front," I said.

33

I woke up the next morning, around seven, and discovered that someone was sleeping in a bed at the other end of the room. I thought it was the major's orderly. It was dark in the room; the only light shone, flickering, through the vent of the stove. My head ached, I felt weak, and I would have liked to go back to sleep. I lay still on my cot, listening vaguely to the murmuring voices outside the room, the soft crumbling of the burned-out coal in the stove, and occasionally the heavy breathing of the man in the other bed. A little while later I heard the door of the next room open; then my door opened and Major Minn tiptoed in. I sat up and he came over to me, looking back toward the other bed.

"How do you feel?" he whispered.

I told him I thought I could get up.

He nodded. "That's your Christian friend over there," he said. "Did you notice?"

I did not understand him.

"He is the minister who came to see you the other day. We brought him in here last night—around eleven, I think." Major Minn explained that a man had come to the hospital about half-past ten at night, asking for me. "He said he was the janitor of the church. His minister had collapsed during a prayer session. Apparently he had been instructed to come to you if anything happened, so he came here. Well, you were in no shape to help anyone. I drove over to the church, since I had just been relieved after a few operations and I had nothing to do at the moment. That church was a mess. You probably know. What are they going to do with all those refugees they have there? I got your minister out and drove him back here and put him in your room. Hope you don't mind. There simply isn't any other room available just now. He was running a high fever. His heartbeat was extremely irregular, and he was dead-tired. I couldn't do much, except give him some sedatives and a vitamin shot. I'll look at him when he wakes up but I am afraid he has TB. He coughed a lot and spat some blood."

"Is it bad?"

"I can't tell until I examine him more thoroughly." He peered at his watch. "He should be sleeping till ten, eleven. Well, what about you?"

I told him that I slept well and that I thought I could go to CIC.

"You have a bad cold and you are quite run-down but I think you can get up and go out if you think you should. Just don't stay out too long and don't overwork." He then suggested that I come over to his room and have breakfast.

As I was leaving my room, I looked at Mr. Shin; he was breathing softly, with his face turned to the wall.

I did not return from CIC until two in the afternoon. Mr. Shin was up. His unshaven face looked bluish. He was sitting near the stove, wearing a white robe over his pajamas; alone in the room, he had been sipping tea. He greeted me with a wan smile.

I sat down on a chair opposite him.

"I never imagined that I would come here in such a situation and in such a state," he said. "I am glad to see you are up. You worried me last night when you left the church rather abruptly."

I told him that I had not been well. "I didn't mean to walk out on your service."

"I understand," he said. "I noticed that you looked ill. You shouldn't have come. I feel much better now. I must have been a bit tired yesterday."

"You should stay here, Mr. Shin, until we leave the city. You need a good rest and a doctor's attention, and you can have both here, at least for the time being."

"But I feel fine, Captain," he said, smiling. "I think I will go back to the church as soon as I see the major. Last night we received a hundred or so more refugees from the North. Where can they all go from here?" After a pause he said, "Those refugees who came last night—they suddenly opened up my memories of the villagers I had seen when I went down to Chinnampo. I thought the time had come at last for me to surrender to the temptation that had been harassing me all my life as a pastor. My despair was too great to bear and there were moments when I could not muster enough strength and courage to love my people. But then I went to visit my friend, an old pastor of a small village church. And there, in the few days I spent with him and with his people, I saw how despair paralyzed their spirits, how it snared them into the dark prison of their weary lives. The village had been bombed, shelled, sacked and nearly razed to the ground twice in three months; they had suffered, Captain. Their young had been lost in the war; their daughters, sisters, wives, mothers had been raped; nothing to eat, nothing to cure their sickness—a hell on earth. I saw how men can come to be beasts without hope, how men can come to be like savages without the promise, yes, the illusion of the eternal hope. Men cannot endure their sufferings without hope, without the promise of justice, if not here and now—and there is none—then somewhere else, in heaven, yes, in the Kingdom of God. And so I returned to the city."

"And *your* hope? *Your* promise?"

"That many will have lived without having been enslaved by despair, that many will have endured their worldly sufferings with a sense of purpose, that many will have died in peace, in faith, and with a blissful vision."

Later in the afternoon Mr. Shin's temperature rose and stayed high. He was too weak to insist on going back to his church. Major Minn told me that he had not been mistaken; the minister was in an advanced stage of tuberculosis.

Around seven in the evening I asked the major to have his orderly stay with Mr. Shin, as I had to go out.

At half-past ten, when I returned to my room, I found the orderly supporting Mr. Shin, who was sitting up in his bed panting. He had just coughed up a great deal of blood. When he recognized me leaning over him, he took away the handkerchief he had pressed over his mouth and tried to smile. The dark hollows under his eyes frightened me. I took his hand. "Your hand is cold," he whispered. "You must have been out."

I nodded.

"I thought I was dying," he said. "Wasn't that foolish of me?"

The orderly and I laid him down and covered him with blankets. Then I told the orderly to go and bring the major if he was not occupied.

Mr. Shin opened his eyes and said, "I was terrified for one moment."

"Try to sleep."

"Can you hear the patients? I heard them crying and moaning. I keep hearing them."

"Please don't let them bother you," I begged. "Try to sleep."

"Are they dying?" he whispered. "Are many of them dying?"

"No, Mr. Shin," I lied. The major had told me that fourteen wounded soldiers had died in two days; twenty or so were in critical condition; half of them would probably die.

He did not speak after that and closed his eyes.

The orderly came back and told me the major was operating at the moment and could not come.

I sat by Mr. Shin's bed for a while then went to my cot and lay down with my clothes on, unable to sleep.

Sometime later I heard Mr. Shin's weak, hoarse voice calling me, and I went to him.

"Should anything happen to me, will you pray for me?"

For a moment I did not know what to say.

"Have you ever prayed?" he asked.

"To the Christian god?" I said. "Yes, when I was a child."

"That will do," he said. "Your voice might be heard."

"I will try," I said. I did not know what else I could say.

34

Upon arriving at CIC the next morning, I discovered that nearly one-third of the detachment had left for Seoul during the night. The unexpected and sudden collapse of our front lines had resulted in chaotic communications between units and between the front and the rear; there were hardly any intelligence reports from the front-line combat units. The atmosphere was tense. I was instructed by the colonel to stand by for our withdrawal at any moment.

When I was able at last to return to the hospital in the late afternoon, I was informed by the major that Mr. Shin had left the hospital in his absence. According to him, a group of ministers had come to see Mr. Shin in the morning and stayed with him for about an hour. Then, shortly before noon the janitor and his wife had come. "I was here when the old couple came," he said, "but then I had to go to the Hospital Command. When I got back the minister was gone. My idiotic orderly, who hadn't lifted a finger to stop him from leaving, said there were lots of people, besides the janitor and his wife, wanting to see the minister, all waiting outside. They were from his church, I think."

The major had sent a sergeant and the orderly to church to bring him back to the hospital. Mr. Shin was conducting a service and the men waited for it to be over, but they were not able to persuade him to come with them.

"So I went there myself," Major Minn said, "I don't really know how I got into this and why I am going out of my way for your minister friend. I can only guess that I must always have been partial to ministers because of my wife. Her minister used to come to our house quite often; he was a jolly fellow and I became a good friend of his, though I never went to hear his sermons. Ah, well. Your friend wasn't at the church, which was packed with those refugees. I am afraid there are lots of sick people there. I found out where he lived from an old gentleman—one of his elders, I think, and went to his house. He was there all right, but the janitor insisted that he didn't want to see anyone. I sent in my name anyway, but it was no use. He simply refused to see me. I asked the janitor what his minister was doing. Praying, he said.

"You'd better go there right now and bring him back here. If he is left alone like that he won't live long. Praying isn't going to help his lungs."

Before I left I asked the major if there would be a hospital train going to Seoul and whether he was sending his patients to the South. He said there was one leaving Pyongyang early the next morning. I told him that I would like to send Mr. Shin on that train, if the major could make arrangements.

"I don't see why not," he said. "He can travel with one of my doctors." He looked at me searchingly. "You don't think we are going to defend Pyongyang, do you?" he said. "You don't have to tell me an official secret."

I told him that, if the worst came, the Army might not defend the city.

"If the worst comes . . ." he said. "And you think the worst will come soon."

I nodded.

"I have twenty patients who mustn't be moved around," he said. "God knows what I am supposed to do with them."

I drove to Mr. Shin's house, hoping that he would see me if no one else. Yet the only reply I received from the janitor, who obliged me by informing Mr. Shin of my visit, was that his minister did not wish to see anyone at the moment.

"Please come back," the old man said tearfully. "I know he trusts you. He is sick but I can't find a doctor around here. There isn't anyone left. I don't know why he made me bring him back here but I do what he tells me to do. I shouldn't have told him people from the church were waiting outside the hospital, wanting to see him. I know he is terribly sick. But the others don't know he is, and that's what worries me."

"You should tell them he's too sick to see them," I said.

"They have been meeting practically every day and night at the church and they want him there. They even come here for special prayer meetings. And then those ministers—well, they come here almost every night, staying so long, talking, talking, when he ought to be in bed. But what can I do? I tell them he is sick, so leave him alone, but they just don't listen to me. They are all scared, you see, so they want him to tell them not to be scared. What can I do?"

I told him he was to keep everyone away until I returned, and I left a note for Mr. Shin about the hospital train for Seoul.

I went to CIC, where I stayed for an hour or so, and then drove back to Mr. Shin's house.

He still would not see me nor give me any reply to my note.

"He said have courage so you can give him courage," the old man said. "That's all he said. I am sorry."

35

I did not see Mr. Shin for the next few days. The atmosphere in the city became tense, the mood of our men gloomier as each hour went by.

One afternoon, on my way back to CIC from a meeting at the Area Command, I was driving by the city hall, where in the wide square I ran into a procession of marchers. They had held a rally in the square and were starting on a tour throughout the city. It was an organized popular demonstration, expressing the people's protest against the Chinese intervention and their entreaty to the United Nations for a speedy retaliation. A Military Police man, who directed the traffic, had stopped my jeep, and I was thus able to observe the marchers as they came by.

Though sunny the day was brisk with a cold wind blowing. Banners of all colors fluttered in the wind. A group of teachers came abreast of my jeep, followed by a long line of high school students, in their black uniforms, who chanted rhythmically: "Down with the Chinese Communists! Long live the Republic of Korea! Long live the United Nations!" The group following them represented the Pyongyang Federation of Labor; and then the Anti-Communist Youth Association group snake-danced by, shouting incoherently; children trotted along, most of them bewildered but some of them giggling, waving Korean flags, American flags and a few U.N. flags; a high school brass band marched by, blaring out-of-tune Korean Army marching songs; women, old and young, quietly followed the band. And then came Mr. Shin.

Ahead of him, two young men carried a banner that read: THE FEDERATION OF CHRISTIANS OF PYONGYANG. Directly behind them, twelve men, all wearing black robes, carried upon their breasts black-ribboned portraits of the martyrs. In the center, somberly flanked by the twelve portraits, Mr. Shin walked slowly, his body erect in a black overcoat. The glasses of the framed portraits reflected the sun in blinding patches of light. Above Mr. Shin and slightly behind the portrait-bearers were two placards held aloft by an old man and Chaplain Koh, reading: IN THE SPIRIT OF THE TWELVE MARTYRS, ARISE! and CHRISTIAN BRETHREN, UNITE AND PRAY FOR VICTORY! Then came the ministers, some of whom I recognized, and their followers. The procession halted briefly. The band now played a Sousa march. They began to move again. I could not see Mr. Shin anymore. A helicopter appeared overhead and sprayed the people and the street with leaflets. The sun flashed. The wind scooped up the leaflets, then hurled them down at the pavement. I got out of the jeep and picked one up; its headline said: VICTORY SOON! OUR FORCES BEGIN COUNTERATTACK!

Later in the afternoon, while I was at CIC, I had a telephone call from Colonel Chang. He had known that I was still in the city.

"I saw Mr. Shin today," he said, "and the chaplain." I told him that I, too, had seen them.

"What on earth are they doing here? And why are they marching down the street like that!"

I explained to him briefly what had happened so far.

"So you don't think they will go, do you?" he said. I said I could not tell.

"It seems Mr. Shin is now the undisputed leader of the Christians here," he said. "That makes it hard for him. Now, mark my words. The CIC will be getting out of here tomorrow morning. I know that for a fact. Get them out with you by all means. Get them out, will you?"

I told him that I would do my best.

"If they won't go," he said, "well, I'll see what I can do."

———

That evening, at CIC, I received official instructions to leave Pyongyang the next morning. I went again to Mr. Shin's house and learned that he had gone to his church.

I found him there, standing in front of his congregation with an open Bible in his hands, flanked by two candles on a small table. The congregation knelt before him. Behind them were crowded the refugees. He saw me as I stood there quietly, and put the Bible down on the table and came to me.

I told him that I was ordered to leave Pyongyang the next morning.

"Then what those leaflets said is not true," he whispered.

He slowly looked about him at the congregation and at the refugees.

It seemed as though all the eyes in the church were riveted upon me. "We lost the battle," I confessed.

"Good-bye, Captain," he said. "I wish you a safe journey." He offered his hand, which I did not take. "Good-bye. I must get on with the service."

He turned away but I detained him, conscious of the people's eyes following our every move.

"Help me!" he said. "Give me courage! Give me courage to say good-bye to you!"

"Tell them to leave," I said. "Tell them we are not winning. Tell them we are not going to defend the city!"

"They all know that," he said.

"If they know, why don't they leave?"

"How far can they go? How long can they endure their suffering? The young people have already left. But the old and the sick, the women and the children—they are too weak."

"And you?"

"My place is at their side. If no one else, then I must make them believe God cares for them and I care for them. Good-bye, Captain Lee."

I gave in to his serene gaze. I took his hand. "Good-bye, Mr. Shin," I said. "Is there anything I can do for you before I leave?"

His pale face seemed to smile. He held both my hands in his. "Help me! Help my work wherever you may be."

I could not bear to leave him like this.

He whispered, "Love man, Captain! Help him! Bear your cross with courage, courage to fight despair, to love man, to have pity on mortal man."

He left me to rejoin his followers. "My brethren, let us pray," he said.

The congregation bowed their heads. Mr. Shin gazed at me and nodded slightly.

I bowed to him and withdrew. I closed the door, leaving behind me the murmuring voices of those who had their god and the one who loved them.

I stopped by CIC to receive provisions for my journey; I was issued a submachine gun and ammunition to be prepared for possible encounters with enemy guerrillas on the way.

I could not find Chaplain Koh; he had returned to the camp a few miles west of Pyongyang, where he was setting up a refugee post maintained by the Christians.

I returned to the hospital and saw that it was being evacuated; ambulances were being loaded with patients. Major Minn, who met me at the entrance, informed me that he had shipped out most of his patients. "But I still have twenty or so who are critical," he said. "If I move them, they will die. I am supposed to use my discretion about them. My discretion, indeed! My God, why don't they just tell me to leave them behind! Isn't that what they want me to do!"

I held his arm. "We will do our best," I said. I did not know what else I could say to him.

"The patients will die anyway," he said. "That's the way my superiors figure."

Snowflakes whirled about, swishing in and out of the light beams of the vehicles. One after another, the ambulances whined away into the dark night.

36

I was in my room when, sometime after midnight, I looked out of the window and saw that the general retreat had begun.

Tanks and guns were rumbling into the city from the North, then clattering through the streets to the bridge across the river to the South. From the southern side of the river, an endless line of empty trucks, with their headlights blazing, crossed the bridge into the city, grinding their way to the North to evacuate the troops. By 3 A.M., two-way traffic, to the South and to the North, reached its highest flux. Trucks from the North began to pass through the city, loaded with troops. The air base across the river hummed on as planes screeched up into the cold, windy darkness; searchlights pierced the black sky, clashing with each other, crisscrossing. More field guns rolled out of the city, their dark long shapes dimly revealed in the lights of the passing trucks. A Military Police jeep zigzagged through the traffic, red lights blinking. In another hour I began to hear the distant rumbling of artillery barrages; the black horizon of the northern sky continuously flashed and boomed. Infantry troops began to appear, slogging along, and now and then a machine gun chattered. Suddenly the whole sky over the city was illuminated by flares. Shadowy buildings, tanks, trucks, guns, troops, lampposts, bleak glass windows in deserted shops, the belfry over the slope were lit up in a cold phosphorescent brightness; searchlights fought with each other; fireballs burst in the sky; the air shook with the hammering barrages of antiaircraft guns; jet fighters swished overhead. Darkness returned once again and with it a sudden hush, then the whining, purring of motors and heavy shuffling footsteps of the troops—all flowing toward the bridge.

I got ready to leave. I rang up CIC to report my departure but received no answer. I cut the wire and destroyed the telephone and the field-radio set and left the room. My footsteps echoed in the dark, empty building as I went down the steps. When I reached the ground floor, I heard a door squeak open from the direction of our former briefing room; a voice whispered, "Captain Lee? Is that you?"

"Yes. Who are you?" I whispered back.

A beam from a flashlight shot out of darkness. "It's me." It was Major Minn.

"Are you still here?" I said. "What are you doing?"

"I am staying as long as I can," he said, coming close to me. "I have twenty-two men dying in there." He pointed to the former briefing room. "I have gotten everyone else shipped out."

"You'd better get out of here," I said, "as fast as you can."

"So we are sneaking out," he said. "Just as we did in Seoul when the whole damn thing started."

"Come, Major, I think you have stayed long enough."

"What has happened to your minister-friend?"

I told him Mr. Shin was staying in the city.

"You never can tell what these ministers are up to," he said. "I can understand what they must feel. My wife's minister stayed in Seoul and got kidnapped by the Reds. I told him to hide or do something but he wouldn't. He just wouldn't run away."

"Now it's my turn to tell you to get out of here," I said. "Come, Major. Come!"

"I am not trying to be holy or brave. I am just trying to be decent."

Suddenly we heard a jeep screech to a halt at the entrance.

"Turn off the light!" I said to the major and pushed him behind me.

Someone kicked the door open and ran into the building, shouting my name. I got the flashlight from the major and stepped out.

It was a sergeant from CIC. "We tried to reach you but the line was cut off. The colonel told me to make sure you had left. We are getting out, sir. We are going to blow up the bridge in a few hours. So you'd better hurry."

After the sergeant left I said to the major, "I think you have been decent enough, Major. We ought to go now."

"Yes, I suppose," he said. "Give me a few minutes. I want to write a letter."

I did not understand him.

"I want to leave a note to my counterpart on the other side. I don't care if he is a Chinese or a North Korean or a Russian. If he is a real doctor he will read it and know what I feel. I have all the records of those men in there and whatever medicine I could scrounge up."

He wanted to take a last look at his patients. I volunteered to come with him but he did not want me to. "You'd better not. At least I can spare you from that. I won't be long." He walked into the room.

When he came out he said, "Six died. Four may survive. I can't tell." He added wearily, "You know, I wanted to pray for them but I couldn't. I felt so damned blasphemous. Treat them decently—that's all I could say."

We left the building in silence. He drove ahead in his jeep and I followed him in mine. The streets were deserted. The withdrawal seemed to have been almost completed. When we reached the bridge, vehicles and troops were still crossing in a congested file. Jeeps, mounted with machine guns, patrolled the streets near the bridge. Refugees had gathered, and Military Police were fending them off the streets. Feet shuffled; motors roared; and voices shouted in Korean, "Civilians to the downstream! To the downstream bridge!" English mingled with Korean. Planes flew overhead in the dark heavens.

Suddenly Major Minn's jeep swung out of the line of vehicles. He shouted to me, "Good-bye, Captain Lee!" Before I had a chance to speak his jeep lurched forward, then roared back into the city. "Hurry up! Hurry up!" an American MP cried, waving a dimmed flashlight. I drove onto the creaking bridge.

While I was still on the bridge explosions down the river to my right shook my jeep; fireballs soared up into the black sky; the downstream bridge was being destroyed. I drove on, squeezed in between the trucks of American units and those of Korean units. We moved slowly. About half an hour later, barely two miles beyond the bridge, we were at a standstill, when we heard a series of shattering explosions. A few parka-clad American soldiers in the truck ahead of my jeep were looking out of the canvas cover. A voice cried out, "There goes the God-damned bridge!" Another shouted, "Oh, Jesus! Look at that!" I got out of my jeep and looked back toward Pyong-yang. The doomed city was in flames.

37

When I reached Seoul I was assigned to a special section of Army Intelligence that maintained direct communications with our agents in North Korea; I was thus able to follow the activities of Colonel Chang, among others, through the clandestine reports he continued to send us from Pyongyang.

Park was somewhere on the eastern front, presumably near Hungnam, where our forces, having retreated from the Manchurian-Siberian border, were establishing a bridgehead, awaiting their evacuation. As for Major Minn, the Hospital Command, which had set up its temporary headquarters in Seoul, could tell me only that he had been officially listed as missing.

Two days before Christmas our troops were successfully evacuated from Hungnam, thus completing our general retreat from North Korea. The next day my request for transfer was granted and I began to prepare myself for my new assignment; I was to report for duty to a Korean Infantry regiment deployed just north of Seoul.

On that Christmas Eve I withdrew early to my quonset hut, where I had a solitary supper of American rations. I was reading a Japanese translation of Aurelius' *Meditations*, when I had an unexpected visitor, an Army captain of about my age, fully equipped for combat.

Following our mutual introductions the captain removed his helmet and rubbed his hands over his sunken cheeks. "I just got back from Pyongyang a few days ago," he said. "I have something for you from Colonel Chang." He produced a small envelope and handed it to me. He explained that he had been engaged in a secret intelligence operation in an area about fifty miles northeast of Pyongyang, which had been overrun by the Chinese shortly before our general retreat had begun. Instructed to return to Seoul, he managed to reach Pyongyang, which he found had already been evacuated, and got in touch with Colonel Chang. He stayed in Pyongyang for two days in a hiding place arranged for him by the colonel, left for a small fishing village on the west coast, then eventually went to an off-shore island held by our Marines; he spent a day there before he was taken to Inchon by a Korean Navy transport ship. "Colonel Chang gave me that," he said, pointing to the envelope in my hands, "and asked me to deliver it to you. So there it is." He stood up; he was in a hurry to go.

When he had left I read Colonel Chang's note:

I am about to send this man through one of my routes, a very safe one. I saw Mr. Shin, whom I could not persuade to go with this man. No reasoning is possible with him; he is determined to stay here, and so is the chaplain. I tried my best, assuring them that my secret passage is absolutely safe. They are still safe; the Reds haven't touched them yet. I'll try again, since it is such a pity not to take advantage of my route, which is guarded by my own guerrillas. Pyongyang is a mess. It has become a Chinatown. Pity! Good luck. Chang.

P.S. Just after I wrote this I learned that the chaplain has vanished from the city. Well, good for him, I say! His followers had forced him into hiding.

38

On the fourth day of January, 1951, a few days after the Communist forces had launched an all-out offensive, we scorched and abandoned Seoul, then retreated further south beyond the Han River. Our counteroffensive began in the latter part of January but it was not until March 14 that the devastated capital city was again in our hands.

I was wounded during the battle of Seoul when my company, having participated in smashing the enemy's bridgehead east of the Han River, engaged in street fighting in the city. I was temporarily accommodated in a field hospital, until I was shipped to Taegu and then finally to Pusan in the second week of April to an Army hospital for convalescents.

Preceding the fall of Seoul all the major governmental agencies had been evacuated to Pusan, which served as the temporary capital; apart from Army headquarters, which remained in Taegu, everything seemed to be concentrated in that city. It was there, while I was still in the hospital, that, one sunny afternoon, Colonel Chang visited me unexpectedly.

Placing a bulky paper bag on the edge of my bed, he said, "It took me some time to locate you, particularly because you had left Intelligence. Well, here we are. I brought you some apples. I thought you might like some." He had traced me through the Adjutant General's Office in Taegu, and decided to pay me a visit, since he was coming to Pusan anyway for a conference with someone at the Korean Marine Corps headquarters. Army Intelligence had decided to evacuate him from North Korea to put him in charge of a new operation. "They sent a PT boat to get me out," he said. "When I got back they told me I was to direct a sort of hit-and-run guerrilla operation against the coastal installations in North Korea and Manchuria. I have North Korean volunteers, Army agents and Marine commandoes in my operation and of course I have the Navy to help me."

I was eager to ask about his operation in Pyongyang but he showed no inclination to touch upon that subject. For a while we discussed the nature of his new operation. Then after he had peeled the skin off an apple for me he stood up and went to the window that looked out over the sprawling city to the sea. He remarked that I had a marvelous view.

When he returned to his chair he began peeling an apple for himself and said, "I am afraid Mr. Shin is dead." He added hastily, "Of course I can't be too sure about that. All I know for certain is that he was arrested and thrown into jail in Pyongyang. As you know I saw him soon after the Chinese came in. He was still allowed to conduct services at his church during the next few weeks." He cut up the apple, munched on a slice. "I tried to see him again. It was too late. He had already been taken away. I found out that the Reds came to his church one Sunday and broke up the service, then took him with them. By that time they had banned all religious meetings. A few other ministers who were still there were also taken away. I had no trouble finding out what happened to them and where they were held. I had my men pass the word around to the Christians as to the whereabouts of Mr. Shin and the other ministers. At least that was something I could do for them.

"Then on Christmas Eve a group of Christians went to the prison where the ministers were and in spite of the Reds who threatened to arrest them, they sang Christmas carols for more than half an hour. The Red guards apparently thought the singing was harmless and let the Christians sing and leave. But the secret police didn't think so at all, and the next day the ministers were moved to another prison, then a few days later, they were sent off to the North. That's the last thing I know of Mr. Shin and the others."

Colonel Chang sheathed his knife, gathered up the apple

peels, and put them in the bag. "He was quite ill when I saw him last. That's why I am afraid he is dead. He couldn't have survived the ordeal. The Reds closed down all the churches and arrested practically everyone else they thought was influential among the Christians. Not only the Christians, of course. So-called people's trials and public executions went on in every square in the city. We could have blown up a few places and even the secret police headquarters but then more innocent people would have been persecuted. So we couldn't do too much to retaliate except to shoot up several high-ranking Reds."

We sat quietly for a while.

Colonel Chang asked me about Park. I had no news of him. He then asked me if Chaplain Koh had been to see me.

"What about the chaplain?" I asked.

"Oh, I am sorry. I thought you knew what happened to him," he said. "He was kidnapped from Pyongyang, as you know. No, no, don't look at me like that. I didn't do it. The people of his congregation did. They forced him to hide, then slipped him out of Pyongyang—heaven knows how. He went back to his brigade after that. Well, he is out of the Army now. Obviously he doesn't know you are here. He is in Pusan. That's why I thought you knew. I am on my way to see him, as a matter of fact. I'll tell him you are here."

According to the colonel, the former chaplain had resigned from the Army after the battle of Seoul and had settled down on a small island just outside the harbor of Pusan, where he tended a church in a refugee camp. Nearly two thousand refugees from North Korea were accommodated there; the colonel thought there were many Christians among them.

"Ah, those Christians," he said, "wherever they may be, they will have their church, even in a refugee camp, and there is always someone to look after them.

"Speaking of their church, by the way," he added, "do you remember the one across the street from our detachment in Pyongyang? The one that clanged its bell all the time? It's gone now and so is the building we were in. Our bombers did a thorough job on Pyongyang the day you got out of it, when the

Chinese were pouring in. Yes. That block is nothing but rubble now." He rose from his chair. "Well, I must leave you, Captain. I am glad to see you are recovering well and I hope the Army will let you go back to your university when you get out of here."

39

Though my condition improved I was not recovering fast enough and I had to remain in the hospital. Then one day, about two weeks after Colonel Chang's visit, Mr. Koh came to see me. When he was shown into my room I did not recognize him immediately. His mustache was gone and he had lost considerable weight. He stood near me at the open window. I asked him if he had seen Colonel Chang.

"Yes. He came to see me at the camp," he said. "I wanted to come to see you before this but I have been unable to leave the island." He had about two hundred Christians among the refugees in the camp and new refugees arrived nearly every day. "They come from all parts of the North. How they managed to escape from there is beyond my comprehension but they keep coming, alone or in small groups, by land and by boat. I am afraid, though, it won't be too long before all the escape routes are sealed off by the Reds."

A cool breeze from the sea rustled the curtains. He looked out of the window and pointed to the eastern side of the harbor. "Our camp is out there," he said. "It is now called the Tent Island because we all live in tents. I hope you will come and visit us. We have quite a few Christians from Pyongyang and they all knew Mr. Shin, of course. But I haven't been able to learn anything definite about him. No one seems to know for sure what happened to him."

"You have heard from Colonel Chang about him haven't you?" I said.

He came back from the window and faced me gloomily.

"Colonel Chang is dead!" he said, and his voice broke. When he was able to compose himself he handed me a letter.

The letter read:

. . . It grieves me to inform you that Colonel Chang has been killed in action while performing his duty for his country and for his people. I know you two have been close to each other through many an ordeal and I know, therefore, how this news will sadden you. As an officer in charge of the operation he did not have to participate in person in the raid in which he met his death. He died somewhere on the coast of southern Manchuria. I am sorry I cannot tell you more than this. But I can tell you that his death was a noble and brave one. When he and his men were ready to withdraw from the beach they were met by a heavy attack from the enemy and it became impossible for the entire raiding party to withdraw safely. Colonel Chang and a few others stayed and held the enemy, while the others made their way to the landing craft that evacuated them. A few days later, through our agents, we learned that the enemy had captured one of our men who died of his wounds later, but Colonel Chang and the others had been killed in the battle. It was a sacrifice on the part of the colonel beyond the call of duty and I have taken necessary measures to see to it that his heroic sacrifice be properly commemorated. I would like you to come to Taegu to see me at your convenience, for I have a certain sum of money that was left by Colonel Chang for you. I have had my officers, those who worked with the colonel, contribute, and I hope you will come to Taegu, so that I may have the pleasure of seeing you again and personally entrusting you with the money. It was Colonel Chang's wish that you use the money to purchase Bibles for your church at the camp, for he had seen that you had very few of them available for your people. . . .

40

By the second week of May I was well enough to be allowed to leave the hospital for occasional brief visits to the city. One afternoon, shortly after I had returned from a walk, a doctor came to my room, accompanied by a young Marine sergeant.

The sergeant had come from Chinhai, a Naval town about three hours drive from Pusan to the west. He was an assistant to the chaplain at the Naval hospital there.

"You have been sent for by the chaplain," the doctor explained.

"It is about Captain Park, sir," the sergeant said. "His records said we should notify you in case of emergency. He was wounded on May second on the eastern front. We finally located you down here, sir, and we would appreciate it, Captain, if you would come to see him."

"I think it would be all right," the doctor said. "You can make the trip."

The sergeant would drive me to Chinhai and back to Pusan.

Twilight was slowly approaching when we arrived at the Naval hospital in Chinhai. The chaplain was not in his office; he was visiting Park. The sergeant took me to the doorway of Park's room, where I saw the chaplain seated beside the bed in the dim light, quietly praying. Beyond his silvery head, I saw Park's dark profile, half buried in the white pillow. I waited for the chaplain outside the room. Presently he came out to meet me.

After thanking me for coming, he said that Park had been unconscious for the last two hours and suggested that we come back later. He was an old man with many wrinkles in his pale face. We walked out of the hospital, side by side, into a spacious garden that looked out onto the bay, where gray warships lay quietly moored. The distant horizon glowed with the lingering rays of sunset. We sat down on the grass.

"I am afraid he won't last long," he said in a low voice. "I heard that they removed three bullets from his chest before he was sent down here. He was all right when he came. One day he sent for me and said he was a sinner as ancient as mankind is. A strange thing to hear from a Marine officer, don't you think? I understood him, naturally, when he told me that his father was a Christian minister. Just that and nothing more. I have talked with him off and on. Meanwhile, his condition became worse and this morning the doctors told me that he might not survive. So I sent for you. I would have sent for you sooner but Captain Park's records came here only yesterday.

"I saw him this afternoon and told him that you were coming. He was hardly able to talk but managed to ask me to write this down for you." He gave me a sheet of paper. "I don't quite understand it but I hope you do."

The words read:

I have been clinging onto the precipice of History, but I give up. I am prepared to take leave of it.

A cool breeze drifted toward the land from the darkening sea. The long shadow of a flagpole stretched up the sloping garden. The grass felt chilly against my palms.

"If he dies," I said to the chaplain, "will you give him a Christian burial?"

"Yes, of course," he said. "That would be quite proper for a minister's son." He lighted his pipe. "Will you do me the honor of being my guest at the officers' club? After dinner we will go to see your friend."

I thanked him and followed him across the garden to the club.

Park did not regain consciousness while I sat beside him that night and he died quietly around three o'clock in the morning.

Late in the afternoon he was buried in the Naval cemetery

on a hill that rose gently behind the town of Chinhai, facing
the glistening, dark-green expanse of the Korea Straits. The
chaplain read from the Bible and prayed. The white cross on
the grave shone harshly in the hot sun. Someone had placed a
few sprigs of blooming azaleas on the moist, dark-brown earth
of the grave. The chaplain's low voice whispered, "Amen."

A few days later, the Marine Corps headquarters sent me
three medals of Park's, together with a citation posthumously
awarded to him by the Chief of Naval Operations, which read,
in part:

> . . . ordered to execute a rearguard action so as to insure a safe
> completion of the tactical redeployment of his battalion, he led
> the survivors of his company in a heroic defense of a critical
> mountain pass, superbly demonstrating his ability as an inspiring
> Marine officer, mercilessly repelling the repeated assaults of a
> battalion of the enemy, until the last man and the last piece of
> equipment of his battalion were established in a new position of
> strength. . . .

41

One late Sunday afternoon, a few days before I was to be discharged from the hospital I took a ferry and went to the Tent Island to visit Mr. Koh. In the midst of the rows and rows of dark-green tents on the flat, barren island, North Korean children ran about barefoot in the choking dust under the glaring sun of the South, slipping in and out of the dark mouths of the sweltering tents, leaping over and crawling under the network of ropes that held the tents together. Voices hummed within the shelters, women hung clothes on ropes between the tents, and a group of old people were gathering in front of one that had a Red Cross sign.

I found Mr. Koh hammering in nails, putting boards together in the oppressive humid interior of one of the tents. He took me outside. "This is my church," he said, pointing to the tent with his hammer. "I am trying to make a floor for it before the rainy season begins." He suggested that we walk down to the beach, where, he said, it might be cooler. "You don't see many men now," he said as we were walking toward the beach. "They all work in Pusan during the day, even on Sundays."

We sat on a flat rock that jutted out above the water. A freighter was gliding out of the harbor. Behind us in Pusan, motors bustled and cranes clanked. The water lapped quietly beneath us.

I told him about Park's death.

He nodded slowly without a word.

After a long silence, he said, "You know, I have been puzzled by this and I am glad I have you here to talk about it. As you know we have many Christians here from practically every corner of the North. I have come to know them all, of course, and I have asked them if they knew anything about what happened to Mr. Shin." He paused, rolling up the sleeves of his khaki shirt. "I have been asking that at every service and of every newcomer. The word got around the entire camp that I was asking about Mr. Shin. The strange thing is that, so far, I have talked with nearly a dozen people who claim to have seen him. There are about three or four from Pyongyang who say that they saw him very much alive. They don't surprise me. For all I know they may be telling the truth. But then, of course, we know what Colonel Chang told us. What puzzles me most is that there are many people not from Pyongyang who say that they have seen him. Some say they have seen a man of his description in a small town on the Manchurian border. Some say they have seen him on the west coast. Some insist that they have seen him on the east coast in a fishing village. It is hard to believe them. But they all insist that the man they claim to have seen fits my description in every single detail. What do you make of that?"

I did not know what to say.

He tapped the rock with the hammer. "Could it be that the Communists have been sort of dragging him around?" he said, frowning. "You know, as an enemy of the people and the state and so on. Most of those refugees say that he was free. Can you imagine? Not only alive but free? If I were to believe all of their stories, well, Mr. Shin is everywhere in North Korea. Of course, in such circumstances as we find ourselves here, refugees are naturally more inclined to remember or imagine many things they have left behind."

"Such as their memories of suffering?"

He nodded, gazing at me. "But last night I talked with a man who just came here. He had left Pyongyang about a month ago. He is not a Christian but he had known of Mr. Shin through newspapers and such. Captain, this man is the only person on this island who told me that Mr. Shin is dead. According to him he was publicly executed in Pyongyang sometime in April."

I asked him if the man had seen the execution.

He shook his head. "That's the trouble. He is not an eyewitness. So . . . which story should one believe?"

"How odd, that people from different provinces should think they all have seen Mr. Shin."

"Yes, and who am I to contradict or doubt what they claim? They have heard the description of Mr. Shin and they think they know him." He struck the rock with the hammer again.

Later when we came back to his tent church he asked me to stay a little longer. I accepted his invitation and said I was sorry that my visit had interfered with his work on the floor for the church.

"Oh, I am not in a hurry," he said. "There is always tomorrow."

I helped him put the boards and nails away, then clean the church. We then sat out in the sun, facing the tents, watching the children play, and listening to the humming voices around us. He was smoothing the rough surface of a wooden cross with a pocketknife. "I made it this morning," he said. "I thought the church ought to have a cross."

Gradually the air began to cool and the shadows of the tents traveled toward us over the ground. Ferries began to bring the refugees back to the island from Pusan. Voices, footsteps, children's shouting mingled with the tooting and chugging of the ferries. People appeared from all directions, many of them heading for the beach where we had been; and there they cleansed themselves. Offshore the gray figure of a destroyer loomed. Wiping the cross with a handkerchief, Mr. Koh invited me to supper. We went into a tent adjoining the church and shared some canned food. Outside, from the other tents, came loud voices, occasional laughter, and the tinkling of pots and pans.

He got up. "I'll go and see if I can get some hot water," he said. "Then we can have some tea."

The dusk fell slowly.

After the meal I went to the church with him and helped him set up folding chairs for the evening service. On the right hand side of the entrance he placed two chairs on which he stacked Bibles and hymnbooks. A young barefoot boy appeared in a white cotton shirt and rolled-up khaki pants. Mr. Koh gave him a brass bell with a wooden handle. The boy went outside and began to ring the bell. After lighting two candles, Mr. Koh took his position behind a table that served as an altar; he held a Bible in one hand, the cross in the other. I sat on a chair near the entrance. Christians were arriving.

So it was that I found myself in the tent church, beneath the dome of tarpaulin in the warm, thick air, in the midst of a congregation of North Korean refugees, listening to their murmured prayers and ecstatic chantings, hearing the impassioned sermon delivered by their minister. I gazed at the two candles twinkling on the table, behind which stood the minister, now with both hands gripping the wooden cross; and I whispered to myself that I had indeed come a long, long way from Pyongyang, while the scenes and the events of the recent past illuminated themselves in my memory like the pictures on a revolving lantern.

The congregation bowed their heads silently.

A latecomer opened the flaps of the entrance and slipped in. The candles flared up and, for a second, the white wooden cross looked red.

Minister Koh said, "Let us pray . . . let us pray for our brethren in the North."

Murmuring voices, rising and subsiding, began to envelop me.

"Our Father," he began.

"Our Father," voices echoed him.

How long, I wondered, how long will the people listen to the voices whispering to them, one from within history, the other from far beyond history, each promising them salvation and justice, each asking them to pledge themselves to its promise? And suddenly, I remembered that night of violence at Mr. Shin's; I saw again, in the light that seeped through the line of guards and Military Police, the cluster of old women kneeling in the snow, heard again their sorrowful dirge, laden with the world's grief. But . . . until it was time for them to chant a dirge for me . . .

I left the church and stood outside, listening to the voices of those who had their god and could say "Amen."

Soon the service was over and the boy came out of the tent to ring his bell again.

I walked away from the church, past the rows of tents where silent suffering gnawed at the hearts of people—my people—and headed toward the beach, which faced the open sea. There a group of refugees, gathered under the starry dome of the night sky, were humming in unison a song of homage to their homeland. And with a wondrous lightness of heart hitherto unknown to me, I joined them.

THE STORY OF PENGUIN CLASSICS

Before 1946 . . . "Classics" are mainly the domain of academics and students; readable editions for everyone else are almost unheard of. This all changes when a little-known classicist, E. V. Rieu, presents Penguin founder Allen Lane with the translation of Homer's *Odyssey* that he has been working on in his spare time.

1946 Penguin Classics debuts with *The Odyssey*, which promptly sells three million copies. Suddenly, classics are no longer for the privileged few.

1950s Rieu, now series editor, turns to professional writers for the best modern, readable translations, including Dorothy L. Sayers's *Inferno* and Robert Graves's unexpurgated *Twelve Caesars*.

1960s The Classics are given the distinctive black covers that have remained a constant throughout the life of the series. Rieu retires in 1964, hailing the Penguin Classics list as "the greatest educative force of the twentieth century."

1970s A new generation of translators swells the Penguin Classics ranks, introducing readers of English to classics of world literature from more than twenty languages. The list grows to encompass more history, philosophy, science, religion, and politics.

1980s The Penguin American Library launches with titles such as *Uncle Tom's Cabin* and joins forces with Penguin Classics to provide the most comprehensive library of world literature available from any paperback publisher.

1990s The launch of Penguin Audiobooks brings the classics to a listening audience for the first time, and in 1999 the worldwide launch of the Penguin Classics Web site extends their reach to the global online community.

The 21st Century Penguin Classics are completely redesigned for the first time in nearly twenty years. This world-famous series now consists of more than 1,300 titles, making the widest range of the best books ever written available to millions—and constantly redefining what makes a "classic."

The Odyssey continues . . .

The best books ever written

PENGUIN CLASSICS

SINCE 1946

Find out more at www.penguinclassics.com

Visit www.vpbookclub.com

CLICK ON A CLASSIC
www.penguinclassics.com

The world's greatest literature at your fingertips

Constantly updated information on more than a thousand titles,
from Icelandic sagas to ancient Indian epics, Russian drama to
Italian romance, American greats to African masterpieces

＊

The latest news on recent additions to the list, updated
editions, and specially commissioned translations

＊

Original essays by leading writers

＊

A wealth of background material, including biographies
of every classic author from Aristotle to Zamyatin, plot
synopses, readers' and teachers' guides, useful Web links

＊

Online desk and examination copy assistance for academics

＊

Trivia quizzes, competitions, giveaways, news on
forthcoming screen adaptations

Printed in the United States
by Baker & Taylor Publisher Services